BOND UNKNOWN

WILLIE MEIKLE

EDWARD M. ERDELAC

An April Moon Books Publication
Published in arrangement with the authors
Edited by Neil Baker
All stories ©2017 the respective authors

All rights reserved. No part of this book may be reproduced or transmitted in any form or by any means, electronic or mechanical, including photocopying, recording or by any information storage and retrieval system, without written permission from the publisher, except for the inclusion of brief quotations in a review.

These stories are not affiliated with the Ian Fleming Estate or Eon productions. They are published in accordance with the Canadian Public Domain laws.
These stories are works of fiction. Any resemblance to actual persons living or dead, historical events or organizations is purely coincidental.

First Edition 2017
This Edition 2022
Published in Canada.

DEDICATION

This story is dedicated to my auld dad, who took me to see Goldfinger when I was only six, and made a memory that stays with me more than fifty years later.

W.M

As an avid reader of James Bond's previously published adventures, which I discovered between the torn, moldy, and water-damaged covers of my father's college-era paperbacks, it is my distinct pleasure to present this story, which I dedicate to him, and to my son Augustus, who I hope will take up the tradition of appreciation, though he is currently content to watch the car chases in the films and earn his prefix shooting scores of enemy agents in the video game. Thanks also to Nathalie Cox, for schooling a Yank on private education in the UK.

E.M.E

CONTENTS

1	Into the Green by Willie Meikle	Pg 1
2	Mindbreaker by Edward M. Erdelac	Pg 44
3	About the Authors	Pg 197

Bond inched as close to the edge of the gantry walkway as he dared to better see what was happening. The globe of light spun faster, and the green washes of color became deeper still, deeper yet somehow more vibrant, more bright...

INTO THE GREEN
WILLIE MEIKLE

I've been a Bond fan as long as I can remember, and back then when the world was young JB was Scottish, hard as nails, and a bit of a bastard. That's how I like my Bonds, and that's how he appears in my story here, which starts with Commander Bond, a British submarine, and a strange research station in Alaska.

Bond went up to the turret for a smoke more than for a chance to see the light show, but his cigarette burned itself out, forgotten where it dangled from his lip as he stood entranced by the sight above him.
HMS CONFESSER had surfaced twenty minutes earlier, a hundred miles north of Vancouver Island off the western coast of British Columbia. The Canadian Rockies glowed and danced way off to starboard, but it was the dome of the sky overhead that really caught the attention. It hummed, crackled, and hissed like a badly tuned radio and blazed in a wash of Turneresque color in greens and blues, like a curtain of shimmering gauze draped over the sea.
"I've been in these climes for years now, and I've never seen it like this," a voice said by his side. Bond didn't have to turn to identify the speaker, Duncan MacDonald's accent betrayed him, as it had for all the years of their acquaintance. "Gie's a fag, Jimmy, lad," the man–the Captain–said. "I'm gasping."
When M had told him he'd be going undercover as Commander Bond RN his heart had sunk. Going back wasn't his style, but Duncan's promotion to Captaincy of the CONFESSOR meant that Bond got

to serve under one of his oldest friends, and that was at least making the trip up the coast from Vancouver that much more bearable.

He passed over a smoke - Capstan, Full Strength, if he was going back, he should at least go the whole hog - and lit a fresh one for himself from the butt of the old. He waved a hand at the expanse of sky and the dancing lights of the aurora.

"It's a nice show, though," he said.

Normally MacDonald would come back with a quip or a curse, but neither was forthcoming this time. Bond realized that the man was worried.

"It's playing havoc with the electronics down below," the Scotsman said. "And have you noticed how warm it is? It's bloody Canada, in bloody January. We should be freezing our baws off here."

Bond had indeed noticed the unnatural warmth of the sea breeze–and so had M for that matter, otherwise Bond wouldn't even be here.

Bond had been called into M's office four days ago back in Whitehall. It was just in time from the Service's point of view; he had been about to head for Monte Carlo for some sun and card play to get away from the drab, gray fug that passed for winter in London.

Moneypenny raised an eyebrow as Bond entered and left his hat on the peg by the door.

"You're late, James. And he's in a bit of a mood."

"When is he never?" Bond replied, only seconds before Moneypenny's intercom crackled.

"I heard that," M said. "Get in here, Bond. There's work to be done, and some of us take our responsibilities seriously around here."

Bond winked at Moneypenny and went through to the opulent book-lined office from where the head of MI6 kept a beady eye on the rest of the world. M sat, puffing on a pipe, staring out of the window over the Whitehall rooftops. There was to be no preamble–M got straight to business.

"I've had your pal Leiter on the phone this morning. It seems there's something going on at a research station in Anchorage. We've had a joint research project with the Yanks running for a few months–some kind of energy production thing I've been told. But it all seems to be going belly up over the past few days–some of the scientist Johnnies appear to be suffering from some strange psychological malady–like sleeping sickness, but when awake, Leiter says. On top of that there's been a spate of dashed peculiar weather for the season, and the bally locals are reporting singing in the sky, if reports can be believed. Now normally we'd put it all down to too much booze and a long Alaskan winter, but one of the affected scientists is the PM's nephew. And now one of the white coats has turned up dead–murdered, they say. So something has to be seen to be done. The local police are on the case, but they've come up empty and Leiter's crew is busy with some nonsense concerning Cuba. We need you to head on over and take a shufti," M said. "I expect a full report by next Friday at the latest."

That had been that, and the same afternoon Bond was on a series of planes heading for Halifax, Toronto, then points west to rendezvous with the CONFESSOR in Vancouver. Now here he was, Commander Bond again, back in uniform, back smoking Capstan–and back sailing with Duncan MacDonald, although this time he doubted there'd be quite as much carousing in exotic ports to be done.
"Tell me, Jimmy," MacDonald said as they smoked. "Do you actually enjoy all this cloak and dagger nonsense? Or is it just that you miss the thrills of the old days?"
It was a question Bond often asked himself. All he knew was that he felt most alive when the stakes were high–whether that be at the card table, or working in the field. But articulating that to an old friend who already knew most of the reasons why proved beyond him just then.
"I'm just doing my bit for Queen and Country," Bond said, and smiled.
MacDonald smiled back. "Just remember, you don't need to do it all yourself. I've got your back–and by that I mean the Royal Navy looks after its own. You could come back in a flash, you know–the First Officer job would be there–it would be like old times."
Some days Bond might have been tempted, but just then the sky hissed at them, and a low hum, a drone like a piper warming up, filled the sky; personal feelings aside, there was a job to be done here, a duty to uphold. Red tendrils wafted through the blues and greens overhead. They looked too much like blood trails–dried blood, from old fights and battles, reminding him, if he ever needed it, that you can't go back, even if you wanted to.
"You got any Scotch in your cabin, Duncan?" Bond asked as they went back below. "That's one part of the old days I wouldn't mind

revisiting tonight."

They brought the CONFESSOR into Anchorage harbor thirty- six hours and two bottles of Johnny Walker Black Label later. Given the time of year, MacDonald's man had left out the winter gear–parkas and oilskin trousers, gloves, and heavy boots. They had need of none of it as they went down out of the sub. Even wearing just his uniform, Bond felt hot, almost to the point of sweating, and most of the crowd who had gathered at the quay to see them ashore was in shirtsleeves.

"Remember," MacDonald said as they walked down the quay flanked by two of their own men, and with four US Marines behind them. "This is an official visit–a ceremonial showing of face on behalf of that Queen and Country we were talking about. So we're on our best behavior–at least in public. Got it?"

"Scout's honor," Bond said. "I'll even leave the womenfolk alone."

"That'll be the day," MacDonald replied, then there was no more time for small talk.

Their destination was a converted warehouse at the far end of the docks. The first thing Bond noticed was the number of armed Marines guarding the facility–a dozen and more–and that was just the ones he saw. M had intimated that this was a civilian operation, but if it ever had been, it was now well and truly under American military jurisdiction. Bond's job to figure out whether anything nefarious was going on had just got that little bit tougher.

The second thing he noticed was the high glass dome that had been fitted to cover the whole far end of the warehouse–tall and handsome, like one of the large atriums at Kew Gardens. But this was on a much grander scale even than those; the structure dominated the skyline of the shoreline community, the glass catching the sunlight and gleaming, almost golden, giving it more of the appearance of a vast church or temple than of any scientific endeavor. Bond couldn't put a finger on it, but there was something not quite right, a subtle feeling, a vibration like a tuning fork struck in an empty room, a feeling that had him on edge before he even saw the interior of the building.

They were met, and shown inside, by an overly officious little man in a white coat; he had one of those bland, false smiles that Bond always distrusted on principle, and a handshake that was like holding a cold, dead trout. He introduced himself, looking particularly pleased to be making the announcement, as the lead scientist for the project, Samuel Kaminski. His smile quickly faded though, as if he had already lost interest in keeping up appearances, and even as they entered the warehouse he looked like he'd swallowed a lemon, obviously unhappy at having to show them around, as if the job was somehow beneath him.

He certainly showed as little enthusiasm for the task as he could politely get away with. Their tour of the administrative area at the near end of the facility was perfunctory to say the least–but then again, there wasn't much anyone could say about office furniture and filing cabinets to make them interesting. Bond was considering making his excuses and striking off for a look around on his own, but the US Marines were making sure that they stood in the doorways, none too subtly blocking any such activity. Kaminski droned on about efficiency savings and proper control systems while Bond wished for a drag at one of the Capstans from his pack.

Matters perked up considerably when they finally left the offices behind and went through into what Kaminski called the Main Hall. Only one thing spoiled it–it felt much warmer still in here, stiflingly so, and sweat ran down the back of Bond's neck under the uniform, making him itchy and even more irritable.

A glance around the hall was almost enough to make him forget the discomfort. It encompassed a huge barn of an area, easily the length and breadth of a football pitch, with steel walls and concrete floor. Everything in sight was brand new by the look of it–and the space was filled with blue crackling bolts of electricity that sparked and crawled around a jumble of tall spiral coils of brass and silver.

There were maybe thirty white-coated scientists on the ware- house floor. But the people were dwarfed under the main feature, the one thing that caught Bond's gaze and held it, almost hypnotically. A huge globe, fifteen yards across, made of what looked to be little more than gas, spun slowly just below the dome, green and blue and shimmering, as if someone had trapped the Northern Lights and caught them in a giant bubble. Even now, in the morning sunlight, the colors were almost too bright to look at directly, and the whole warehouse hummed and buzzed in an electrical drone that sounded like a choir with their voices muted, as if chanting into a wind. Bond also noticed that everyone in the group was now staring at the spinning globe, slightly slack jawed and wide eyed, as if trapped by its spell.

The Scotsman was first to, somewhat reluctantly, drag his gaze away. "Aye, it's very pretty and all that. But what in blazes is it?" MacDonald asked, echoing almost exactly what Bond had been thinking.

"It's an electrically neutral medium of unbound positive and negative particles," Kaminski said, and again he seemed inordinately proud of himself, until MacDonald spoke again.

"Aye–I can see that," he said dryly. "But what is it for?"

"It's a plasma–for want of a better word–we have succeeded in bringing a natural plasma–the aurora if you like–down to our level. We're drawing ionized particles from the upper atmosphere via the Tesla redactive effect," Kamninski said. "Once we have drawn them down with the coils you see around us, we contain them in a magnetic field, which alternately contracts and expands and, in doing so, provides us with a continuous flow of electrical energy."

"Oh," Macadam replied, with only the slightest hint of sarcasm. "Is that all?"

Bond managed to hold back a grin as Kaminski walked them over to stand under the spinning globe. The hum got louder, a vibration washing through them–it was not entirely pleasant, like a dentist's drill running along bone. Bond had to force himself to concentrate on what the scientist was saying.

"As you say, it looks very pretty. But it is much more than that–this may be one of the scientific discoveries of the century. What we have here is a completely new source of cheap energy," Kaminski said. "And it appears stable enough to be put into mass production across the planet."

It all sounded too pat, too rehearsed–and Kaminski, rather than giving the appearance of excitement you might expect from a man at the center of such a project–showed little more enthusiasm than he had when describing the filing system earlier. Bond was starting to smell a rat–and a bloody big one at that.

"What about the weather effects?" Bond asked.

"What weather effects?" Kaminski replied. His smile was almost as fake as his enthusiasm. "If you're talking about the unseasonal heat– that is just a local phenomenon, a peculiarity of this winter where the jet stream has been pushed north and east of us from its usual run, bringing warmer air up from the tropics. It has nothing to do with us or our experiment here, regardless of any gossip you might have heard to the contrary."

"And I've got a bridge in London I can sell you too," Bond said, but held his peace when that got him a sharp glance from MacDonald.

The globe spun slowly above them, and Bond felt it, as if it was a huge weight, ready to fall on them at any moment. He reached up his hand, intending to see if there was any reality in the sense of heaviness that he felt. Kaminski immediately reacted, stepped forward and pulled Bond's arm down.

"I would not suggest breaking the plasma boundary," the scientist said. "Have you ever seen a lightning rod being struck? The effects on a human body are rather more severe–we had a poor chap killed just a few weeks back trying the same thing."

"It was an accident then?" Bond said. "We heard there were suspicious circumstances."

Kaminski's smile never reached his eyes.

"It would only look suspicious to the uninitiated," he replied, and stared at Bond, as if the phrase should mean something. When he didn't get a response, the scientist turned away, and Bond realized that there had been a test, and he had just failed.

The rest of the day was more prosaic–they were given an extended tour of the remainder of the facility, but nothing they were shown matched the awe and strange splendor of that spinning globe under the dome. Kaminski led them among ranks of storage batteries that might well have been wonders of modern science inside, but was just row after row of squat, rather boring, gray boxes in a second warehouse adjoining the first. There were more US Marines on duty here too, all of them armed, none of them smiling. So far Bond had counted a total of twenty armed guards–that was a lot of firepower for something that worked so hard at pretending to be dull and ordinary.

The tour seemed to go on interminably and despite some probing, both of Kaminski and the accompanying scientists, Bond got nowhere with any of his questions. Kaminski in particular proved adept at fielding anything put his way, deflecting all answers into explanations of the science which were both dull and incomprehensible, a combination that had Bond again longing for a smoke and a drink long before the tour finally came to an end. He finally got his wish at lunchtime. They left the facility by the same door they had come in and were shown across the main square to the Excelsior Hotel. The sky was as clear and blue as any summer day, and once again Bond felt stifled and overly warm in his uniform–not as warm as it had been under the globe, but uncomfortably hot none the less. He looked forward to divesting himself of the uniform at the first chance he could get.

They stopped on the short flight of wooden steps that led up to the frontage of a hotel that had been there considerably longer than the warehouse opposite.

"We have arranged a quiet lunch to welcome you to Anchorage," Kaminski said with another smile that was anything but welcoming. "Several of your compatriots from the team will join you, and will answer any further questions that you might have. It was very nice to have met you both." And with that the scientist turned and walked away across the square. He took the Marine guards with him, leaving Bond and MacDonald alone on the hotel steps.

"I don't think he meant that, Jimmy. Do you?" the Scotsman said. He had obviously been of similar mind to Bond, for on entering the hotel, he made straight for the bar and ordered up doubles for each of them. Bond passed a Capstan, and lit them both up, old style, striking a match with his thumbnail.

They sucked strong smoke for a minute before MacDonald spoke again.

"Well, Jimmy, lad? Did we learn anything?"

"Only that Kaminski is a bit of a bastard–and that he's trying damned hard not to show that he's hiding something."

"Aye, I got that far myself. Yon big green ball fair gave me the willies though, I'll tell you that for nowt. If that's a power supply, then I'm bloody Harry Lauder."

Bond laughed.

"You don't have the legs for it. But you're right–I don't know what in blazes it is, but it's a damned sight more than a power unit–despite what they're saying."

"Did you spot anything else?" MacDonald said, helping himself to another of Bond's smokes and ordered them another double each. Bond was surprised to see that he'd finished off his drink without really noticing—being around Duncan MacDonald could have that effect, and Bond knew he'd have to watch himself- slipping into old habits might be seductive, but it wouldn't make for very efficient field work if he did.

"Not yet," he answered, not lifting the new drink straight away when it was put in front of him. "They were too bally careful by half. But I'll have a better look around on my own later, after dark."

"You did see all those Marines, didn't you?"

"They won't be a problem," Bond replied.

"Remember, Jimmy lad, best behavior. And I'd best watch your back a wee bit closer too—just in case."

They didn't get a chance to talk further—four men entered the bar and made straight for them, their accents on introducing themselves making it apparent that they were the 'compatriots' that Kaminski had mentioned. But despite their shared heritage, these four proved to be every bit as tight lipped as their superiors when it came to anything of any import. They were the least enthusiastic scientists Bond had ever met—normally men of this background couldn't be stopped from explaining, in the tiniest detail, their work and its importance. These four seemed more interested in talking about storage batteries and paperwork, and how much they missed black pudding and tea. They did agree that, yes, there had been an accident where one of their number died tragically, and they also agreed that some of the staff had been laid low—stress related issues seemed to be the official line. Beyond that, Bond got nothing out of them.

At least the air conditioning in the hotel was working—most definitely a plus, given that the temperature outside was still rising, showing no sign of abating for a while yet.

MacDonald had already finished off his drink and was ready for more. Bond declined anything stronger than a beer—it looked like the Scotsman was working himself up to a session, and Bond knew from long experience that could last for hours—hours of fun that he couldn't afford at the moment. The promised dinner was too-tough steak and more of the too-bland beer, and Bond excused himself from the dessert course to try the public bar at the front of the building, looking for someone who might have more to say than the scientists.

He found several more than willing drinking companions around a well-used dartboard–hardy, bearded types in clothes that had seen too many washes. He didn't have to ask to realize that these were local workmen. After dazzling them with his prowess at the game– a misspent youth had some advantages– then buying them a round of drinks, the men were only too happy to expound on the state of the weather–and the research facilities part in it.

"We thought it would be the making of the town," one of the men said as he chugged a beer down. "New jobs, good money– that's what we were promised anyway. But the warehouse was there already, all of the building work was contracted out in Vancouver, the workers are all scientists–and the guards are all Marines. We've seen precious little of any benefit from the damn place."

And it quickly became clear that the locals were far more certain than Kaminski of what was behind the current heat wave.

"It gets warmer every time they ramp the thing up," one old timer with a seemingly inexhaustible thirst for beer said. "First we get the humming, then the lights, then the singing–and then the weather goes funny. And every time it's the same story–local weather anomalies. Anomalies my ass. I've been here for sixty years and more and it was never like this before they came. If the folks in that building aren't doing it, you tell me what is?"

The old man's opinion was shared by all of the locals. Three men in the corner watched the conversation, didn't disagree, but left quickly when it was clear that feelings were running high against the research station; Bond guessed they were station workers on a day off. And he also guessed that Kaminski would be getting a report from them in the very near future. He was going to have to be careful not to blow his cover before he got a chance for a closer look at the site.

He bought more beer, asked more questions, but beyond suspicions and guesses got no more concrete answers for his trouble. He did however get an idea of the night guard operation, and a stern warning–from the old timer again–to stay well clear if he knew what was good for him.

"There's been a couple of inquisitive young un's gone in for a look around," he said. "They came back sure enough–but they came back wrong."

"How do you mean? Wrong in what way?"

"They're not quite living in the here and now, always distracted by

something or other; wrong in the head, mostly," the old man said. "And they get worse, just like the weather, every time the boogers ramp that damned machine up."
Bond had plenty to think about as he went back through to the dining room to find Duncan MacDonald.

He'd missed the Captain in the dining room–Bond had been longer in the bar than he'd realized and the dinner party had already left. It wasn't until he got back to the sub that he caught up with the Scotsman in his cabin.
"I thought we'd lost you," the Captain said. "I saw you at the dart board and then buying a round. I was mightily tempted to join you–those scientist lads are a dour sort, and not much for drinking. I did get one of them to let something slip though."
"You shouldn't be the one asking questions, Duncan," Bond said, helping himself to some Johnny Walker from a freshly opened bottle on the table. "You need to keep your nose clean on this–representative of Her Majesty, remember?"
The Scotsman smiled broadly.
"Then who would have your back, Jimmy, lad? Anyway, as I said I might have something. One of the four chaps was a newcomer–only been here a couple of days, but he thinks there's something rather dodgy going on–he caught me at the bar, and seemed a bit squirrelly, but smart enough, if you know what I mean? Anyway, he thinks that the experiments aren't all as up front as Kaminski would have us believe. He said that there's some moonlighting going on, as it were–in the early hours of the morning. There are hints that the show of force from the Marines is to protect these other, secret tests–and there's talk of it being a new kind of weapon–a stonking big weapon."
Bond answered with a thin smile of his own.
"I suspected as much from the beginning–M isn't in the habit of sending me half way round the world after an electrical supplier. And now there's all the more reason for me to have a closer look tonight."
"In that case I'm coming with you," MacDonald said.
"Not this time, Duncan. I work best alone–you know that. I'll be careful–I promise. I think this is merely a case of one hand of our Government not knowing what the other hand is up to. Somebody's in bed with the Yanks on this one, and if they haven't told M about it, there'll be hell to pay in the corridors of power. But I don't think

there's any real danger here."
"Famous last words," the Scotsman said, but didn't press Bond any further.

They spent the rest of the sultry afternoon trying to find respite from the heat–below decks was better, but the air felt too hot, too dry, and Bond was thankful when nightfall brought with it a lowering of the air temperature. Fog rose up from the bay and drifted over Anchorage, a strange light glowing through it where it picked up hints and washes of color from the glass dome of the research facility.
Bond changed clothes–black slacks, black roll-neck pullover and black, rubber-soled plimsoles. He pulled on a dark wool hat that could be pulled down into a Balaclava if required, and strapped his pistol in a holster below his left armpit. MacDonald came into his cabin just as Bond was making sure his cigarette case was filled, and raised an eyebrow when he saw the holster.
"These are friendlies, remember, Jimmy? Don't go shooting the Yanks–Her Majesty wouldn't like it."
"I'll keep that in mind," Bond replied. "And don't be such an old woman–you know how I operate; I always come back, don't I?"
"Just make sure you do. And before midnight too–that gives you five hours. Anything after that, I'll be coming in after you."
"Anything after that, and I'll let you," Bond replied with a grin. MacDonald walked through the sub with him, and went out onto the turret to see him off. The fog was getting ever thicker, so much so that most of the dock was now obscured. That suited Bond just fine; it would prove to be extra cover for what needed to be done. He shook MacDonald's hand as they parted.
"Don't drink my share of the Scotch–I'll be back before you know it."
The Scotsman returned his grip.
"Take care, Jimmy. I'm getting used to having you around again."
Bond nodded, and dropped silently off the boat and onto the quay.
Nobody saw him, nobody tried to stop him, and in a matter of minutes he had made his way out of the docks to arrive in an alley at the back of the second warehouse. A round of beers had bought him the fact that this was the least protected part of the facility; he was about to put that to the test.

Bond found a dark corner in the alleyway and pressed himself into it, pulling the Balaclava down over his face to better merge into the shadows. He wasn't sure he needed to hide at all, for the fog was rolling up into the streets of the town now, blanketing everything in a moist cotton wool that dampened all sound and hid all sins. Bond even felt hidden enough to have a smoke, although he was careful to cup the cigarette in his hand to avoid anyone detecting his inhalations.

The fog was hindering in some ways–even as it hid him in the corner, it also obscured the area between the high wire fence and the warehouse where the guards patrolled. He tried to time their passing, but every so often thicker fog rolled through and obliterated the scene in front of him entirely; he wasn't at all sure that he hadn't missed one of the patrols in the murk.

But lurking in corners wasn't getting him anywhere. He put out the cigarette, rubbing the butt to fragments between his fingers and blowing them away so as to leave no trace of his presence. He waited until the fog was at its thickest, then made for the high fence, climbing up and over with practiced ease to drop silently on the other side. A quick left to right check showed him that his entrance had gone unnoticed–nothing moved but the fog. Wasting no time, he ran for the rear of the warehouse. He was prepared to have to unlock a door or smash a window to gain entry but to his surprise the handle of the nearest entrance turned in his hand and the door swung silently open to allow him access. Either someone had been slack on the security check–or they just didn't care.

Or they're expecting me.

In any case, he was going in–that was why he was here. He stepped inside. The door shut with a soft click that sounded suddenly too loud now that he was out of the dampening effect of the fog. Only once he was sure that he had again gone unnoticed did he turn to have a first look around.

The long warehouse was only dimly lit with a high row of soft night lighting strung from the ceiling, but it was enough for him to see that he was alone among the long-ranked rows of batteries he'd been shown earlier. Whereas then they'd seemed like mere dull gray boxes, now, in the quiet dark, they seemed almost alive, as if expectantly waiting to be called into action. The air was filled with a constant drone, a hum that sounded almost musical, and there was a vibration beneath it that set Bond's teeth on edge and made his skin crawl. A haze hung in the air, as if he'd brought some of the fog in with him, but this mist was faint and glowed green and blue and yellow and cold, a rainbow aurora shimmering above and between the batteries.

Bond admonished himself for his too vivid imagination and hurried along the nearest row–he was sure there was nothing whatsoever to fear, but something about this area made him want to be clear of it as soon as he possibly could. He heard voices at the far end of the storage area where it adjoined the main part of the facility, so he headed quickly in that direction.

There was a great deal of activity in the other warehouse–he was able to see much of it through the window of an adjoining door. But his position was too exposed to be tenable for very long–all it would take would be for one person to approach the door or even just look in his direction and he'd be spotted immediately. He looked around for other options, and spotted a high metal gantry that ran around the whole circumference of the main warehouse some twenty feet off the floor. It was time for a calculated risk. He slipped through the door and quickly moved away from it to his left. The spinning globe of green plasma hung above an otherwise darkened floor area, and he was able to keep mostly to the shadows it generated as he sidled along the wall. His luck improved further when within ten yards he came to a set of steep stairs that led directly up onto the gantry walkway. He went up them quickly and a quick check left and right reassured him he had the walkway to himself. He inched forward until he had the best possible view of the proceedings down on the facility floor.

Now that night had fallen the full extent of the aurora created by the spinning globe could clearly be seen. The whole warehouse was a wash of shimmering color, an aurora brought low, but not tamed–it seemed to prowl the warehouse, like some caged beast. Bond had thought the hum and vibration from the ranks of batteries had been bad enough, but here in the main facility the effect was far worse; a deep throbbing pounded in his gut and his head span, giddy, as if he'd taken too much of MacDonald's Scotch. The vibration did not seem to bother the workers on the warehouse floor–they came and went, taking measurements, reading meters, making notes. It all seemed innocuous enough–scientists doing science, incomprehensible to the non-initiated, but Bond felt something else in his gut other than the throbbing–he'd been feeling it ever since they arrived in Anchorage–there was something off here, something wrong. But it looked like he was in for a long night on the gantry if he wanted to find out.

He found the least uncomfortable position on the walkway that afforded him a clear view, and tried to relax. What he really wanted– needed–was another smoke, and more of Macdonald's Johnny Walker. As he watched the scientists do their thing, he thought that it might not be too long before he could have both–it was looking more and more like his gut was wrong and that everything was as it appeared to be–an experiment–albeit a most peculiar one. He had just about convinced himself of that conclusion when the shimmering light glowed stronger than ever, sending a darker wash of olive green through the building. That was the signal for the workers to stop whatever they had been doing and gather in a rough circle below the spinning globe. Four workers wheeled in a gurney. On it sat a large, sharply angled stone about the size of a child, slightly longer and wider than it was tall–a dark polyhedron with many irregular flat surfaces that seemed to suck in the light. Thin red threadlike striations ran though it–once again Bond was reminded of blood, trails of it, dry now long after it had been spilled.

Bond inched as close to the edge of the gantry walkway as he dared to better see what was happening. The globe of light spun faster, and the green washes of color became deeper still, deeper yet somehow more vibrant, more bright. The vibration in his jaw and gut went up another level, and the gathered people on the warehouse floor set up a wordless chant that rose in the air and joined the swirling colors and the ever-growing hum. Wispy tendrils, scarcely of any more substance than the fog outside, trailed out from the southernmost aspect of the globe and wafted over the dark stone polyhedron. The assembled scientists moved closer. Their chant rose higher, echoing around Bond's position in the gantry, as they eagerly plunged their hands amid the color around the stone. More green fell out of the spinning globe, fell around the stone–the scientists washed themselves in it, taking it inside them, sucking it in, until all trace of the green was gone and there was only the dark stone once more.

The chant stopped. The globe slowed and the wash of color dimmed and settled, until once again it was only a faintest glimmer, one that cast the warehouse in shadow. Bond took the opportunity to stand and back away across the walkway so that he could not be seen from below should anyone inadvertently look up. It was only as he turned to make his escape that he found his way was now blocked.

Two burly Marines stood at the top of the staircase that led back down to the warehouse floor. Each was armed with a pistol that pointed directly at Bond's heart. But that wasn't what had got his pulse racing. When they raised their heads to look at him there was no white to their eyes–green color danced in there, as if their heads were full of the stuff.

They didn't speak, just motioned with their weapons that Bond should make for the stairs. He was trying to decide which one of them to attack first when he heard a soft whistle from behind the guards–two tones, one high, one low. He hadn't heard it for many years, but knew immediately what it was–and who had done it. As instructed, he went left. He dropped his shoulder and lunged–risky at the best of times, but the two men, although armed, hadn't shot first, so chances were they'd been instructed not to kill him. That gave Bond all the advantage he needed. He hit his man, hard, at the same instant as the guard finally decided to fire. He missed, but the sound of the shot rang long and loud in Bond's ears even as he put the man down with a punch to the gut then two to the chin.

By the time Bond stood up, MacDonald was making sure his own man stayed down by giving him a swift kick in the head.

"I told you I had your back, Jimmy, lad," the Scotsman said, and smiled. He was still smiling as the green color swirled up out of the body at his feet and danced around his legs, up to his waist before he could move, "What the hell is this?" he said, and that was all he had time for before the green was at his face, his mouth, diving inside him as he drew a sharp breath. Bond stepped forward, unsure what he could do to help.

But it was too late, both for the Scotsman and for Bond himself.

MacDonald's eyes filled up with green. Bond was about to swing a punch, intending to put the man down and drag him out of there. But as he did so he caught a glimmer of green from beneath him, and when he looked down it was to see swirling color rise up from the man he'd knocked out. Green fog rose up and filled him with a cold vibration that drove everything from his mind.

Bond went elsewhere.

Consciousness became little more than ragged fragments of quick cuts and meaningless scenes; for a very long time all Bond had were these snippets and dream sequences, and those he did remember were annoyances that disturbed his long languid dance in the green.
"Welcome, Commander Bond," Kaminski said as they stood beneath the spinning plasma. "Be one with the one and dance with us here." When Kaminski raised his hands to wash them in the glow from the stone, Bond joined him and felt the dance fill him, infuse into him, every bone and fiber of his being humming and singing and dancing in the green.
Later, Bond and MacDonald–they had other names now, but the old ones were still useful when dealing with those not yet green– returned to the submarine. As the sky sang and cavorted, those of the green shared its dance. Everyone was welcomed; everyone danced, all the way to Vancouver. That first leg of the trip took three days. Bond's cigarettes lay untouched on his bedside table, and the level of Scotch in the bottles of Johnny Walker did not drop. Those needs belonged to other people, people who had not known the dance, people not of the green. Now they were not required. The green provided, and was enough–was more than enough. The peace was deep, the calm unbroken–whatever the green wanted, Bond was prepared to give, if it meant he could keep dancing.

Bond and MacDonald left the sub in Vancouver, hid the dance deep inside so that it would not be seen before it was ready, and made their way to the airport for a trip that would take them back to Britain via Toronto and Halifax. They danced in the green all the way. When they reached London, the Scotsman and Bond parted company at Charing Cross Station. Bond was left alone in the green. But inside, he still danced.

In the early days after his return Bond traveled around London uncontested. He did not go to Whitehall, but spent his time moving between his flat in Knightsbridge and a site near Temple in the City. He worked–he must have worked hard, for in the evenings on his return he was always dirty, and dog-tired. He remembered nothing– nothing but the green and the dance. It was enough.

Once, two weeks after his return, he took a train out to Oxford and spent a weekend with a group of scientists. He met others of the green there, and it was always a joy to share the dance again whenever they were together. They called to the sky in an open field, and the sky sang for them, there under the stars. They all danced together.
Back to London, back to Temple. He worked. He was helping with the plan for the dance, not knowing his part in it, not knowing the final goal, only knowing that he danced, and that he mattered.
The dance grew stronger, and Bond felt peace in the green.

He had been back for a month before he noticed he was being followed–three men in a black Rover with a slight wobble in the front wheel on the passenger side. He saw it outside his flat, then again at the entrance to the Tube station. It was back outside his flat that evening when he got home. Even from inside the dance, deep in the green, he had enough left of his training to spot one of his own.
He was more circumspect after that. He didn't return to Knightsbridge the next night, but took digs near Liverpool Street Station in a dingy bedsitting room above a bar. There was to be no more use of public transport either. He walked down to Temple each morning to do his bit to serve the needs of the dance, returning to the bedsit only to sleep and to keep himself clean and tidy enough to pass muster out on the streets. He worked, harder than ever. Only the green kept him going–that, cheap sandwiches from street vendors in the city, and sleep so deep that he could scarcely distinguish between it and the dreams in the green. He took care going to and from the site in Temple, using all the trade craft he could muster to make himself small and invisible.

But it was to prove too little, too late–the damage had been done– MI6 was onto him, and they finally caught up outside the Bank of England on a wet morning as he was making his way to the Temple site. It was a standard pick up–one man stopped him and asked for a light while two came up from behind and held his arms–or at least tried to. Bond kneed the first man in the groin, hard enough to double him up, and enough that a kick to the head put him down. He swung, hard, to his left, dragging the man on the right off balance, tumbling into the third. Bond wriggled and went low–almost got clear, but the men were well trained and efficient–the heavy one fell on Bond as he tumbled, his weight keeping Bond pinned while the others regrouped. The same black Rover, wonky wheel and all, pulled up to the curb and Bond was bundled ignominiously into the boot. It smelled of diesel, but he didn't have long to worry about possible fumes– they pumped a syringe of something cloudy into the vein at the back of his hand, and the green started to fade as they rattled away and off through the London streets.

It had all been over in less than ten seconds. And ten seconds after that Bond was out for the count, lost in blackness.

There was no green, no more dancing.

He came out of it sometime later. He sat–hands tied tight behind him– on a hard chair in a damp room that was little more than four stone walls and an overhead light bulb. He knew immediately where he was– he'd been here often, standing where the man standing over him now stood–an underground cell, four floors below M's office in Whitehall. It was a place the public didn't want to know about, the place where bad men got asked questions until there were no more questions to ask.

They'd taken his shoes and socks–the stone floor felt bitterly cold under the soles of his feet–and stripped him down to his underwear, which was already soaked through with cold sweat. His jaw ached as if it had been recently punched and he tasted blood in his mouth, felt it run down the back of his throat from his nose. It seemed the interrogation had already started, but Bond couldn't bring himself to care.

"Where have you been, Bond?"

"What happened in Alaska?"

"Where is Captain MacDonald?"

Bond didn't answer any of them–he was somewhere deep in the green, lost to the dance. Nothing else mattered. The figure standing over him got increasingly frustrated.

"We can do this for as long as we want," the man said, and punched Bond, hard, in the gut.

Something flickered. A memory, a taste–two tastes actually, Johnny Walker and tobacco. Bond realized he wanted more of both. He looked up at the man standing over him.

"Hit me again," Bond whispered as the green flowed back, offering peace and calm if he would only forget. "Hit me harder."

The interrogator was only too happy to oblige. He smacked Bond in the face with his open palm, the jolt knocking Bond's head back. He tasted more blood.

The green faded away.

Bond wanted a smoke.

"Again," Bond said. "Harder. I'll tell you what I know–just keep hitting me."

The next blow was on his chin, rattling his jaw and sending a white flare of pain through his skull. It did the trick–Bond felt his head clear, lucid, for the first time in weeks.

"Get M in here, right now," he said. "This can't wait."

Before M could be fetched, Bond had to get them to hit him again. He saw confusion in the interrogator's eyes, but the man– scarcely more than a lad–did as he was told. He seemed to pull his punch slightly, but it proved at least enough to keep the green at bay for a time.

M stayed back in the doorway when he arrived, but he allowed Bond's hands to be untied so that he could have a smoke. The nicotine hit was immediate, threatening to take off the top of his head, but this was a floating sensation he knew how to control. The green was still there too, still lurking. But he knew its weakness now as well as he knew his own. He sucked on the smoke until the tip was red and glowing then, before anyone could stop him, applied it to his skin at his left wrist, at the tender point. He grimaced against the pain, but when he finally removed the cigarette from the burned circle of skin, he was fully himself. M had stepped further into the room to watch more closely.

He looked into Bond's eyes, and nodded, as if he'd seen something that pleased him.

"Would you mind telling me what in blazes is going on, Bond?" he said.

"It's a long story, sir, what little I can remember of it; I'll need you to fill in some stuff for me. But we'd best get the explanations over and done with fast–it's trouble. Big trouble."

It took some persuasion on Bond's part, but they eventually let him get dressed and get out of the cell. He made his way upstairs to the relative comfort of M's office. Two armed guards with pistols in hand stood at the door while M poured them both a stiff measure of the MacAllan.

"After your report, we waited for you to come back," M said as he handed over the glass. "But you never did."

Bond knocked back the Scotch in one gulp, feeling the heat run down to his gut, chasing any remnant of the green away. He held the empty glass out and M poured another without any retort. Bond sipped at the second one while trying to decide what to tell his superior.

"I made a report?" he asked to buy himself more time. M nodded, and after getting his pipe lit, continued.

"You said there was nothing to worry about, that it had all been a big misunderstanding, and that you'd brief me on your return. Then you and MacDonald buggered off with the CONFESSOR. We thought we'd found you at your flat, but of course you gave us the slip and we didn't hear another peep–until you were spotted near Bank tube station on Monday. I had you brought in, you let us punch you around a bit until that green shit was gone from your eyes–and now you're here, drinking my Scotch. That's as much as I know–now it's your turn."

Before answering Bond took a smoke from the box on M's desk and lit it with a match. When he wasn't chewing on his pipe, M favored long Black Russian cigarettes that produced an almost toxic level of nicotine–just what Bond needed at the moment. He sucked it down greedily, and extinguished the match by placing it on the skin on his wrist next to the existing burn. The pain was white hot–but far preferable to the alternative. The green was still there, still dancing, somewhere deep inside him–he could feel it. And it was insidious, offering him something he couldn't admit that he desired, calling him back to the dance.

"007?" M said sharply, and Bond dragged himself out of the fugue. He pressed his right thumb on the burns, bringing a fresh flare of pain.

"I'm okay, sir. I have it under control."

"I would be happier if I knew what you were talking about in the first place," M replied, but relaxed back in his chair, puffing away at his pipe as Bond started his story.

It took some time. He laid out the tale of what had happened in Alaska, and as much–which in truth was very little–of what he knew of his time back in London. When he mentioned Oxford and his weekend there, M had him stop for as long as it took to make a call and get a team sent out West. Bond had another smoke lit–and another burn mark at his wrist, by the time the call was done.

"Captain MacDonald?" M asked when he settled back in his chair. "Any idea where he might have gone?"

"Last I saw of him was at Charing Cross–I have the impression he was heading north–going home. I'd like permission to go after him, sir."

"I'll consider it," M said gruffly. Bond got the feeling that he was being appraised, that M was testing him out to see if he was ready–and capable–of being put to work. "What about the business at Temple? What were you up to?"

"Not a clue, there, sir. I spent a lot of time in manual labor–I know that much–I moved a lot of stone of some sort, and I was in some kind of vaulted chamber. But the city is riddled with such underground structures–it'll be like looking for a needle in a haystack."

"I have three teams on it," M replied. "We'll get to the bottom of it. We'll have to–if what you say happened in Alaska is true. Some kind of bally mind control on a mass scale if I'm not mistaken. Any idea what we're looking at? Is it Soviet?"

Bond shook his head.

"Further away by far, sir. As you know there's been rumors and loose talk for years that the Yanks have had contact with something from out in space. I think that's what we're dealing with here–they pulled it down from the sky, and we are as alien to it, as it is to us."

"What does it want, man?"

Bond shrugged. "That's not clear yet. Has anything happened in Alaska while I was out of it?"

"Apart from it getting dashed hot over there, and more reports of the strange aurora, it's all been bally quiet. And now that I've heard your story–I think it might be too quiet. But don't you worry about that–I'll get the Yanks onto it."

"We have to find our sub–and our best chance at that seems to be in you finding its Captain. Are you sure you're up to it, 007? I must admit I'm loath to send you back out into the field–I'm not a hundred per cent sure that you're trustworthy in this matter."

Bond pressed his thumb against the burn on his wrist and grimaced before answering.

"I'm all you've got, sir. I know how this thing does what it does–I know the taste and the smell of it; I'm the only one who does. Besides, it's Duncan. I owe it to him, if nothing else."

M nodded. "Just try to find out what you've both been up to since you came back from Alaska—and where you've parked that bloody submarine. That's the most important thing right now. Moneypenny will get you on a first train north. I want reports twice a day, Bond. If you go off the grid again, we'll be forced to take you out of the game for good. Do you understand me?"

Bond understood only too well.

Bond's train booking meant that he had no time to even go back to Knightsbridge. He had a shower in the basement locker room, and changed into a spare dark wool suit he kept there for just such purposes—along with a pack of Chestertons, a box of matches, a new holster and pistol, and a sheathed knife that he strapped to his ankle. Once fully dressed he felt much more like his old self, and he found that by pressing firmly on the fresh burn every few minutes he was able to keep the allure of the green far enough at bay to be able to ignore it completely.

Moneypenny hadn't needed to be asked his destination—she was good enough at her job—and knew his history well enough—to send him where he needed to go. He caught a cab up to Kings Cross and half an hour later was settled in a first-class compartment on a train heading for Edinburgh—four hundred miles and almost twenty years ago away. He smiled when he looked up—a suitcase, his own suitcase from the flat in Knightsbridge—was already in the rack above his head; Moneypenny had showed her worth yet again.

It being a weekday afternoon, it was quiet—he had the carriage to himself for most of the journey and got through half of the Chestertons before the train pulled into Waverley Station. He also had some new burns on his wrist, but he was able to cover then up with his shirt and jacket, and although he could still feel it dancing somewhere deep down inside him, the green stayed at bay.

It was mid evening by the time he checked in to the North British Hotel above the station under one of the Universal Exports cover names. After a wash and shave he treated himself to a quick supper of oysters and Bollinger, neither of which were as good as they could have been, but which did more than enough to restore his palate after the abstinence of the last few weeks. What with that, the smokes, and the fact that the green now seemed to have faded almost completely he felt back to his old self as he went out into the city, into his past, looking for a lost friend.

His search began in the Cafe Royal–the old ornate bar hadn't changed despite his many years' absence, but the clientele was too young for MacDonald–or Bond himself for that matter–to feel comfortable there for any length of time. Bond didn't even wait to be served a drink for old time's sake–he turned on his heel and left in search of something closer to an old sailor's tastes.

He spent the rest of the night visiting a series of bars and clubs in the old part of town–MacDonald's favorite place in the word he'd always said. He didn't find anyone that knew the Captain, but, posing as an old friend in town unexpectedly, Bond left his card, and a few pound notes, with the barmen, ensuring that word would be spread. He visited a dozen bars in all, but as they started closing for the night he was no closer to finding his friend.

It was midnight by the time he got back to the North British, and although he felt tiredness wash over him he refused to give himself to sleep lest the green creep back and overwhelm him unexpectedly. He sat fully clothed in a chair by the window–he had a bottle of Laphroaig sent up, and he sipped at it, smoking, and playing solitaire with a tattered pack of cards while looking out over Princes Street and the old castle beyond. Light played on the crags and old stone, silver and white as the moon shimmered, alternately veiled in thin cloud, or exposed fully to beam down the cobbled parade of the Royal Mile. Bond only had to burn his wrist once over the course of the night– but even than he was almost too late. He looked up from a losing game as he shuffled the cards–and saw the old castle bathed, not in silver but in shimmering, dancing green, the sky above threaded with crimson filaments–dried bloody trails through the stars leeching from a blood red moon. Without conscious thought he stood, too fast, knocking the chair over with a loud thud. It was only the cigarette in his hand that brought him out of the fugue–it had burned down far enough to scorch the skin between his fingers when he moved. The sudden jab of fresh pain did the trick–Bond stabbed the stub of the smoke into his wrist, hard, angry at himself for falling into a doze. The pain swelled and flared–and once again the green faded and retreated. When Bond looked out the window it was to see silver moonlight washing over the castle rock. That was as close to sleep as he allowed himself to come in what proved to be a very long night indeed.

A shower did little to improve his mood in the morning. The jet of water stung at his new burns, and was too tepid to make him feel fully cleansed afterwards. He decided against dressing in the wool suit–he had a feeling that something more rugged might be required if he was successful in finding MacDonald.
Moneypenny had also second-guessed him here too–he left the room wearing a dark tweed overcoat above a black sweater and slacks. The weight of his pistol felt snug and comforting where it nestled under his left arm; that single small feeling of familiarity did much to anchor him in the here and now, away from the green, apart from the dance.
The phone rang as he was about to leave the room–it was a report from M on a scrambled line, and it wasn't good news– Leiter had led his team to Anchorage, but the site had been cleared and the warehouse emptied–there was nothing to find. And MI6 had no better luck in Oxford–there was no trace that anything untoward had ever happened. The scientists Bond had met there– and the green with them–had gone to ground. M was none too happy to hear that Bond, so far at least, had no better luck with his own search. Bond felt slightly better still on receiving a note from the receptionist as he went down to breakfast. The pound notes he'd distributed in the bars the night before had indeed paid off. The note wasn't a report of the whereabouts of his friend Duncan MacDonald–but it was the next best thing. A submarine had been spotted heading up the Firth to Rosyth–a vessel that glowed, a strange, green glow that seemed to dance and shimmer in the night.
After a quick breakfast of just coffee, a smoke and some too-dry toast, Bond headed down to the railway station. He had a lead. He only hoped he'd be on time to do something about it.

If he'd thought seriously about it, Rosyth should have come to mind sooner. Bond and MacDonald been billeted here back in the old days–it was where they had first met, first shared a smoke and a drink, first realized that they were fellow travelers, forging a bond that would last through many scrapes and dangers. If the green hadn't had him so befuddled, it would have been Bond's first instinct to head to the old port.

When he arrived on the quayside mid-morning he found that the dock hadn't changed a great deal since his days in the service–there were more merchant boats now and fewer of Royal Navy vessels, but it was still busy–thriving even. And he'd found what he was looking for– one part of it at least–the CONFESSOR lay docked at the main quay. In the thin morning sunlight it looked like any other vessel, but even from his vantage in a disused warehouse some one hundred yards north of the quay Bond felt the vibration and hum. It buzzed in the soles of his feet, thrummed up his spine, echoed in his head, offering peace and joy in the dance. He had to press his thumb, hard against his burns, causing the ravaged flesh to weep thin watery blood. The pain cleared his head again, enough to let him take note of what was happening down on the dock.

Crates, each four feet on the longest side, and a great many of them, were being brought out of the vessel and put in the back of a line of trucks waiting on the quayside. Bond watched for several hours, and still crates were being brought up out of the sub–he now understood why Leiter hadn't found anything in Anchorage. At one point a darker cloud obscured the sun for a minute and Bond saw a faint– but definite–aurora of green haze hang over the quay, mostly directly above the boxes going into the trucks.

Over the course of the next ten minutes he crept as close as he could to the trucks–nobody spotted him or tried to stop him–in fact, the loaders of the trucks seemed singularly intent on their purpose. Bond thought he knew why–they, as he had been–were lost, deep in the green, lost in the dance. Whatever was going on–it was spreading.

There was no sign of MacDonald, but Bond knew that his mission was more now than just finding his friend–he had to know just where these crates were going–and why. As the last of the crates were brought up out of the sub and loaded, Bond crept alongside the line of trucks and pulled himself into the rear, dragging a tarpaulin down to cover his body.

The trucks set off minutes later. Once they were moving Bond was able to take a chance and open one of the crates. He had to use the knife from his ankle-sheath, and he had to put a lot of pressure on the lid to force it open. And once he had done so, and had a quick look inside, he closed it again immediately. A chrome and brass coil–probably one of the same ones he had seen on the warehouse floor in Alaska–lay in the box like some sleeping pet. It hummed and buzzed and somehow seemed alive, giving off a distinct shimmer of green aurora that was faintly visible even after the crate was resealed.

Bond kept as far away from it as he could get, sitting at the rear of the truck with the tarpaulin lifted just enough to allow passage of air. He had to press constantly against the wounded flesh of his wrist, welcoming the pain and the clarity it brought him, for the green was strong here, and in danger of overwhelming him all over again.

Fortunately, the journey was a short one. Scarcely ten minutes after leaving the dock the trucks pulled to a halt. Bond heard the distinctive, unmistakable sound of a large steam locomotive, and by process of elimination hazarded a guess that they had pulled into a goods yard at Dunfermline Railway Station. He chanced a look out of the gap in the tarpaulin; the first thing he saw was one of the trucks, already being unloaded and the crates getting neatly stacked in a long carriage, one of twenty or more attached to the chugging locomotive.

He slipped silently out of the truck–once again the guards were not doing much in the way of actual guarding of any note, seemingly completely focused on the task of getting the crates onto the train. Bond was able to find a safe spot behind a coal bunker from which he could watch proceedings.

It was clear that they were preparing the goods train for transport of the crates–and they were doing it quickly, with a score or more workers tirelessly employed in the task of shifting crates into carriages. If Bond was right, and the coil he had looked at had indeed come from Alaska, then it looked like the whole content of the warehouse–and probably even the stacks of batteries–were now here in the crates, having been transported on the sub.

So now he knew what–but he still had no clue as to why.

Five minutes later he saw an instantly recognizable figure walk along the tracks–Duncan MacDonald seemed to be in charge of the loading. The Scotsman made his way to the front of the train and entered a passenger carriage that had been hooked up just behind the tender. Bond looked around–nobody was paying the least attention to him. He jogged quickly over to the train, took his pistol from its holster, and stepped up into the carriage.

Any hope he'd had of getting MacDonald alone was immediately quashed–it was gloomy inside the carriage and Bond's sight didn't quite adapt quickly enough as two burly figures approached from his left. He saw green where there should be white in their eyes. He fired, twice, getting one of the attackers full in the chest–he hoped he hadn't just shot MacDonald. Then there was no time for thought as the second attacker barreled into him and caught him, tight, in a bear hug, slamming Bond back against the wall. Bond cracked the pistol against his opponent's skull, over and over but the man's grip refused to lessen, and a gray mist–tinged with green–started to seep into Bond's mind. He only had seconds of consciousness left before he'd be lost again. He didn't want to do it–he knew his attackers were not themselves, knew they were under the influence of the green. But self-preservation won out. He twisted the pistol in his hand, turned his head away, and blew a hole in the side of the man's head.

The pressure on his chest immediately lessened, and Bond stepped aside as the body fell to the floor. A wisp of green, almost smoky, rose up. Bond held his breath and rubbed at the burn on his wrist as the shimmer dissipated and broke apart in a light breeze.

Bond finally remembered to breathe.

The first man he'd shot lay on the floor, not moving. Bond stepped toward the body, thinking to check for life, just as the carriage lights came full on.

Duncan MacDonald stood at the far end of what was obviously a club compartment for the better off traveler–all mahogany fittings and leather chairs. Bond might even have felt at home– had it not been for the green that shone in the Scotsman's eyes when he spoke.

"Jimmy, lad. Jimmy, lad. What are we going to do with you?"

Bond didn't hesitate. He stepped forward, and shot his friend, just once, high in the left shoulder. MacDonald stumbled, but didn't fall, and was still upright when Bond reached him. The green faded from the Scotsman's eyes.

"That's it, Duncan," Bond said, holstering his weapon and taking the man by the shoulders so that he could stare into his eyes. "Use the pain. Fight it, man. You can beat this thing."
The Scotsman grimaced, put a hand to his shoulder and showed Bond the bloody fingers when he lifted them away from the wound. His eyes were clear, white showing around the pupils as he spoke again. "You've got it all arse over tits as usual, Jimmy. Why would I want to beat it? Peace and quiet, no fighting, no war, just calm and dancing, forever and always? You cannae beat it." Green mist swirled, filling the Scotsman's eyes, and he smiled. "You'll see, Jimmy lad. You'll see soon enough. I've got your back."
The carriage door behind the Scotsman opened, and the scientist, Kaminski came through, with two more armed guards. When MacDonald reached for Bond's weapon, Bond let him take it. Fighting now risked getting them both killed, and he wasn't ready to give up on his best friend.
Not yet.

They didn't tie him up, and they let him sit in one of the club armchairs–they even allowed him to smoke and poured him a drink–some smooth single malt–from a well-stocked cabinet on the long side of the carriage across from Bond. And although they kept his pistol they didn't search him, and he still had the knife in the sheath at his ankle. It seemed that Duncan might be happy in the green, but it had certainly robbed him of much of his sense.
They had cleared the two dead men out of the carriage–there was still the faintest hint of green miasma above the floor where they had fallen. But, as yet anyway, the green inside Bond was still held at bay by the simple act of rubbing a thumb on the burns on his wrist.
"You will need to sleep sometime, Mr. Bond," Kaminski said. He sat on the opposite side of the carriage from Bond in another of the armchairs.
MacDonald completed a threesome in a third chair. Now that the lights were up, there was no sign of green in either of the men's eyes–but Bond didn't have to see it to know it was there. "I'm not in the slightest bit tired," Bond replied casually. "But if you have something to be getting on with, don't mind me."

He heard the sounds of carriage doors being shut along the length of

the train, and the huff and puff of the locomotive engine as it worked up a head of steam. They were making preparations to get underway.
"I take it Alaska was too cold for you?" Bond said, lighting up a fresh smoke. Normally MacDonald would be joining him– but his old friend was far from being normal. Bond had shot him in the shoulder mere minutes before but if the man was in any discomfort at all, he didn't show it. He hadn't had any medical attention since taking the wound, but there was no sign of blooding, and he did not seem to be in any pain.
Kaminski eventually answered Bond's question.
"What do you think, Mr. Bond? After all, you were with us in the dance all that time, and did your duty, as we all have. Surely you retain some hint of what is to come?"
Bond laughed. "If all you are about is digging around in musty vaults, then I may as well go home, for there is nothing for anyone to worry about."
"Jimmy, lad," MacDonald replied. "There's definitely nothing to worry about–I told you that already. But you'll see soon enough. The whole world will see–Alaska was merely a test run. What happens in London will bring the dance to you all."
Before Bond could ask another question, the train lurched violently, then started to move, gaining speed as it headed out of the goods yard. Kaminski rose without another word, and taking the armed guards with him left Bond and MacDonald alone in the carriage.
Bond blew smoke at his friend.
"So, London then, Duncan? A trip to Soho then back to the club for canasta and a cigar is it? Maybe take in a show?"
The Scotsman laughed lightly. "Oh, there'll be a show all right, Jimmy. A show such as this country–this planet–has never seen. The last dance, if you like?"
"I don't like. Come on, man–use your brain–fight this nonsense," Bond said. He crossed his legs, as casually as he could manage, bringing the sheathed knife within reach of his right hand as he continued. "Get it out your system and let's have a smoke and a drink and stop it, right here, right now."
MacDonald laughed again.
"I've already told you, Jimmy–I like it this way–and I think most right-minded people will agree with me; there will be no aggression, no war. We will all, every one of us, be at peace in the green, all

equal, all free from worry, free to dance."

"That sounds suspiciously like the kind of thing we've been fighting against since we were boys, Duncan," Bond replied. He slid a hand under his trouser leg and freed the blade, feeling the weight of it nestle in his hand.

"If it is, then I regret every minute I spent in that fight," the Scotsman replied.

"And I regret having to do this," Bond said.

With one smooth movement he drew back the knife and threw it, straight and fast, hitting MacDonald high on the shoulder near the bullet wound, getting up out of the chair even as the blade met its target.

The Scotsman didn't flinch. He pulled the knife out–the last inch was bloody–and let it drop to the floor even as Bond was on him. Bond threw a left hook and a right jab, both hitting their target, but still MacDonald barely registered the blows. Bond stepped closer and stuck a thumb in the man's wounded shoulder, and this time he saw a grimace of pain in the Scotsman's face. He dug his hold in deeper.

"Come on, Duncan. Fight it. Fight it for me."

MacDonald smiled, and took Bond by the shoulders. The pair grappled, like kids in a playground, staggering backward and forward across the swaying carriage as the train shuddered and slowed, coming to a halt. Bond kept digging at the fresh wound with his thumb. There was no green in his opponent's eyes, and there were signs of pain in his eyes and at his mouth, but he did not stop fighting against Bond.

"Just like old times, Jimmy lad," the Scotsman said as he tried to trip Bond, sending them both staggering, almost falling.

"Not quite," Bond replied. He took advantage of their slight loss of balance and heaved them both toward the rear of the carriage. "This time, I've got your back."

They hit the carriage door, hard and continued on through it to fall, still wrestling, into the space between the cars. Bond's back hit the guardrail to their left, and their weight was enough for it crumple behind them as they tumbled the four feet down onto the side of the track. They turned during the fall itself, such that the Scotsman took the brunt of the impact on the rough stone and gravel. But if it pained him at all he didn't show it–for a man that had been shot, stabbed then slammed to the ground he still had a remarkable amount of fight in him. The pair of them rolled and tumbled, each looking for the grip that would bring the fight to a swift end.

After several frantic seconds it was MacDonald who gave way. He went limp under Bond and stopped struggling.

"Okay. Uncle. You've got me."

At that same moment the train above them got underway again, and Bond, for the first time, noticed where they had stopped. They were on the Forth Bridge, high above the river, the train obviously having come to a halt at the points before the small passenger station at South Queensferry. And now the locomotive was on the move, picking up speed fast.

MacDonald still lay on the gravel, and he laughed when he looked up at Bond.

"This is an apt spot, don't you think? A symbol of all you are fighting to keep hold of–the might and strength of the old Empire. But think on it, Jimmy–how long will it really last–it's already rusting. It will be long gone in just a few short years. And we will still be here, in the green, in the dance, while the very planet itself goes cold and turns round a dying sun, we will still be here, dancing, lost in the green."

Bond saw it in the man's eyes again, the misty flow and swirl of it as it filled him. He had lost his friend–and was in danger of losing everything as the train picked up speed, heading off across the bridge. If he lost it now he might never find it again.

The Scotsman saw him looking.

"So what's it to be, Jimmy lad? Are you going to keep battering me to try to save my soul–or are you going to do your duty and get after yon train?"

"A bit of both, if you're lucky," Bond replied, and hauled the man to his feet.

In the end they had to run alongside the carriage for long seconds before finally pulling themselves back up and into the compartment, falling, panting heavily, on the floor. Kaminski stood, looking down at Bond, smiling, the green dancing in his eyes.

"Welcome back, Mr. Bond. Nice of you to drop in."

It proved to be the start of a long, long afternoon and evening. The train picked up speed near Edinburgh, then headed southward with no sign of slowing for any station stops–London again was Bond's best guess at the destination. He was left in the club carriage with the two guards, neither of whom showed any desire for communication. Bond's knife and pistol were sitting on top of a bureau in the far corner, but the guards had pistols of their own trained on him the whole time– MacDonald might have allowed him some leeway, but these two looked like they meant business. Bond sat in the same armchair as before, smoking a succession of cigarettes–the smokes had survived the rough and tumble at the Forth Bridge, although several were bent and misshapen. He smoked them anyway, and when they got down to the butt he ground them out on the flesh at his wrist. The guards didn't stop him when he went to the drinks cabinet and poured a stiff measure of Scotch–he limited himself to just the one, aware that drinking and smoking on an empty stomach wasn't going to do much to help his levels of alertness if they were needed.

He had plenty of time to ponder the earlier events. He was at a loss to explain Duncan MacDonald's behavior–if it had been him he'd have had no hesitation at taking a chance to leave the influence of the green–the fresh burns on his wrist were testament to that fact. The friend he knew–the man he thought he'd known– was not a blind follower, not a creature of faith. So what was it about the green that MacDonald found so damned alluring? Bond still hadn't formed any firm conclusions as the light went from the sky in late afternoon and dusk fell.

It was only then that he spotted it–a faint, but definitely present luminescent green that hung in the air everywhere he looked. He rose and went to look out of the nearest window–the guards' grip tightened on their pistols, but they didn't stop him as he pressed his nose to the glass. The shimmering was even more distinct outside. It looked as if the whole carriage–possibly the whole train–trailed green phosphorescence in its wake. Indeed as they turned into a long curve Bond saw the locomotive at the front streaming green, glowing, smoke in a high plume as it snaked through the countryside like a fire breathing serpent from some long-forgotten myth.

He didn't see MacDonald again until later in the evening as the train slowed to make its way through the numerous sets of junctions and points needed to traverse London. The Scotsman entered carrying a plate of sandwiches, and handed them to Bond– white bread and stale cheese, but Bond wolfed it down, suddenly aware how hungry he had become.

MacDonald laughed.

"That's a boy, Jimmy. Get it down you–you'll need your strength, for it's going to be a long night."

"Where are we headed?" Bond asked as he finished off the last sandwich.

"The same place where you spent your time in the dance," MacDonald replied. "I hear you did a fine job getting the place ready. Remember that symbol I was talking of back at the bridge? Well we've found an even better one. And later the world will see just how petty and impermanent the works of man can be. Tonight we shall all dance in the green."

"Nobody really talks like that, you know?" Bond said, trying to get a rise from the man–and failing, for MacDonald merely smiled.

"You'll see. You'll all see, soon enough."

The Scotsman showed no sign of discomfort from the wounds in his shoulder. Bond considered tackling him again, having another try at bringing the man to his senses, but he was coming to understand that his old friend wasn't actually under any kind of involuntary influence–and that would make any attempt at separating him from the green that much more difficult. Bond was on the inside now– and it was probably for the best that he stayed there, at least for as long as it took to get to the bottom of whatever plan had been hatched.

The train came to a halt around eight o'clock. Bond tried to peer out the window to get his bearings, but they had stopped in a tunnel, all he could see was red brick and green luminescence. Just judging from the time it had taken, and the lines they had crossed, he knew they had to be somewhere in central London– and still on the north side of the river, for they had not crossed any bridges. And given that he had his vague memories of rooting around in the vaults near Temple, he could hazard a good guess that they were in that general area. It was enough to be going on with, for now. They sat there for some time as the sounds of carriages being emptied and doors slamming echoed around them before eventually going quiet almost an hour after the train had come to a halt.

"So, what now?" Bond said as MacDonald stood up.

"Now we go and dance in the green," the Scotsman replied. "You are welcome to join us–but only if you dance."

Bond smiled thinly and lit up a new smoke. "I'll sit this one out, thanks anyway," he replied.

"That's up to you, Jimmy lad–but you'll change your tune later, when London–and the world–sees what we can accomplish together."

"Go on, surprise me," Bond said. "What's the big show going to be?"

MacDonald tapped the side of his nose.

"That's for us to know and you to find out. Patience, Jimmy– it'll all be clear soon."

"Fight it, Duncan," Bond said. "No good will come of this."

MacDonald smiled again, turned his back, and left the carriage. Bond realized that he'd never seen the Scotsman in such good humor for so long a length of time.

He waited for the time it took him to finish the smoke to see if the guard on him would be relaxed now that they had reached their destination, but the two armed men still stood between him and the door, each with a weapon in hand. Bond stood, showed them his empty glass, raised an eyebrow, and motioned toward the drink cabinet. Neither of the men so much as twitched, so Bond stepped across the compartment and poured himself a large Scotch. He kept the bottle in his right hand as he poured, then downed the liquor in one gulp. Without any pause he threw the glass in one smooth continuous motion at the nearest guard, at the same time jumping forward, bottle raised, aiming for the other.

They were caught completely unawares. The glass distracted the nearest one as he raised his weapon to swat it away. That also gave Bond enough time to step forward and smack the bottle on the other one's head, twice before it broke, but more than enough to drop the man insensate to the floor. He turned just as the first guard regained his composure and raised his weapon. Bond was close enough to knock it away with his left hand and step inside, bringing the jagged shards of the bottle down and into the man's neck, severing the jugular as he pushed it home.

Blood spurted and the man fell away. Even before he hit the floor a wash of shimmering green rose from the body and hung in the air. Bond held his breath, dropped what little was left of the whisky bottle, and pushed his thumb, hard, into the burned flesh of his wrist as he felt his head spin and float, felt the green inside him surge and sing. The pain brought clarity, of a sort.

He was able to step over to the second, unconscious guard and snap his neck; he couldn't afford to leave anyone alive who might give him away. Taking the two pistols—one in hand, one in his overcoat pocket—Bond stepped out of the carriage and finally felt able to take a breath.

He climbed down onto the tracks alongside the carriages, looking along what was obviously an old railway tunnel of some age—Victorian at a guess, and not used much in the intervening years. There was no sound save the ticking and cooling of the locomotive engine, and no movement apart from swaying shadows where a line of naked bulbs strung overhead swayed in the slightest of breezes.
The breeze seemed to be coming from Bond's left, so he headed in that direction, keeping close to the carriages in case he had to duck under quickly. As it turned out he didn't need the stealth as it seemed he was the only person in the tunnel. The breeze got slightly stronger as he went further along, and when he reached its source—a passageway leading off and up to the right—he heard faint murmuring, as of voices in the distance, and felt again the wash and flow of the green surge inside him. It was getting stronger, and he lit a smoke just to etch a new circular burn on his wrist before heading into the tunnel offshoot.
The air was warmer in here, damper too, carrying with it the smell of the river, a smell that thickened as he kept going up a slight incline. The brickwork was recent—very recent, as was the floor underfoot, and Bond had a flash of memory as he came to a set of stairs—he'd put down some of these stones himself, while he was deep in the green. Whatever his destination, it seemed he was getting close.
The sounds from above got louder as he ascended—a hollow, echoing sound that told him the passage was going to open up into a larger space. He slowed, checked that the pistol he carried was loaded, and, keeping to the walls as much as possible, crept silently up the last short set of steps to look out over what was indeed a much bigger chamber.
And again it was a space that he half-recognized. It had until recently been a vault—a crypt of sorts judging by the stone coffins and carved stonework. But all that was old about the site had been shifted right back against the walls to make way for the long ranks of gray batteries—probably the very same ones Bond had walked among in Anchorage. What he had taken for murmuring or talking had been in fact the hum

and throb of the gathered boxes. The sound filled the vault and, along with a recurrence of the glimmer and gauze of the green aurora, once again threatened to wash Bond away into the dance until he jabbed his thumb, hard into the new burns on his arm. His wrist was starting to look like a lump of steak that had been cooked too fast, charred on the outside, red and weeping where cracks showed in the skin. The pain was almost unbearable–but it was better than the alternative.

Bond set his gaze straight at a set of stairs at the far end of the vault– there was a wash of light coming down from there, and the breeze, what there was of it, seemed to originate in that direction. Besides– it seemed to be the only way out apart from going back down to the train, and he'd had enough of sulking in tunnels for one night.
He made his way quickly through the batteries. The green inside him rose and sank as if in time to a beat only it could hear. He felt light-headed, as if he might float away at any second, and his footsteps fell into the same rhythm as the swell of the green inside. Bond had partaken of –or been forced to take–many drugs, licit and illicit, over the years, but he'd never felt an effect as strong, as alluring as this. He heard the high chant rise up inside him, saw a green miasma wash over the ranks of batteries.
If it had been any further than a few more yards to the stairs, he would never have made it. He hit the steps at a run, and got halfway up a flight of thirty before realizing that bursting out into another open area might not be wise. At least here in the passageway the effect was drastically lessened, and he was able to pause, catch his breath and, by pressing against the burns again and again, regain some of his calm and composure. He still felt the green though, swimming around inside him, filling up all the empty places. He was starting to understand how MacDonald could find it so compelling. But understanding and agreeing were two different things–Bond wouldn't–couldn't–give in to the call; it went too far against everything he believed in.
He took a tighter grip on the pistol and inched up the steps in the passageway to see what he could do about it.
It was only as he neared the top that he realized where he was. The passageway opened out into a huge open area inside a building. Wooden pews and benches had all been moved against the walls to make way for the coils and generators familiar from the experiment

in Alaska–but it was on looking up that Bond finally understood what MacDonald had meant about a symbol.
The equipment had been set up under the huge span of the dome of St Paul's Cathedral, and high up there, almost dead center and hanging in space, a globe hung–only basketball sized, but already growing–shimmering, green, spinning and dancing.

There was plenty of activity on the wide expanse of floor of the cathedral beneath the green–white coated scientists scurried among valves and coils, electricity sparked and hummed, and the old stone walls seemed to thrum and shiver in anticipation of what was to come. There was no sign of MacDonald though–or Kaminski for that matter–and Bond had business to finish with both of them before the job was done. He sidled around the wall in what shadows he could make use of–but nobody was paying too much attention–all eyes were either on the spinning globe of green, or on the equipment beneath it. For the first time Bond noticed something else–there seemed to be no wiring supplying current to any of the equipment–and he'd seen none coming from the batteries either. Whatever was powering this whole shebang seemed almost be coming out of thin air.
Or out of the green itself?
He kept to the walls until he reached the staircase that led up to the whispering gallery and the top of the dome. Still no one paid any notice to him, and he reached the first gallery with no problems. At this height he was level with the green globe, which spun lazily–four feet across now–suspended in the air below the center of the great dome. The vibration beat through Bond again, and the green in him responded, surging up in a wave that threatened to wash him away.
He needed clearer air, a clearer head. He took the stairway up, climbing steeply all the way to the top of the cathedral and out onto the platform that enabled visitors to stand on what seemed to be the roof of the city. The effect of the green was lessened greatly here, and Bond breathed deeply, having never been so glad of the smells and sounds of the old town. But even as his head cleared Bond saw that the green was already spreading. The faintest of shimmers rose up from the dome, reaching high above the cathedral before spreading, like an opening umbrella, a sizzling aurora of greens and yellows and golds, mushrooming out, covering an ever-greater area as the globe

inside the dome spun and grew. . . and danced.

As he watched the aurora spread over the city, the green swelled inside Bond again. He lit a smoke, alternating between taking a deep drag and pressing the glowing tip against his flesh. Slowly– too slowly–the green receded, but now it was never too far from the surface of his thoughts, its influence getting stronger as the globe in the dome grew larger still. The city shimmered and danced beneath him, and the aurora covered the sky, from Hammersmith away to the west to the Tower and beyond to the East. MacDonald had spoken of a symbol–there was little more potent than a city that had stood against the might of the Nazis in war only to fall now, peacefully, calmly, to the green. Even the old dome below him, the structure that had stood proud so famously during the blitz, was taking on a green glow, shimmering and swaying as it too joined the dance.
It had to be stopped, and quickly at that.
He flicked his smoke away with thumb and forefinger, watching the glowing tip as it fell away into the night. On following its path Bond saw that the steps and concourse in front of the old cathedral were packed with people, all with their faces raised up to the sky, all standing, silent. Even from the heights on which he stood he could clearly see their eyes, shining, shimmering, as green as the skies dancing above them.
The chanting started as Bond went back down to the whispering gallery to see what was happening inside the dome itself.

The globe was many yards across now, a spinning ball of gas and plasma, shimmering and shining and glowing and dancing, calling Bond to join it. He pressed the cold barrel of the pistol against the burns on his wrist, hard enough to make the wounds weep. His head cleared–not completely, but enough that he could resist.
The chanting rose up ever louder from below. The scientists had all stepped forward, surrounding the same dark stone polyhedron that Bond had seen in Alaska. Long tendrils of green miasma wafted down from the globe, before the stone sucked them into itself, developing a shine, a glow that was brighter than the globe itself.
The whole cathedral hummed and throbbed, and the green swirled everywhere. Bond saw Kaminski at the front of the group of scientists, the first to reach for the stone and wash his hands, arms–his whole

torso–in the glowing green. Duncan MacDonald was right behind the scientist waiting his turn and Bond knew that if he let his old friend approach that shining trapezoid he would never be able to free him from the dance–the green would have him forever.

The walls of the great dome of St. Paul's took on the aurora's shimmer, and Bond heard the chant rise up louder from outside. The people on the steps, on the concourse–perhaps even everyone in the old city, all sang, all danced, all lost in the joy of the green. He didn't have to see it to imagine it–the same aurora he'd watched from the deck of the CONFESSOR now hung over old London.

The sky danced–and London danced with it. Bond raced for the stairs.

He was almost too late. Kaminski backed away from the glowing stone before Bond got down the final flight. MacDonald stepped forward to take his place. He plunged his hands, all the way up to his elbows, into the green.

"No! Duncan!" Bond shouted, and leapt down the last four steps in one jump, almost over-balancing on the stone floor. He ran across the cathedral floor, knocking scientists out of the way like ninepins, knowing already that he was too late as the green washed over MacDonald's whole upper body.

"Duncan!" he shouted again.

Kaminski moved between Bond and the Scotsman; the green shone, livid in his eyes. Bond didn't slow, didn't hesitate, He put a bullet in the man's face and another in his heart to be sure, and passed the body before it had fully fallen to the ground.

The chant swelled around him, the cathedral hummed and throbbed in time, and the green inside surged and rose up, demanding to be noticed. He extended his pistol arm and grabbed the burned wrist with the other hand, feeling the pain push the green away, grimacing at the white, almost joyful heat of it.

Duncan MacDonald turned to face him, the green shining in his eyes. He raised his hands and green tendrils wafted like smoke from his fingertips.

"Join us, Jimmy, lad. It's truly glorious. Join us and be free."

Bond raised the pistol again. MacDonald laughed, the green escaping from his parted lips.

"We both know you're not going to shoot me, Jimmy, lad."

"I'm hoping I don't have to," Bond replied. He shifted his aim to a point over MacDonald's left shoulder and emptied the pistol into the dark crystal stone.

The effect was immediate. The left part of the stone blew apart like a dropped light bulb. High above them the green globe stopped spinning, started to falter, and dissipate, losing cohesion. The chanting cut off as if a needle had been lifted on a record player and even the hum and throb from the electrical equipment seemed dulled and muted, the quiet in stark contrast to the cacophony that had filled the cathedral just seconds before.

Bond felt the green inside him sink and subside. He dropped the gun and took the second pistol from his overcoat, taking aim at the largest remnant of the crystal. He pulled the trigger, twice– just as MacDonald stepped in front of him, both bullets taking the man high in the chest near his previous wounds. The Scotsman fell aside, giving Bond a clear shot–he took it immediately, emptying the second weapon, blowing the remains of the black stone into a cloud of tiny fragments in an explosion of green that shimmered briefly then faded as if taken by a breeze. The globe of plasma hung in the dome for a second, hissed and puttered with a discharge of electricity that set Bond's hair on edge, then it too merely faded and died and was gone. The electrical equipment sparked–green flashes that smelled of ozone before, after a final loud throb, they too went silent and still. White coated scientists wandered, confused, on the floor of the suddenly quiet cathedral, and Bond heard shouts of confusion from outside on the steps and concourse, but by then he was at MacDonald's side, kneeling over the man's bleeding body.

"Jimmy, lad, Jimmy lad. What have you gone and done this time?" MacDonald said, and coughed. There was no green at his lips now, just red, far too much red.

"Don't speak, Duncan. I'll get help."

"Dinna fash yersel, big man," MacDonald said, reverting to the accent of their youth. "I'm done here. I'm off to the last dance. It's a crying shame, so it is–we could all have danced together–we could all have had that peace you keep fighting for."

"The cost would be too great." Bond said, but his friend was already gone.

Later, as the sun came up and the MI6 cleanup crew removed the evidence from the cathedral, Bond stood on the steps having a smoke, pondering MacDonald's last words. He knew he had done the only thing that he could have done in the circumstances. He watched the people of London go about their business. He had saved their way of life for them–and they would never know of it. He was sure he had made the correct choice– right up until the point a van delivered the daily papers to the newsstand on the corner. He only saw the headlines– but that was enough for him to finally realize the full import of Duncan's words.

Anti-Castro Units Land in Cuba; Reports of Fighting at Beachhead

He smoked the cigarette down and flicked the butt away as he strode down the cathedral steps.

M would have need of him.

BOND UNKNOWN

In the midst of that ancient, broken vessel, something yet more dark than all the black of this stomach-like chamber rose. Bond shined the light briefly on it...

MINDBREAKER
EDWARD M. ERDELAC

50 years after the passing of Ian Fleming (almost to the day), Mr. Taro Suzuki, a colleague of mine associated with the Wilmarth Foundation with whom I became acquainted during my compilation of a certain renowned academic's personal papers (published elsewhere), and knowing well my fondness for certain esoterica (and perhaps, of my willingness to publish), passed this manuscript to me with the assurance that the information contained within was no longer classified under the strictures of the Official Secrets Act. After prolonged legal consultation, the manuscript has been necessarily altered in and fictionalized, both to avoid the possibility of reprisal from relevant parties and to conform to the requirements of international law. Any errors stemming from these alterations must necessarily be my own. The events, as they stand, are officially unconfirmed.

1. The Princess No Knight Would Save

It was no easy thing, to be a princess.
Girls the world over pined for the title and the life they imagined went with it, but Anne knew better. It was a staid, mostly joyless routine of pomp and conformity. Every dress had been picked for her from the day she was born. Every nuance of speech and step had been drilled into her by her dour governess, Ms. Peebles. Under that woman's instruction, Anne felt little different from the show ponies

she loved to ride. All Ms. Peebles was missing was a crop to correct her gait.

Many days she had spent looking through the window of a humming motorcar at the wide-eyed girls her age standing alongside the road, peering in, wondering about her. It was the only time she got to see regular girls. She had always envied them. They could jump in mud puddles at their leisure, wipe their hands on their clothes, wear mismatched stockings any day of the week. No one was in danger of losing face if they did.

Most people toiled their whole lives to attain a modicum of what Anne had merely been born into. She wanted for nothing. When she was nine years old she had read an article about the Girl Guides and asked her mother if she could join them. The 1st Buckingham Palace Company had promptly been re-formed, consisting of twenty girls, all daughters of the Palace staff. They convened regularly in a summerhouse in the garden and Captain Bayliss led them on hikes around the grounds and taught them stitching and woodcraft, and told stories about Boudicca the queen, and they had held skits where Anne was both director and star and thus, doubly insufferable.
In hindsight, it had been somewhat ridiculous. None of the other girls had wanted to be there, or ever even talked to her without her speaking first. They did whatever she bid them to within reason, and if ever a girl resisted some petty chore she had delegated, a quick, private talking to from Captain Bayliss put them shortly back on track.
The year before she'd come to Bendenen for school, she'd learned the 1st Buckingham Palace Company had originally been formed for her own mother's benefit. Sure enough, upon her departure, the company had immediately disbanded, much to the relief of the other girls, no doubt.
Something in that discovery had changed Anne. While bossing the others about she had naturally entertained the notion that she was their sole reason for being there, and often held this above them. But discovering it was true, just as it had been for her mother, it got her thinking. Had none of them attended Girl Guides because they'd wanted to? Had they really forfeited every Saturday for five years solely for her benefit?

Why?

She had come to the Kent countryside and Bendenen School, where she had begun her independent studies. Something in one of her textbooks had made her come to the realization that every one of her childhood friends from the Girl Guides had been compelled to accompany her because of their parents' employment at the Palace. This saddened her.

She soon found too, that at Bendenen, she could not carry on as she had, ordering girls about. Oh they had deferred to her rank well enough to begin with, but now, two years in, she had no real friends. She was never sought out to attend birthdays, and the girls her age clammed up when she came around.

She did not know what it was like to not be a princess. She had never really thought of herself in such terms. Yet the other girls her age averted their eyes when she spoke to them, and fifth and sixth years even curtsied to her when she passed in the hall, though Anne was well aware of the peals of shrill laughter and whispers when she turned the corner. Once in history class during their studies of Roman Britannica, she had found a note in her desk with a drawing of a long-maned horse in a tiara and toga with the words 'Princess Epona' scrawled beneath.

She had spent that day crying softly in the lavatory stall. She had always suspected she was homely, though none at Buckingham would ever dare tell her so. She was awkwardly thin and pale, and like her brother, her teeth were too large for her mouth. Her boring brown hair was as flat and lifeless as her boyish chest. Meanwhile there were girls her own age that looked like they had bounced giggling out of a Carry-On film.

She came to realize that she was, like Rapunzel in the old fairytale, a kind of a prisoner. A princess in a tower, but the tower was built by her own hubris. She was a princess no one cared to save. She was isolated by class and peerage. She had been too wealthy to ever run and tumble in a field with screaming playmates, and now that she was too old for such things, she found that she was too separated by her station to even walk with friends or do whatever fifteen-year-old girls were supposed to do. She said little outside of class and dressage team, which remained her greatest pleasure. She felt quite at home around horses. Perhaps, since it was the only time she had ever been encouraged to care for something other than herself,

she cleaved to it. It was the one time she felt whole and connected to another living thing outside herself. She loved the bellows of the horse between her knees, the spatter of lather, the wind on her face. Outside of practice and class, she listened to records and studied alone in her dormitory, always with her pudgy old security man, Sheffield, somewhere within earshot. Cilla Black was her favorite. She listened to her over and over, and hoped in her heart for a prince to liberate her from her ivory prison.
Nevertheless, she had not looked forward to the social ball with the boys from Tonbridge.
She had little experience with boys outside of her brother Charles, and he had always been an imp. She wanted nothing more than to stay in her dormitory.
However, attendance was mandatory, and so she'd put a ribbon in her hair, piling it as best she could, ironed her best yellow dress, and set out with her lumpy, gassy bodyguard rolling in tow, ensuring the night would be an unmitigated disaster.
As she had expected, the girls stood against one wall like pigs in a market, and the fervent, ungainly boys in their pressed trousers and maroon blazers and ridiculous straw barges had strode up and down the line in groups like knots of restauranteurs seeking a deal, selecting the choicest cuts beginning with the usual Carry-On girls and proceeding in descending order to lead the lucky, blushing, but middling ones to clumsy but oh, so lovely stomping on the scintillating dance floor. Only the most unattractive girls were let to silently watch the swirl of skirts and toe mashing with piteous envy, and await the tortuously slow revolution of the merciless clock, until such time as they could be released to flit back to their pillows and soak them in bitter tears in the dark.
The Princess sat prim, her hands clutching her pocketbook, knees together, imagining herself in the box at one of her mother's appearances, assuming the prisoner's disconnect, even as the music turned to Cilla Black's It's For You, her favorite song, the song John Lennon and Paul McCartney had surely written for her somehow, though they had never met.
When she opened her eyes, a smoky-eyed, dark young man stood before her. There was no mistaking it. He was not simply loitering about. He looked down at her with hopeful expectancy. He was quite a beautiful boy; older, and not English. There was a swarthiness to

his skin, and his hair and eyebrows were blacker than black. His straw barge was set back on his head, like a cowboy.

"Pardon me," he said, bowing slightly at the waist as none of the other fidgeting rogues had done. His accent was Middle Eastern, somewhat like the actor Omar Sharif's. "But if you will do me the honor, I should very much like to dance with you."

He held his arm out, smiling.

Anne rose from her chair almost before she knew what she was doing, and was surprised to find her hand on his arm. Had she sprung up like an overeager jackrabbit? She couldn't be sure. He placed his warm hand over hers and led her out onto the dance floor. Yes, he was lovely, up close, like something from Arabian Nights. Who was he? Where was he from? She had never thought Cilla Black would ever be an intrusion, but now her high, soulful lament was a nuisance. She wanted to hear this boy's voice, to know his asking her to dance had not been some sort of trick or a mistake.

He led masterfully, never once treading upon her toes. Ms. Peebles would have approved. He smiled. His teeth were very white and even.

But over his shoulder, she saw the other boys and girls lingering on them both. Though they turned, they were like curious owls, their heads ever swiveling back to her and her companion. Were they shocked that she, a Royal Princess should be dancing, or that so handsome a boy had chosen so plain a girl? She suddenly felt ashamed, and stumbled slightly, losing the rhythm of the song.

Her partner's smile thinned, and he bowed his head and guided her from the dance floor.

Like a clumsy horse, she had ruined everything, as surely as if she had thrown a shoe or bucked her jockey. Damned fool!

He led her away from the music, to the outer hall, where it was quieter.

"I am so sorry if I have offended you," he said hastily.

"What?" Anne exclaimed, baffled. "Offended me?"

"I should never have asked you to dance," he said, bowing again.

"Why did you?" she found herself asking. "Why did you ask me to dance?"

"Why?" the boy said, looking puzzled. "Because it seemed a shame to see you sitting there, a lovely girl, all by herself."

Lovely? Was this some cruel prank? Had one of the Carry-Ons put him up to this charade?

"Do you know who I am?" she demanded, with all the imperiousness of her mother. If this was a trick, well, she couldn't have his head off, but she could come close. Sheffield would put him out on his arse if she asked him to.

"I know your name is Anne," he admitted. "I heard some of the other boys talking."

"And you knew I was a princess?"

His face split once more into an uncontrollable grin, and he chuckled.

"Well confound it, what's so funny?" she demanded.

He shook his head, composing himself. "I was thinking how fortunate I am, or might be, could be." He slapped his hand to his lips as though to catch the words. "That is, should you. . . I mean. . ." He bit his lip and bowed solemnly once more, running through his next words mentally. "That is, I am not surprised. You have the bearing and the beauty of your title."

Anne folded her arms through his blathering, but when he said the last, she could not help but smile too, and splayed both her white gloved hands across her lips to hide it.

He looked up at her, and took her gently by the wrists, lowering her hands. "Don't cover your smile."

"I'm hardly a beauty," she mumbled.

"You are. I see it in you. You're like an orchid before the dawn. Would you like to take the night air, Princess?"

His name was Anwar Kulthum, and his father was an Egyptian consul. He hated Tonbridge, he said, from the fools who attended it up to the administrators who allowed so barbaric a practice as fagging to continue. The first time his arrogant housemaster had tried to cane him for refusing to warm his toilet seat, of all things, he had snatched up the older boy's stick and broken it against the floor. This had earned him a serious beating and months of humiliation and petty disciplinary action.

"I am thinking of running away to Heathrow and flying home to Cairo." This saddened and thrilled her all at once. She almost begged him to take her with.

"But you see, Anne, that is why I have shamed you. To my bastard schoolmates I am an upstart wog, soiling the reputation of their princess."

"Oh," she said, pulling his arm close and putting her ear to his firm shoulder. "I hate them all. I think you're a hero to have done what you did."

"A hero? For breaking a stick?"

"No," she said, smiling at him, looking into his deep eyes. "For rescuing me."

Without a word, his head darted in quickly and she felt his warm, soft lips touch hers. Her face burned so hot she thought her eyes would melt, and she lowered her head and touched her fingers to her own lips. Her first kiss.

She felt lightheaded.

The Kent air was cool, and she thought to warm her chilled fingertips on the latent, fast-fading heat there.

"Now I have offended you," he said miserably.

"No, no, not at all," she assured him, squeezing his hand. There was a queer tattoo on the back of his hand; a mark like a crusader's cross, but with a loop at the head. It was an ankh, she knew, from a trip with her family to view the Egyptian exhibit at the British Museum. It meant 'life.' Yet it was inverted when his hand hung at his side.

His other hand went to her chin, and gently lifted her face to the country stars, which wheeled about his lovely head.

"No?" He asked. "Then why do you cry?"

She brushed at her eyes. How to tell him? How to tell him that she wished this moment could be set in a frame and hung in some antechamber of the Palace where only the maids would disturb it with a light dusting. Where her mother wouldn't be angered to see it and turn it to the wall? But she was thinking of the faces of her schoolmates, disapproving not only of him, but of her too.

They were two separate people.

And he was perfect.

And they could never be together again, past this wondrous evening. They had strolled far from the light of the school, across the grounds, almost to the edge of the Twenty Acre Wood.

"We really must be getting back."

"So soon?"

"Regrettably."

"Stay a while longer," he said quietly, as if he understood. "Smoke with me under the stars."

"Alright. Just a bit more."

He produced a black lacquered cigarette case, opened it, and extended one of the two remaining cigarettes inside to her.

She had snuck fags in the girl's lavatory before. She took the cigarette. It was black tipped. Exotic. She put it between her lips, and he lit it with a lighter.

The smell of the tobacco was strange, and she wondered with a thrill if it might not be hashish. Didn't Egyptians smoke a good deal of the stuff? It was earthy, but sweet in her lungs. More pleasant than a regular cigarette.

"What is this?"

"Black Lotus," said Anwar, rubbing her shoulder. "Are you cold?"

"No," she said, giggling a bit. "No, I feel quite warm."

She took another drag of the black-tipped cigarette. It was like candy. So smooth. When she exhaled, the blue cloud that rolled across the stars seemed tangible, as if she and Anwar could pull themselves up on it and float away like in an Arabian fairytale.

Anwar smiled and took the second cigarette. When he struck his lighter, the flash of the ignition showed a tall man standing behind Anwar.

She shrieked and jumped uncontrollably, sure it was Sheffield and that she was in for it.

The man lunged and grabbed a hold of her upper arm. It was not Sheffield.

This man was taller, broader, stuffed into a too small double-breasted suit of evergreen. His head was obscured in a dark headdress. His fingers were hard and cold, his grip solid as a machine's.

She tried to pull away, but he drew her closer. She opened her mouth to scream, and a hand slapped over her lips.

"Sleep," said Anwar, and her eyes rolled up on her, as the black tipped cigarette tumbled from her fingers.

She fell into the arms of the giant in the suit and wine-red keffiyeh. They turned toward the tree line.

George Sheffield had of course seen the dark boy and his charge dance. He knew it was inappropriate, but what the hell was that to him? He was a bodyguard, not a governess. The poor, skinny little thing had had a hard time of it since coming to school. He knew she was aware of the contempt the other girls had for her. Envious bitches, they were. Maybe Anne had been no angel, but she was a sight better than most of the hens in this coop.

God, how he hated this assignment. He had told himself the country living would make the time fly by, but he longed for London. In the winter he was cold and in the summer his hay fever acted up. Country living was not his sort of thing.
Then he had to stand by and watch Anne stumble through the awkward years. He had no children. His Meg had been barren, and she'd died before they ever decided to adopt, but he pitied the poor thing, learning the hard way the rules of the game.
So he hadn't overreacted when the wog boy had asked her to dance, even stepped in when one of the disapproving chaperones had made a move to part them. Let the girl have a bit of sunshine. He'd trailed them across the grounds of course, watched them kiss, likely her first. It had warmed the cockles of his fluttery heart. Everybody deserved a bit of happiness. The cigarettes were nothing. He knew she smoked, of course. What the hell kind of bodyguard would he be if he didn't know that? Watching them made him pine for a fag himself.
But when the big chap in the dark keffiyeh stepped out of the tree line and grabbed her, that was when he pulled his Browning, flicked off the safety, and shifted it across the field.
"Hold it!" he yelled, and to show he meant business, he brought his automatic up and blew the branch off a sapling just to the big chap's left, leaving it quivering. It was against all his training, to fire without killing, but the girl was there.
Anwar cringed at the sight of the lumbering old security man huffing across the field toward them, aiming another shot.
"Take her," the large man demanded in a deep, French accent, pushing the unconscious girl into his arms. "I will deal with this one."
"Don't be long!" Anwar hissed, springing into the woods. The big man drew a blocky revolver and returned fire.
Sheffield groaned as a bullet pierced his thigh, and stumbled, but his Browning crashed three times in the night, and while one shot went winging off into the trees after the boy and the Princess, he was positively sure he hit the larger of the two kidnappers in the center of his chest. Nevertheless, the big man's aim proved just as true, and Sheffield was knocked flat by the next shot and laid wheezing and bleeding in the grass, unable to feel his extremities.

The man in the evergreen suit trudged off into the dark forest. The boy, Anwar, should have been engaging their getaway, but he heard no motor. As he increased his pace through the forest, he became aware of the sound of weeping and moved toward it. He found the girl, only half-conscious, mewling under the body of Anwar. The fat old man had caught him in the back. A wild, unlucky shot, really. The man in the evergreen suit grunted and pulled the body off the bloodied girl. He briefly checked her. The blood was all Anwar's. With a grunt, he scooped her into his arm, where she lolled drunkenly. He hissed for her to be quiet and started off.

Sheffield did not know how long he lay there. Over the ragged sound of his own breathing, he heard girlish shrieks and adult cries of alarm from the direction of the school. Somewhere from the direction of Cranbrook Road, the warble of a police siren began to sound.
Then he heard a mechanical spluttering somewhere on the other side of the woods. The sound of the engine surprised him the most out of the bad turn of events that had occurred thus far this evening. It surprised him because he knew it well, and hadn't heard it since his RAF days, when he'd worked calibrating Chain Home radar stations in 1940. It was an old Civet-1, a 7-cylinder. Sure enough, moments later he heard the familiar whup-whup-whup of a rotor beating the air, and watched the shape of a two-man autogiro rise above the trees. It almost delighted him to see the little old bird in the air. He hadn't seen one in flight in twenty years. But the pain in his chest reminded him of the slug of hot lead the pilot or co-pilot had left him with, and that his charge,
Princess Anne was trussed up in the ungainly thing.
It turned slowly south and burred away, skimming the tree tops.
George Sheffield lay his head down and prayed he'd live long enough to tell what he'd seen.
At least do that, you old fool!

2. 008

James Bond stepped out of the London drizzle into the gray building off Regent's Park and caught the lift as a deep rumble of thunder shook the windows and made a few of the girls in the lobby glance outside.
He found himself sharing space with a gentleman quite singular in appearance; early thirties, mop haired, black, prodigious horseshoe mustache dusted with premature streaks of grey. He wore thick dark spectacles, a navy, pinstriped Edwardian jacket and slim matching pants. Wine red ruffles poked out of the edge of his sleeves, matching socks above his patent leather Chelsea boots, and a garish yellow marigold sprang from his breast pocket. The chap was fairly bursting with colors, like a rainbow that would not be contained within an expiring thunder- head.
The old one-armed liftman had retired, and the antique lever control had gone with him.
Bond excused himself, reached past the man for the shiny automatic panel, and found the ninth floor had already been lit. "Sorry," he said, thinking there'd been some mistake. "What floor?"
"Ninth," said the man, in a soft Northern accent.
Bond pressed the eighth for himself, straightened, and shuffled back into place beside the man. As the doors slid closed and the lift began its ascent, Bond worked his jaw muscles.
He glanced sidelong at his lift mate. The hands were manicured and soft looking. A ring on the right third finger bore a strange symbol he didn't recognize. Some kind of circled, warped star set in jet, with something else, a complex eye or pillar aflame in the center, with a sprig or branch motif. His mind raced through catalogs of various organizations he had encountered in study and practice, but nothing came up.
He stood listening to the character's nasal passages whistling. Evidently the unseasonable chill and the rain had gotten into him. He exuded a peculiar scent, Bond identified as sandalwood.
What in the hell was this Earl's Court dandy doing heading for the top floor? And for that matter, where had he come from? There wasn't a spot of rain on him, and he hadn't preceded Bond into the lift. The only explanation was that he had come up from the basement, but there was nothing down there but the shooting gallery,

and there wasn't enough sandalwood in creation to disguise the acrid smell of cordite from Bond in close quarters. Had he ridden the lift down by mistake and gotten turned around?

Well he wasn't lost now.

The doors slid open, and Bond stepped out into the green corridor, only to be intercepted by a devilishly good looking, broad shouldered man with a trim beard and smooth, unblemished African features. He was William Ibaka, 008, a good agent; good enough to have outlived three successive chiefs of Section J.

"James," the man said, flashing a bright grin and slapping Bond's shoulder heartily as the lift doors closed behind him. His slim gray suit fit him like a barracuda's skin. He had his pipe in hand, a gift from M after a particularly hard run in with SMERSH somewhere between Peenemünde and Berlin a number of years ago.

"Hello, Bill," Bond said, genuinely pleased to see his old office mate. The nature of their work afforded little time for fraternization between agents. The 00s were always coming and going on assignment, or being replaced. Though he had shared office space with 008 and no less than three 0011s, they had rarely occupied the same space for more than a day or two in the past ten years of service. Yet they were both Navy men. They'd dined together with M at Blades, shared drinks at Bond's Chelsea flat, and partnered up a few times at Crockford's. Three and four years from mandatory retirement respectively, they were the old men of the section. Bill Ibaka was a friend.

"Are you just now back from Jamaica?"

"Just now," Bond confirmed.

"You've still got your tan. Spot of bother with Pistols Scaramanga, I'd heard."

The latent stiffness in his side where Scaramanga's golden Derringer had planted a poisoned bullet was all the reminder of that affair Bond needed.

"Nothing I couldn't handle, in the end."

"Not like Mary Goodnight," Ibaka leered wolfishly.

"What the hell does that mean?" Bond said gruffly.

"Only that I heard you convalesced up by Mona Dam in her villa the past two months, and that you even moved out of the spare room for a time. But then in an unhappy reversal of fortune you were forcibly evicted altogether."

"Bloody clishmaclaver," Bond muttered, using one of his housekeeper's expressions. Of course, Bill was spot on, damn him. "Where are you going?"

"My eyes only, James," he said, calling the lift. "Say, who was your friend in the lift?"

"That's a good question," Bond said, his previous curiosity briefly returning. The man's odd dress had reminded him somewhat of Fanshawe, the antiquarian they had consulted during the ousting of the KGB Section Chief last year. But something about him didn't quite fit a jeweler. He was too young, and his taste in bijouterie was off.

The lift chimed and the doors opened. Empty.

"Well, fair weather, James," Ibaka said in parting, then, as an afterthought, he caught the doors with his hand and flashed another mischievous grin. "Speaking of fair, have you seen our new secretary?"

"No," Bond sighed. "Pretty?"

He already knew the answer. He had come to suspect the 00 Section secretaries were selected as much for the mental distraction they provided the operatives as for their ability to collate.

"She makes Goodnight look like a spaniel. Better get in there. 006 is already making time. You're going to lose the sweep again."

"Go to hell, Bill," Bond quipped as the doors slid shut on his chuckling friend.

He unbuttoned his dripping topcoat and made his way to his office, where he found 006 sitting on the edge of Mary Goodnight's old desk.

Ibaka's remark about losing the sweep had been anything but innocuous. Goodnight's arrival in the section had put the 00 agents in a lather, and a five-pound sweep on who would bed her first had been initiated early on, with 006 and Bond himself in a dead heat until he had withdrawn upon meeting Tracy.

Tracy. God, to think of her sober on a stormy afternoon... he liked to remember her as they had met, her roaring past him in her Lancia on the N.1, that little pink scarf flapping in the wind behind her like a beckoning, or perhaps her scowl as he bailed her out at the baccarat table at the Casino Royale, or her skin in the dark later that night. But always his mind drifted to their wedding day, to blood on the

shattered windscreen, the flash of the gun muzzle out the window of the speeding cherry red Maserati, and dark blossoms blooming on her grey Tyroler dress with the green trim.
Hell.
It had been Goodnight's discovery of the wager that had signaled the end of his extended recuperation in her villa over-looking Kingston Harbour. Maybe his slip of the tongue had been deliberate. She had become less of a girl and more of a mother hen in the latter days, nesting all about him, fussing. He had begun to feel the leash tightening, and so had slipped it.
It was for the best.
He leaned in the doorway and got a good look at Goodnight's replacement.
She was young, a real blossom, with a sweep of full red hair and an upright, proud chest, a pouty pair of lips and eyes too big and bright to be obscured by the glasses she wore. She was enraptured by whatever 006 was saying, but her dark lashes batted like butterfly wings at a window pane when she looked over his shoulder and saw Bond.
He gave her an easy smile.
006 looked back and straightened. He was a young Turk, ex-Royal Marine Commando, and knew well his own worth with the girls.
"Hello, 007."
Bond didn't acknowledge him, but moved past and shouldered out of his coat.
The girl pushed back her chair and stood.
"Let me get that for you, sir," she said, clicking over to take the coat.
"Thanks," Bond allowed. "And it's Bond. James Bond. James is fine."
"Dolly Bird," she smiled, extending her hand. He took it.
"I hope this is the beginning of a rewarding professional relationship," she said earnestly.
"I'm sure it will be. Any messages?"
"Oh yes. M asked you to report in as soon as you're settled, sir."
Bond held up his finger in a tut tut gesture. "James."
"James." She smiled.
Bond nodded as she eased back into her chair. She had a lovely way about her. He turned toward the door and saw 006 fold his arms as he went off down the hall to the lift.

3. Seconded To What?

Bond pushed through the green baize door, made his way down the corridor to the end office, and entered to find Moneypenny setting her phone back on the cradle.

Moneypenny started at his entrance. The Jamaica sun had been favorable to his skin tone. She'd seen him this bronze color before. At a glance it suited him, but she didn't like how it made the scar on his cheek, the Cyrillic Sha cut into the back of his left hand, stand out like paint scratches. It was a reminder to her that the life of mundane holidays and beach strolls could never be his; that in turn, such a life with him, no matter how badly she might pine for it, would be forever beyond her reach. She wouldn't let him see that of course. She put on her best facade; a smile she put on for all of them, but just a little more, something she kept in reserve just for him.

He would need every bit, this time around, maybe even as much that little girl would need him.

"How could you refuse knighthood, James?" she scolded. "I was looking forward to calling you 'sir'."

"Oh please," he smirked. "I've got a new secretary I've got to break of that habit already."

"I'm sure you'll cure her of her respect for you in no time."

"Not if 006 has anything to say about it. Lady Moneypenny. Now there's a..." He looked at her sharply then. He knew the variety of her teases as well as a flautist knew the tonal scale, and he could read the eyes above that pretty smile like the back of his own hand. She was taking him in ruefully. The pretty smile was cracking. "What's the matter, Moneypenny?"

She turned to her filing cabinet to compose herself, then turned back to him, laying some random docket on her desk.

"You don't know yet?" she said, nonchalantly.

"Know what?"

"She's so very young, James," she said, and was not entirely successful in keeping the whimper from her voice.

"Any sign of 007, Miss Moneypenny?" came the gruff voice of M from the intercom.

She keyed it, thankful for his interruption. "He's just arrived. I'm sending him in now, sir." She looked up at him and nodded. It was more than a 'go on in.'

He nodded back, and that, he knew, was a silent promise. He went into M's office and found the old man seated and smoking as ever behind his wide desk, a queer looking file sitting on the red leather. Black with a red star meant top secret, of course. He was all-too familiar with that clerical code. This folder was entirely red, a black star on the cover. He had never seen one of those in circulation.

Standing at the window, soft hands clasped behind his back, looking down on the London traffic circling the park, was the queer fellow from the lift.

"Sit down, James," M rumbled.

James. That was an appellation the old man usually reserved for special, unofficial favors.

Bond sat down.

"This is 007?" the younger man at the window said, with a decided lack of etiquette. Bond was used to M initiating conversation his own office.

"Yes," said M "James Bond."

"Born the eleventh, November, nineteen twenty?" the man at the window said. Bond looked at M querulously. M raised his eyebrows and nodded.

"That's right," said Bond.

"Scorpio. Controlling. Independent. Faithful. Magnetic. Forceful. Sensual," the man said, as if ticking off some internal laundry list. He turned from the window. He had overlarge, womanly eyes, blue as slate, with small black irises. Bond couldn't tell if the comparative brightness of the window had caused them to dilate or if they were perpetually reacting to some falsely perceived light, which perhaps the lenses of his spectacles kept somehow in check.

"Also compulsive. Obsessive. Obstinate."

Bond said nothing. The man sounded like the astrology page of some tabloid rag. He wanted badly to ask if he would beware a fire or a dark stranger, if love would bloom or wither in June.

"After your last mission to Japan, you were captured and succumbed to mind conditioning at the hands of the Soviets in Leningrad," said the man, not accusingly, but matter-of-factly. "You tried to assassinate your superior officer. You underwent psychological treatment at The Park, and by all accounts, managed a complete recovery. How's your mind, Bond?"

"Just fine. How's yours?"

"Answer him plainly, 007."

An official order, then.

"No more lingering thoughts of eliminating the warmongers of the West in the name of peace?" the man pressed.

The words were familiar to Bond, but only just. Like something he'd read in a novel a long time ago.

"Who are you, sir?" Bond asked, more slighted than truly irritated. The 'sir' was generosity on his part.

The man stared at him a bit with those direct, sensualist's eyes, then straightened, nodding. "No sign of agitation," he muttered, but whether it was to M or to himself was anybody's guess.

He went back to the window and clasped his hands behind his back again. "You were personally recommended by a member of my branch, 007," said the man to the windowpane.

"What branch is that?"

"O Branch," said the man. "You may address me as D."

He had never heard of an O Branch. Who had recommended him?

"D is chief of O Branch," said M "So you'll afford him all deference, 007."

That rankled him a bit. Did this 'D' even have a rank? It didn't matter.

"What's this about?" Bond asked, looking to M.

"Two nights ago the Princess Royal was abducted from her boarding school in Kent," M said, "this has been withheld from the general public. Only the Queen and the Duke of Edinburgh have been informed."

Bond frowned. And Moneypenny, of course. That was the reason for her distress. Maternal instinct, he supposed. The Princess Royal was what? Fifteen? Sixteen? A mousy little thing, he recalled. "Has a ransom note been received?"

"Not yet," said M

"There will be no ransom demand," said D.

Bond looked over at the head of O. "What makes you say that?"

D looked at M

M opened the red file on his desk and spread out the papers until he found a pair of photographs, which he pushed across the red leather at Bond. Bond took them.

The first depicted a line of cars parked at the curb in a circular drive, each disgorging boys in maroon jumpers, toward the front of an old stone building. Parents embraced their sons. A mother, tearful. The focus of the photograph seemed to be on a handsome Middle Eastern boy departing for his first day at boarding school. A hulking attendant in a dark green suit, face obscured by dark glasses and a muted keffiyeh, was carrying his bags. The man must have been over two meters tall, and broad as a bridge.

"New arrivals at Tonbridge School in Kent. Just down the road from Benenden. Given the proximity to a Royal, and the possibility of fraternization, they're photographed every year. Note the big man lugging the suitcases. No name on him, but the boy was registered as Anwar Kulthum, enrolled by his father, a consul at the Egyptian embassy in London."

Bond looked at M.

"Anne's bodyguard saw her leave a social ball with the boy, and tailed them. He saw the same man in the photograph snatch her. The kidnapper escaped in a gyroplane with the Princess. Anwar Kulthum was shot dead."

M slid another stack of photos from the file to the middle of the desk. They showed the same handsome Middle Eastern boy from the admittance photo lying in a forest clearing, dead and staring from various angles, a bullet hole in the center of his back. There was a single shot of a tattoo on the boy's hand, an ankh. It didn't correspond to any organization Bond was aware of. Odd spot for such a tattoo, as it seemed to be upside down when the hand was hanging in repose.

"Unusual mode of transport," Bond remarked, meaning the gyroplane.

"Hard to track. It was found near Lydd. We assume they left the country from there, probably in an air ferry to Le Touquet. Likely he hid her in the boot of a car."

"What about the bodyguard?"

"Died this morning. They pulled 11mm slugs from him, and he described a Chamelot-Delvigne Model 1873."

"That's an antique," Bond said. Then it occurred to him, and he tapped the school photo of the living Anwar in his hand. "Sir, this photograph is a year old?"

"Yes," said M, striking a match and lighting his pipe. "This has been in the works for quite a while."

"What about the boy's father at the embassy?"

"He was questioned. He has no son. Not even married."

Bond frowned. No one had ever bothered to contact the consul before? "Did the bodyguard get any rounds off against the big man?"

"Two."

"Did he hit?"

"I'm sorry, M," D interrupted, "I'm afraid that's above your clearance."

Bond scowled at D. Above his clearance? The head of Intelligence? Just who the hell was this D?

M puffed his pipe and raised his fingers off the desk to surreptitiously quell Bond.

Bond went to the next photograph M had handed him. It showed a stylish, blonde-haired woman with bright red lipstick seated at an outdoor café, not quite Parisian, with a smartly dressed, rather hefty man, balding, with a bulldog's sleepy eyes.

"Do you recognize the woman in the photograph?" D asked.

"Yes. Beatrix Treat," Bond said, ruminating. "Trixie, to her friends. Involved in Hearts and Minds during the Malayan Emergency. Psychological warfare, interrogation, mind control. She defected to the Communists and was recruited by the Special Executive Department of the MWD in '61."

M looked hard at Bond. "She left the Soviets last year," he said. "She was last seen in East Germany. Did you ever meet her?"

"Yes." He answered quickly, though he had to think hard to recall where.

"How?" D asked, arching an eyebrow. Bond frowned.

"We weren't intimate, if that's what you're asking, sir. I don't think we even exchanged names. I seem to recall meeting her at a conference early in 1960."

"Your assessment?" D asked.

"She never should've made it past psychological screening. She was a bit of a kook," Bond said, looking directly at D, "she got involved in LSD experimentation and mysticism. If she hadn't defected, she would've been ousted from the service. Ran with some cult or something. Order of The Golden Dawn."

"It was The New Isis Lodge, which was later absorbed into the Typhonian Order," D corrected him. "Do you know anything else about Ms. Treat, Bond?"

Bond shrugged. "No, sir."

D and M exchanged looks. What the hell was that about?

"The man is Marius Domingue," said M, taking back the photograph and indicating the man at the table, "high in the Unione Corse and, at the time of operation Thunderball, number seven on the board of S.P.E.C.T.R.E."

Bond could not entirely hide his discontent. S.P.E.C.T.R.E. again?

"That picture was taken last month in Bastia."

"What's the connection?" Bond asked.

"One of Treat's known associates matches the description the bodyguard gave of Anwar Kulthum's overlarge accomplice," D said.

"It's possible," said M, "that Treat and the kidnappers are working as sub-operators for Domingue and a resurgent S.P.E.C.T.R.E. An investment of capital extorted from the Royal Family could greatly aide in resurrecting the organization."

Bond looked down at his hands, trying to tactfully verbalize his dissent. S.P.E.C.T.R.E. had died with Blofeld and Blunt. But the organization had stuck in M's craw. Bond didn't want to waste time chasing ghosts. It was possible that Domingue was involved in the kidnapping, but he doubted S.P.E.C.T.R.E. had anything to do with it. It was a bold move for the Unione Corse. Not their style at all. They earned all the money they needed from their heroin trade via Marseilles. Why attract unwanted attention with a kidnaped royal?

"Once again I must respectfully disagree," said D, to Bond's surprise. "I don't believe a ransom demand is coming. Treat's motives extend far beyond the material. It's not S.P.E.C.T.R.E. we need to worry about her resurrecting."

M's jowls flexed and Bond though his pipe stem might snap in two, but the old man said nothing. He hated deferring to this man, but somehow, he was bound to. Who was he? What was O Branch?

"This brings me to my purpose," said D, not waiting for either of them to voice any disagreement, or perhaps sensing the imminence of M's boiling point. "Two of my field researchers at the Philae Temple Complex outside Aswan in southern Egypt have not reported in."

Bond could not hide his puzzlement.

M cleared his throat, as if he did not relish his next words. "007, I'm seconding you to O Branch until further notice. You're to contact and if necessary, extract those field researchers."

Bond leaned forward. Seconded? To what, exactly?

"Sir, with all due respect, after all this, shouldn't I be on the kidnapping case?"

"It is likely that the two cases are related," said D, moving from around M's desk and going to the door. Bond noticed he did not leave the red file folder for M to put in his out tray, but tucked it under his own arm and took it with. He pulled the door open. "Follow me if you please, 007."

Bond looked at M.

M looked away.

He rose from his chair and left the room, sparing Moneypenny a frown as he and D went out into the hall.

As the door shut behind them, Moneypenny bit her lip. She'd been privy to many secrets in her time in this office, had seen James leave for certain death and return, sometimes the worse for wear, but always with a smile for her, too many times to count. But the man in the garish suit, the strange, aloof man who never said hello and whom the old man resented, twice she had seen him pass through the 00 Section with his red folders, and twice the men he had requested had never returned. She didn't know who D was, and couldn't ask, but she dreaded him as a mother hen dreads the hatchet.

She saw M standing in the doorway of his own office with his fists in his pockets, glaring at the green baize and huffing his pipe like an idling locomotive.

4. Darkheart

Bond followed D into the lift. When the doors closed, D ran his finger down the control panel, then pressed his ring to the blank metal beside the basement button. There was a snap as it was apparently magnetized to some device behind the panel. The lift began to descend.

Bond said nothing, but watched the floor indicator count down to the basement. They continued past that for quite a while, then the lift halted, and the doors opened.

A portrait of an austere, slim, and delicate looking old gentleman with a broad forehead and oval face, his person festooned with medals and fruit salad from various nations, greeted them as they stepped off.

Bond recognized the man from the annual Twin Snakes Club dinner at Blades, that depressing gathering of Old Boys from Intelligence, once vital agents and spymasters, now drifting blearily through forced retirement and their own murky memories towards the grave. He had been a French born duke and soldier of fortune who'd done a good deal of work for Churchill and Sir Pellinore Gwain-Cust since the early days of SIS. Bond had seen him always off in a corner drinking with Sallust. He'd had something of a reputation as an eccentric, possibly brought on by dementia, and had died of a heart attack on a flight from Ceylon about four years ago.

It was a shame that men were more like milk than wine in the end. They did not ferment and grow sweeter, they curdled and expired.

D led Bond down a red carpeted corridor that seemed to be bereft of personnel. They passed several office doors, each marked not with numbers, but odd symbols. Circled stars, mysterious sigils, all of them meaningless to him. He spied a lone man, obviously a guard of some type, thick necked and unimaginative, standing beside a black door at the end of the passage. The man opened the door and D went inside. No reception area, no pretty secretary. The door opened right on D's office. It was dim. Being underground, there was none of the natural light of M's window. There were shelves on two of the walls, holding a substantial collection of leather-bound books. A low table on the back wall displayed a collection of statuettes, dim shapes petrified in mid cavort. Bond couldn't make them out. A single green glass desk lamp on the corner of D's polished black desk lit the room.

D sat down in black leather chair and fumbled in a drawer. He didn't invite Bond to sit, but he did anyway.

D produced a ticket and slapped it on the desk, pushing it across with a swift whisper, forcing Bond to catch it.

"Ticket to Daraw International for one via United Arab Air- lines. The operatives you're seeking are Dr. Petra Bottoms and Dr. Farad Sadat. Archaeologist and photogrammetrist, respectively. Their cover is that they've been assigned by the British Museum to study and measure the Temple Of The Black Pharaoh at Philae, before the entire complex is removed to Angilkia Island."

"Their cover? And what are they really doing?"

"Need to know. Do you know of Philae?"

"Do I need to?" quipped Bond, looking at the tickets, feeling stupid and thus aggravated.

What was he doing here? Was he to be a distraction from the real rescue mission? Was that the assignment 008 had landed? And what was that damned business about his S.ME.R.S.H. brainwashing? He had thought that was all behind him.

"Philae," D began, pyramiding his hands and settling back into the chair, "as denoted by the plurality of its name, properly consists of two islands in the middle of the Nile, just above the First Cataract. In ancient days it was known as the resting place of Asari, or Osiris, if you prefer."

"Indeed I do," Bond muttered, setting the ticket back on the desk.

"Birds did not fly over it," D went on, ignoring him, "nor did beasts of any kind attain its shores. No fish swam in its shallows. It was known as The Unapproachable, forbidden to all but priests. The people ignored this taboo of course, and the priests petitioned Ptolemy VIII to enforce it, to no avail. Merchant ships braving the rapids on their way north used it as a debarking area, and its proximity to the granite quarries along the Nile made the edict quite unenforceable. The smaller island of Philak is a priceless historical record, crowded with marvels of ancient architecture. It has been home to temples and shrines dedicated to the Egyptian pantheon as well as to Trajan and Christ. Garrisons of Egyptians, Macedonians, and Romans have all guarded the southern approach over the years. Napoleon's men visited it during his Egyptian campaign. In 1906 the British constructed the Aswan Low Dam, which has steadily flooded the complex. UNESCO has been working to relocate the ruins for the past four years, though the island of Senmut is nearly lost to time and progress."

"This is all very fascinating, D," Bond lied. The whole thing had sounded like narration for a slideshow. "I still fail to see why you need me for this."

"The work of Dr. Bottoms and Dr. Sadat has been of a most sensitive nature. And as I said, you came recommended."

"By whom?" Surely not M

"Simone Litrelle."

Solitaire. Bond had long wondered what had become of her. He leaned forward in his chair.

"She's not here, 007," D said, with a hint of amusement. "She is assigned to one of our forward divinatory stations. She only half believed in her abilities when she was recruited, but O brought out her powers quite admirably."

Bond blinked. Divinatory?

"In answer to your query, you were selected partly because you have a favorable birth sign. And your code number, 007. Did you know that 007 was how the celebrated magus and intelligence agent John Dee signed his secret correspondences to Queen Elizabeth? The double 0's represented his eyes, which he dedicated to her. And seven. A very fortuitous number. A god number in ancient Egypt. Seven days, seven seas, seven heavens, in antiquity, seven planets."

"Yes and seven sins," Bond said. He shifted in his chair, frowning.

"There are no coincidences, Bond," said D evenly. "Prior events in your life, as well as events prior to your life have been ordered whether by human or preternatural design to place you into a unique confluence of destinies. Have you studied your family history closely, Bond? Did you know that John Dee's daughter Madinia emigrated to France and herself had a daughter named Marie by one Charles Peliot, a privy maid to Queen Henrietta Maria?"

"What in the hell are you talking about?" Bond exclaimed. He was babbling like the book-rabid fellow at the College of Arms, Griffin Or.

D leaned forward, his eyes fervent behind the lenses, fingers interlaced now, that damnable ring glinting in the lamplight.

"Lineage aside, Bond. The death of your parents when you were eleven, your expulsion from Eton, your education at Canterbury and

Fettes, and Geneva, all uniquely qualifying you for acceptance in the Special Service. Which brings us to your career thus far. Your encounter with agent Litrelle in New Orleans, her subsequent recruitment and suggestion of you for this mission; the little bits of esoteric wisdom you've unwittingly picked up over the years from your first secretary Loelia Ponsonby and your housekeeper. The death of your wife and your subsequent brush with mental collapse. Yet through your reconditioning at the hands of the Russians and your unlikely recovery, you have proven yourself possessing of a remarkable mind, both malleable and resilient. All of these things have led you here. You truly are a blunt instrument, yet I believe you can also be attuned for more delicate work if need be. I have on occasion required the service of men of your ilk. Other 00 agents have sat where you are. I've never seen any of them again."

"What is this?" Bond said finally, gesturing to his surroundings. "What is all this?"

"For as many years as you have been privy to the secrets of crown and country," said D, "did you never suspect there were secrets even you, even your beloved M, weren't told? O Branch has existed in its present form since 1940, when my father convinced British intelligence that the war, like other wars before it, was being fought on multiple planes of perception, not only with modern technology, but with ancient tools which man has utilized since first he heard the word of God through His angels, and was tempted away by darker, older powers. This is Occult Section, Bond. 00 fights in the shadows. O fights the shadows themselves."

Bond smirked and rose from his chair. He badly needed a cigarette. "Ridiculous," he chuckled.

"*Orbis non sufficit.*"

"What?" Bond started.

"The World Is Not Enough. There are worlds within worlds, Bond. Can you peer outside this one? Will you shrink from what you see? I wonder. . . "

Bond turned and went to the door. This was madness. M could have his resignation if he for a minute thought he'd put his own life in the hands of this basement-dwelling, moon-eyed lunatic.

"Another photo for you, Bond," D called from the door, and Bond heard the undulation of a glossy being brandished. He looked back, against his better judgment.

D was holding it up beneath the light for him. It was the giant in the green suit and the dark red keffiyeh, his face obscured by sunglasses. The angle was overhead, as from a balcony looking down on a crowded street, somewhere in the Middle East.

"Dr. Sadat sent this to us yesterday through channels. He took it on the streets of Aswan. It was the last communication we received."

Bond glared at the photo, and released his grip on the door- knob.

5. Deaf Ears and Blind Eyes

The blistery smell of jet fuel and the whine of the silvery Il-62 streaking overhead, combined with the April heat of the burning sun over Aswan, could not entirely induce Bond to remove his linen jacket, lest the stitched pigskin holster and its tenant Walther PPK attract attention. He would have to suffer the sweat until he checked into a hotel or made contact with the eminent doctors, whichever came first. He slipped on his Foster Grants against the glare and hailed a taxi to the curb to take him into town.

The half hour drive north to Aswan proper was prolonged once by the crossing of a camel driver and his groaning, spitting charges, and Bond was afforded a prolonged and contrasting view of the custard cream of the dry Sahara out the left window and the green fringed blue of the Nile on his right. The ancient and the modern overlapped like the confused recollections of a man long past his prime. Electrical towers sprouted like a strange bare crop in the trackless sand, and uncouth motorboats puttered along beside the graceful, drifting feluccas.

The driver took them under the faded blue painted steel archway with its 'Bien Venue' and 'Welcome' and presumably matching sentiment in fanciful and utterly incomprehensible Arabic script. They crossed the river over the Khazan Aswan, the Low Dam erected by the British back before the revolution. The old dam would be a quaint reminder of British influence in the region once the Russian and Egyptian crews completed the massive modern dam further south.

The pink limestone mausoleum of Aga Khan III rose over the jumble of the Nubian precinct on the west bank hill, a rich sultan regarding its shabby subjects from on high. Bond saw the ancient temple structures clinging to sandstone islands in the middle of the reservoir to the south. One of those must be Philae, the object of O Section's attention.

They turned from the verdant neighborhood of shaded palms that had sprung up north of the dam and down one of the narrow streets that cut through the pastel houses on the east bank. One of these was the rented house where Sadat and Bottoms made their daily reports. He wondered briefly whether the two doctors were a couple. It was natural for two agents in such close proximity to fraternize. There had been much speculation about Strangways and Mary Trueblood, and of course there had been his own time with Goodnight. A dalliance with Dolly Bird seemed almost inevitable.

He'd only looked at the photos of Sadat and Bottoms long enough to mark them. He was looking for an older man, mid- fifties, mustache, slicked graying hair, thin. Perhaps he was a bit too old and scholarly for his partner. Dr. Bottoms was in her early thirties, attractive without much effort in the manner of a woman given over to intellectual pursuits and eschewing the cosmetic. Her unsmiling dossier photo had presented an unenhanced face. No lipstick or makeup, her black hair tied back into a serviceable ponytail, dark rimmed glasses. Like Sadat, she had the Egyptian coloring and features that were so striking in young women of the region. But that name, Bottoms. Petra Bottoms. It amused Bond, and took him back to the town in Canterbury where he'd lived with his aunt following the death of his parents.

He frowned slightly, thinking back to D's assurance that there were no coincidences.

That he was more than an eccentric was evident. He was a nutter. No doubt he had inherited his position from his father, though what that position was in the Service, Bond couldn't begin to guess. If nepotism was running so rampant at Headquarters that a lunatic like D could be allowed to hold court in some abandoned sub-basement like a delusional asylum patient lording over a day room satrapy, perhaps it was time to think about retiring early. Particularly if D had been granted the power to lure him from his own section on some errand. He bitterly thought of M, and wondered why the old man had let D get a hold of him. Punishment for refusing a knighthood?

Still, there had been the promise of the Princess' kidnappers, or at least one of them.

He kept his eyes open.

He told the taxi driver to stop a few blocks from the house and walked the rest of the way down the broken little street, which was flanked by potters, bodegas, and spice shops. The sparse motor traffic pulled aside for a robed boy driving a tractor wagon pulled by a mule, and an old man on an orange and yellow motorcycle took the opportunity to buzz ahead, eliciting angry, musical sounding epithets. Shaking fists protruded from the windows, but he paid them no heed.

Bond circled the block when the bright yellow stack of houses on the corner came into view. Sadat and Bottoms shared the two-bedroom bungalow at the top of the stairs. The curtain were drawn, the iron shutters closed. Against the heat of the day? Bond couldn't be sure.

Bond went to the little store across the street and bought a cold coke. He sipped it in the shade and watched the place for a bit, then noticed a boy on a bicycle pull up outside a Nubian eatery down the street and go inside. A minute later he came out with a grease spotted paper bag in his teeth and zipped away.

Bond walked over to the eatery and smoked, waiting.

Three Senior Services later the boy returned, and Bond hailed him. He explained his situation. He was seeing a woman in the yellow upstairs house, and wanted to know if her husband was home. He guaranteed the boy a five-pound note if he agreed to go up there under the pretense of delivering a bag of kofta to the wrong address, allowing Bond to observe who answered the door.

The boy readily agreed, and Bond paid him to order the minced meat and a bottle of coke, leaving him a hefty tip, and waited.

The boy emerged soon after and dutifully walked it down to the yellow house.

Bond found a spot across the street where he could readily observe, and watched the boy climb the stair to the balcony and *whap* the flat of his hand on the red door.

After a bit the door opened a narrow slit, and Bond watched the boy chatter at someone through the crack, gesticulating with the bag.

To Bond's surprise, a brown hand snaked out of the door and shoved money at the kid, then took the bag of food inside. The door closed. The boy fairly skipped back down the steps. He was making a killing. Bond intercepted him.

"The man was home, *sahib*," the boy said. "And hungry!"

"Yes I saw. Was he an older man, thin, with glasses and a mustache?"

"No, sahib," the boy said slowly and warily, as if he thought Bond might demand his money back. "He was not thin, but not fat, and he had a beard and no glasses."

"That's fine," said Bond with a reassuring grin. "Many thanks."

The boy bowed his head, the bright smile returning, and scuttled off down the street to resume his work, though he had made more in the past ten minutes than he would make all day.

Bond, meanwhile, felt the silencer in his pocket. What did he have here? Not Sadat. A famished stakeout man, stranded in the hot afternoon in a dead man's home, grateful for the boy's mistake? Or was Sadat or Bottoms still alive in there with him?

He climbed the steps, setting his sunglasses in his pocket and glancing to see if anyone took any note of him.

The Egyptians went about their business. No one seemed to be paying attention to the house.

Bond slowed as he reached the top of the stairs and gingerly touched the handle of the door. Locked.

He looked around. The house next door was empty. Eye level across the street, a shapeless woman in a black chador finished taking down her washing from the line and carried the bushel inside, closing the door behind her. From the direction of the center of the city, the tinny speakers atop the El-Tabia Mosque began to send the melodious adhan out over the rooftops, calling the faithful to the dhuhr prayer. Bond inspected his Rolex. Just a bit past noon. Down below, a few men on the street lowered their heads, and some of the shopkeepers went indoors.

Bond slipped the suppressor from his pocket and hastily screwed it into the barrel of the Walther. As the noon prayer summons reached a crescendo, he swung out in front of the door and kicked it with a swift, forceful motion. The door banged open, and Bond slid inside, bringing up his automatic.

A bearded man in a short-sleeved blue shirt sat on the couch, the bag from the eatery torn open on a coffee table before him. The coke bottle was in his left hand, and a fork of kofta was in his right, poised before his open mouth. A revolver of some sort lay in front of him. The man's eyes, squinting against the sun spilling across his face from the door, went to it.

Bond would never know if the man saw his pistol or not. He dropped the kofta and grabbed at the gun, and Bond planted a 7.65mm hole above his right eye that sent him jumping back against the couch. He sagged into the cushions; his overturned soda bottle trickled on the rug.

The PPK had made no more sound than a child's cough and the metallic clink of a pair of steel whisky tumblers.

Bond pushed the door shut with his foot and proceeded to sweep the rooms, directing the smoking barrel of his gun into corners, and finding only one other person, Sadat, lying dead under his sheets in one of the two back bedrooms, his mouth slack in a silent scream.

A dark hole in the blood-soaked coverlet over his chest showed where the gunman had shot him from the doorway. One arm dangled from the bed, the fingertips brushing the floor where his spectacles lay. It could have happened in the middle of the night, or early morning. His eyes had been plucked out, possibly after he had been killed. A fit of rage, or some strange fetishism on the part of the killer? The hollow, bloody sockets were densely packed with twitching flies that had wandered in from the open window.

He'd been briefed on the location of the wireless set, hidden behind a front of false book spines in a cabinet in the corner, but so had someone else, as he found the equipment had taken two bullets more than Sadat. If this was a listening station, it was deaf now.

There was a good deal of photographic equipment laying about untouched, including an underwater camera. Conversely, Sadat's file cabinet had been ransacked, and various photos and geometric diagrams of what looked to be ancient Egyptian structural components, pillars, blocks, statues, architraves, and the like, were scattered all over the floor. He found a lanyard bearing some official looking Arabic script and a UNESCO emblem, with Sadat's face. He tucked it into his pocket.

Bond went back into the front room and examined the dead gunman. He must have been waiting there for Dr. Bottoms, whose bed was still made. There was no identification on his person, just a wad of Egyptian pounds and an admission stub from Philae island. He noticed a faint tattoo on the back of the man's left hand, an Egyptian ankh, upside down. Just like Anwar's. Bond went into the girl's room. It was simply arranged, bare of personal knick knacks – the room of a traveler, used for sleep and nothing more; certainly not for liaisons with her housemate, he could surmise. The dresser had been emptied, and a shelf of various archaeological textbooks had been dumped on the floor. After sifting it idly with his foot, he found nothing more than Sadat's killer had.

On a whim, he knelt on the floor and peered under the bed. There was a brochure there, for the Nubian Museum on nearby Elephantine Island. Flipping it open, he found a name inscribed in pen next to the museum phone number, Dr. Suphi.

He found the telephone in the living room, and dialed.

A voice answered in Arabic and Bond cleared his throat. "Excuse me, I'm calling for Dr. Suphi."

"This is Dr. Suphi," the voice on the other line said, switching smoothly to English. "Who is calling?"

"Dr. Suphi, I'm actually calling to see if a colleague of mine has been by the museum. Dr. Bottoms. She's working at the Philae site."

"Yes, she's been here for the past two days, looking over our collection. Are you with the British Museum?"

"Yes," said Bond. "I'm just in Aswan this morning, from London. Can you tell me where she's staying?"

"I believe she was staying in the Nubian quarter, but she was heading back this morning. She left here about a half hour ago."

"Ah, thank you, Doctor. I suppose she'll turn up shortly."

Bond hung up the line and unscrewing his silencer, slipped it back in his pocket, holstered his PPK, and slipped on his sunglasses before going back out into the sun and pulling the broken door shut behind him.

He hastily descended the steps and moved down the street toward the river.

6. Petra

Down on the wharf, Bond hired a motorboat from a reluctant owner whose misgivings faded as his rental fee increased. He soon found himself cutting through the Nile, bouncing across the wakes of tour boats and feluccas, toward the shrub lined island of Philae.
It was hardly an island really. The dam had rendered the place into a kind of archipelago in the middle of the Nile, with only the tallest and highest structures breaking the surface, along with rows of tall palm trees, their roots submerged.
Colonnaded temples stood high and dry upon piles of Syenite, while others seemed to rise from the gleaming water itself, like a sunken city. The water-stained pillars and obelisks of the ancient site seemed sturdy and solid though, defiant of the ignominious threat of progress, even as hardhat wearing workers swarmed over them and groaning cranes atop anchored barges labored to carefully disassemble what had weathered the millennia. The reliefs were still bold and vivid, depicting animal headed deities and rows of deeply engraved hieroglyphs, barely softened by the years, and stately sphinxes watched the measured desecration with dignified aloofness. Here and there, Bond saw the graffiti of the Ancient Greeks etched boldly over Egyptian pictograms, as if denouncing the old gods. He also saw the unmistakable crosses of Christian defilers. Old gods giving way to new. As the boat neared a patch of high land ringed by purple blossomed bougainvillea bushes, an official looking Arab in a white hard hat turned from his surveying equipment and flagged him down. Bond stood in the boat and held out Sadat's UNESCO lanyard, thumb over the picture.
"I'm here with the British Museum!" he called over the roar of the cranes, hastily dropping the ID card into his shirt with practiced nonchalance. "Where's the Temple of The Black Pharaoh?"
"Follow those trees to the southern tip!" the official called back, waving him on toward a quiet part of the ruins.
Bond drove the boat south, the clusters of workmen and machinery dwindling as he passed a Roman hypaethral and came at last to a rickety makeshift dock adjoining a low stand of boulders, on which stood a remarkably old looking, partly collapsed temple, fronted by two broken obelisks and a vigorously mutilated pylon, the original carvings obliterated. It was as if someone had assaulted this

structure. It was in worse shape than any of the others. Unlike the other temples, the emblems of the newer religions had not been carved over the old. The old had simply been hacked and scratched away, forever lost. The obelisks had been dragged down. The material of this temple also differed from the others. Whereas the majority of architecture were hewn from granite and limestone that glowed in the sun, this was of some non-indigenous material. Black basalt, maybe, brought in on some ancient barge.

The whole thing put Bond off.

He circled the temple once, found no other boats, and then dropped anchor behind the temple, wetting his socks on the partly submerged shore and clambering over broken stones to the dark entrance, which plunged down a flight of carved steps.

He passed from the sun into the temple, and found much of the floor beyond the stairs slanting underwater. Lights had been rigged with a generator, but he did not engage it. A table bore a pair of waterproof torches and two sets of SCUBA gear. The inner chamber amplified his breath, and was strikingly cool compared to the hot sun.

He waited there in the darkness. An hour, hour and a half, two. He was fairly biting his lip for a cigarette when to his surprise, a white robed figure appeared noiselessly in the doorway. He had been certain he would hear a boat motor. He touched his PPK as the figure descended the steps, unfurling its headdress and shrugging from its robe as it came.

Bond relaxed and was reaching for his Ronson instead of his gun. The curving figure silhouetted in the sun posed no immediate threat. Her stifling outerwear shed, she skipped girlishly down the last few steps and called out; "Sadat! I know where it is!"

Bond lit his cigarette, illuminating his own face in the dark, causing the girl to stop short at the bottom step.

"And where is it, Dr. Bottoms?"

She stood stock still, lips parted. What she saw terrified her. The man that slid from the shadows as though from an old coat was dark, but not Egyptian. The blue eyes in his face were bathyal and the face in which they rode was as cold. There was the hint of a scar on his cheek, and his expression bore a kind of primal cruelty, no, not cruelty, danger; the kind of danger one feels in the eyes of a strange animal unexpectedly encountered. The air of danger and attraction

that says a chance meeting can go only one of two ways; seduction or death.
She assumed she was about to die.
"Who are you?" she hissed sharply, taking one step back up the stair. "Where's Dr. Sadat?"

Bond smiled thinly.
She was indeed an attractive thing. The desert sun had brought out the amber inherent in her silky skin. Traveling in Aswan she had modestly donned a robe and chador, but beneath she wore a short beige jacket over a white undershirt, and a pair of brief khaki shorts which barely contained her ample hips. She had fine, strong limbs, a modest but not unworthy chest, and a slender neck. Her face was much as her dossier photo had captured her. Without her glasses, her eyes were big and wide, the lashes pronounced. Her oil black hair was bobbed, the prodigious curls turning inward towards her chin. Her mouth was bowed and small, the lips pronounced, giving her an aloof, coquettish look, like a Betty Boop cartoon come to life.
Her accent was a pleasing mélange of English and Arabic, cultured and musical, at once reassuringly familiar and yet exotic.
"Excuse me," said Bond. "I'm tired and I'm just looking for a place to sleep. Any recommendations?"
It was the code phrase D had taught him.
She stood poised on the stair, and her shoulders drooped a bit, though she still looked ready to run.
"Sleep is overrated." Her white teeth showed even between her parted lips.
"Unless it's a sleep without dreams," said Bond.
She sighed and came down the stairs.
He moved toward the light so she could see him clearly.
"Who are you?"
"Bond. James Bond. I was sent to find you. Why weren't you at your post?"
"I moved to the Nubian Quarter two days ago to be closer to the museum on Elephantine Island. I was looking for the Seed there, as we'd learned the original location was underwater. I wanted to see if it was among the artifacts uncovered during the dam construction."
"And was it?" Bond asked, not knowing what she was talking about.
"I believe so. It was photographed by the archivist at the Aswan

Museum."

"So you have it?"

"No. It was transferred to the archives at the Cairo Museum months ago. Where is Sadat?"

"Dead. He was killed in your bungalow last night."

She sucked in her breath. "I noticed men," she said, looking over her shoulder. "Men from the construction. Watching me as I sailed here. I just assumed..."

"How many?"

"Six or more."

"Where's your boat now?"

"Tied at the dock."

"I didn't hear it."

"I rented a felucca."

That would do them no good on the open river against anything with an engine.

"You're going to lose your deposit, I'm afraid."

She started to say something in reply, but Bond held up his hand for quiet. There was the distinct drone of a boat motor, increasing in volume.

"What are those SCUBA tanks for?" Bond whispered.

"Many of the carvings we needed to study were in submerged passages."

"How deep do the passages go? Is there a way out on the other end?"

"Yes," she said, stripping off her jacket and going to the table. She hefted one of the tanks on her back and Bond did the same, dropping his linen jacket and shirt in the water and swapping his Guccis for a pair of flippers.

As she buckled in, he checked her gauge. "When was the last time you used these?"

"They are overdue for a refill. We've mainly been photographing this chamber the past few days."

Her tank was only a quarter full.

"Check me," he said, turning around and watching the stair as the engine cut out.

"You have a half a tank."

"Get down there," he urged. "Go as fast as you can. My boat is anchored at the back of this island."

"But what about you?" she asked with concern, as she fit her diving mask over her face.

"I'll be right behind you. Go."

He heard the hiss of her aqualung, and the liquid swirl as she descended into the deeper part of the chamber. He saw the light of her underwater torch flicker and shrink.

Bond went to the side of the chamber and engaged the generator, then kicked the plugs out so the lights winked out one at a time. Maybe the noise would cover the sound of Bond's boat.

He was about to dive after Bottoms when a shadow slid across the patch of light from the door.

Bond crouched in the dark and drew his Walther. The silencer was gone now, sinking to the bottom of the chamber with his jacket. Surely the intruder's accomplices would hear the report of his pistol.

He watched the shadow pause in the center of the sunlit doorway. Then something small, round and bright red spun through the air.

An Italian 'Red Devil' hand grenade.

Bond sprang from his corner and dove into the black water. He had no time to properly adjust his mask or stuff his regulator into his mouth before the dull thud of the explosion lit the water and flung him hard forward, end over end into the black tunnel beneath.

The side of his head ground against stone.

7. The Sunken Pharoah

Bond tumbled end over end through the cold blackness, ears ringing from the explosion, head bleeding a graceful trail of crimson from where he'd scraped it.

His shoulder collided with hard rock, and he shuddered, disoriented, but shook his head, primed the torch he'd managed to hold onto, and jammed his Walther back in its holster.

At first he was struck with panic, that the grenade had caused a cave-in and enclosed him in some inescapable pocket. It had brought the rock down the way he'd come, blocking the way back to the temple entrance. He checked himself all over. There was a slash on his left hip and the back of his right hand was bleeding, but no shrapnel from the Red Devil had planted itself in him.

His tank had saved him from a fatal chunk of shrapnel, but it had given its own life for his. Or had it? The last of the air was bubbling fast from the hole in the tank.

He sucked greedily at the regulator, then let the whole affair sink through the broken hole in the collapsed wall beneath his feet.

How far was it to the rear passage Petra had described? Against all his screaming instincts, he pushed further down.

He found himself in a vast, pillared chamber. This had once been the main sanctuary, and was immense compared to the deceptively small structure the ruins seemed to suggest. Bond could not see the bottom of the chamber. Yet rising from the gloom was the rotted remains of an intricately decorated Egyptian barque, its broken hull festooned with lapis lazuli and tarnished bronze fittings, the ghostly rags of what had once been a great square sail of silk streaming hypnotically in the dark.

And in the midst of that ancient, broken vessel, something yet more dark than all the black of this stomach-like chamber rose. Bond shined the light briefly on it. It was a tall sculpture of the same midnight hue as the rest of the temple. It was the form of a man in royal trappings, a regal, pleated nemes headdress and rearing, fanged uraeus.

But it was the face of the cult figure that caused Bond to shudder. It was not by the carelessness of some long-ago plunderer or the natural wear and tear of the ages that the huge statue had no face.

Instead, the black stone there had been polished to an almost mirror sheen which reflected the light of Bond's torch, and burst across its surface in such a way that it suggested a supernova, or a white flash of dark intellect.

He half expected the thing to lunge up at him.

Then, immediately across the huge chamber, he spied another light.

There was Petra, paused at the broken opening of some ascending tunnel, waving her light back and forth.

He surged toward her, pulling himself across the murky room for all he was worth, the blackness of the place seeming to assail the perimeters of his vision.

When she saw his distress, she left the hole and kicked off the wall towards him. They embraced, and she took the regulator from her mouth and pressed it into his. He didn't know how much she had left. Didn't want to take it. But he couldn't stop himself. He allowed himself a quick gulp of air, then passed it back to her. She pointed to the hole in the wall. He nodded.

They swam together for it, leaving the sunken Pharaoh to eternity.

They had to go one at a time up the passage, and Bond went first, undulating up toward the flickering spot of sunlight until his nose broke the surface, then his face, and cautiously, his head. He was in a little pool in the rock, and recognized the jumble of stones to the east as being the same that he'd steered his boat past.

Petra surfaced beside him, peeling off her mask and regulator. They were close, of necessity, and he helped her out of her harness.

"You're bleeding," she whispered. He nodded, kicking off his flippers.

"My boat's just over toward those rocks. Be quiet. When they hear the engine, they're going to come after us."

He slid out of the water and crept over the hot stones. The boat was bobbing where he'd left it.

He could hear the chattering of the men at the front of the temple bouncing off the rocks. They were arguing.

He got to the boat and climbed in, glad to see Petra had kept up. When she was crouched behind him, he handed her his automatic.

"What are they saying? Can you understand them?"

"They are scolding the one who threw the grenade. They are supposed to verify we are dead and are arguing over which of them will haul away the rocks. They want to radio in one of the construction crews."

Bond raised the anchor and kicked the boat off the stone. The current caught them, and the boat slid to the north, turning idly. Bond watched the ruined temple dwindle, and thought for a moment they would be able to slip away unseen, when a shot rang out and blew a piece of the bow to splinters.

He engaged the engine and ordered Petra to lay flat as a fast boat with three men emerged from the shallows and cut towards them.

One of the men in the boat had a carbine, and cut loose on them again, smashing the windscreen.

"Can you use one of these?" Bond yelled back at Petra, not waiting for her answer but sliding the gun across the bottom of the boat.

He thought that she nodded. Maybe she was no field agent, but if she was in the Service she had to have some kind of range experience.

In a minute he heard the familiar report of his Walther tentatively answering the bark of the carbine. No bodies splashed into the Nile. Bond looked back and saw a second boat come from around the broken blocks of the sunken temple. Four aboard that one, and it was faster, gaining quickly.

He took the boat between islands, weaving behind the stony little piles that jutted up suddenly and infrequently along the course of the Nile for cover, but soon both of their pursuers were close behind and Petra hadn't accounted for a single man.

"Give me that!" he yelled thrusting his hand out at her when they had put a jut of rock between themselves and the boats behind.

She passed the pistol back up apologetically and he reloaded with his spare magazine.

Their motor had taken a hit and was leaking a greasy trail of oil. They were out of the relative shelter of the rocks now and coming into open water. The dam he had ridden over that morning was in sight, and the water was suddenly crowded with traffic. Feluccas, tour boats, and all manner of pleasure craft glutted the artery here.

Bond hoped the influx of witnesses would discourage fire from the two boats, but he was disappointed when the faster boat opened up with a chattering submachine gun, walking a row of bullets across their stern, and causing Petra to shriek.

Her scream was echoed by several horrified passengers on the other boats, and he saw tour guides racing to bring their slow-moving boats about and head for shore.

Bond fired back and was pleased to see the machine gunner tumble over the side and disappear in the white foam wake.

The boat roared closer, and Bond saw a figure rise up in the back, a flash of red in his cocked fist.

Probably the same grenade-happy fool who had tried to bring the temple down on their heads. He'd learned nothing from his superior's scolding apparently, and Bond whipped the wheel starboard and, like an old war galleon, gave his equivalent of a broadside and a lesson the bomber and his crew would never forget. He caught the would-be grenadier with two shots and the man fell into the bottom of the boat. One man managed to leap clear as the others scrambled to follow, but it was too late. The grenade exploded and the boat burst apart in a flash of fire and black smoke.

He tried to open the throttle again, but the damaged motor only spluttered as the second boat accelerated and the rifleman took careful aim.

Bond dove down beside Petra as a bullet snapped over his head.

To his surprise, a volley of returning fire chattered from the north followed by a snarl of Arabic through a tinny bullhorn.

"It's the river police," Petra gasped at his side.

8. *Zdravstvuyte*, Mr. Bond

The basement of the Aswan jail was a relief from the heat of the day, but when Bond's cell clanked open and he looked up from his bunk, the flushed face of the crewcut wearing man in the drab suit with the nickel-plated eyes suggested there was more heat to come.

This was no Egyptian. He was Eastern European, and no policeman. At least, no ordinary policeman. There was a manila docket tucked under his arm, and the bulge higher up suggested the presence of a Makarov, the Eastern Block counterpart to his own Walther, which the police had confiscated.

Bond let his cigarette fall to the floor between his feet and ground it out.

He had dealt with men like this many times. They weren't called SMERSH anymore, but this one was old enough to have been called that in the past. Bond had been aware of the danger of deploying in Egypt, seeing as how President Nasser was so close to the Soviets. Either the KGB had been keeping tabs on the British UNESCO archaeologists, or Bond's name had turned up on the teletype and simply raised an alarm. There'd been a death sentence against him for years, and last year's outing of the London Director of the KGB had surely exacerbated the Russian's attitude towards him.

The man nodded to the sweaty Egyptian policeman who had opened the cell and the door clanked shut behind him.

"*Zdravstvuyte,* Mr. Bond," said the Russian, confirming all Bond had suspected with his words, which practically embossed themselves in Cyrillic in his ears. "You were apprehended just south of the English dam with a half-caste archaeologist from UNESCO, whom we have suspected as being part of your British intelligence service since their arrival. *Spasiba* for confirming it for us."

"*Pozhalusta,*" said Bond. "Glad to be of help."

The Russian smiled. "I suspect you will be of more help than you know. We don't quite understand what your archaeologist has to do with anything. Of course you found the photographer and liquidated his assassin earlier today. We matched the 7.65mm round in his head to your Walther PPK. The men in the second boat killed three policemen before they were gunned down, and all bore the mark of the inverted ankh which you are no doubt aware of."

Bond said nothing. It was certainly something to ask Petra about.

"Well my friend, you may think you are in a great deal of trouble here, but I do not intend to deport you and your lovely companion to Moscow. We are aware of your target in this region and will instead assist you in acquiring her to the best of our ability."

He opened the folder and showed Bond a glossy photo of Trixie Treat, on an unidentifiable cobble street crowded with Arabs. She wore a modest topcoat. It was night, the light of a street light flaring, overexposed.

"Here is a recent photo. We have reason to believe that Comrade Patricia Treat is operating in the Cairo city limits, though we have not yet ascertained her precise whereabouts. You will be issued two tickets to Cairo aboard this evening's train. We believe Treat's associates keep a watchful eye on the airport. We will provide you both with traveling papers and a change of clothes."

Of course, the Russians wanted Treat dead as sure as British Intelligence. No intelligence service of repute could take kindly to fickle women alighting from their ranks like pollen-laden honeybees. Still, it was strange that they should afford him such amenities. Was she really more of a threat to them than he was? It bruised Bond's ego considerably to think that. So they thought he was here to eliminate Treat.

"That's very considerate of you," said Bond.

The Russian shrugged amiably. "We are practical. We know you above all men are highly motivated to eliminate Treat given your shared history."

Shared history? Bond didn't know what the Russian thought he knew, but he surely wasn't going to burst his bubble by admitting he hardly knew her.

"You are doing us a favor," he went on, "and whatever the result, the cost to us will be minimal." He said the last with a slow grin.

"I see. You'll be releasing us then?"

"Not I, Mr. Bond. I was never here. In an hour the charges against you will be dropped and a policeman will come to take you to your belongings. I assure you they will all be accounted for. In addition, there will be a fresh magazine for your pistol. They have been instructed to drive you to the train. *Do svidanya.*"

Two hours and a pack of cigarettes later, Bond was escorted from police headquarters in a no doubt deliberately ill-fitting suit and met an anxious looking Petra at the curb.

"Oh my goodness, James," she sighed when she saw him. "I didn't think I'd see you again. No one will speak to me. What's going to happen to us?"

"It appears we're taking the train to Cairo," he said, taking her by the elbow as the two Egyptian policemen ushered them towards a waiting car.

She looked tousled, but unharmed.

"Well, that's something. I intended to go to Cairo anyway, to the Museum. Are we being watched?"

As the police car pulled out into the crowded street, Bond turned in his seat to peer out the back window and saw a sedan leave the curb a few feet behind. He couldn't make out the driver clearly, but the distinctive crewcut silhouette of his friend from earlier was just visible in the passenger's side behind the glare of the windscreen.

Bond settled in.

"Yes. By our estranged cousins across the Iron Curtain."

"No one ever asked me anything. How much do they know?" she whispered.

"I don't think they're onto the Seed," Bond said, still not knowing just what the Seed was. "Their idea is that I kill Trixie Treat."

"Who in the world is Trixie Treat?" she giggled uncontrollably. "Gods, what a moniker!"

"That's fine talk from a girl named Pet Bottoms," Bond quipped.

"Petra is where my mother and father met and fell in love," she countered, with a hint of haughtiness. "They were both archaeologists, researching the site."

"Charming," said Bond. "You should be thankful they didn't meet at Chew Stoke."

"You still haven't told me who Trixie Treat is."

Bond looked at her. "She's an associate of the big man in the green suit and black head wrap."

"Fesche?" said Petra immediately.

"Fesche," Bond repeated. The Princess' kidnapper. "Who is he?"

Petra looked like she'd swallowed a brick. Her big eyes moved to the two policemen. "We shouldn't talk about him here."

"Alright then what do you know about the men who came at us this morning? These men with the inverted ankh tattoo?"

"Worshipers of Nephren-Ka, the Black Pharaoh," she whispered.

"Worshipers?" Bond repeated. "You mean, they're some kind of cultists?" He hadn't dealt with that sort since the Black Widow Voodoo Cult. "Is Fesche Nephren-Ka?"

"No," she chuckled nervously. "You saw Nephren-Ka down in the temple," she said. Then she looked at him pointedly. "Didn't D brief you on any this?"

"I was given a lot of the old 'need to know'."

"Well, you need to know some of this, if we're to prevent Fesche and this Treat woman from getting the Seed. Nephren-Ka was the last king of the Third Dynasty. Some say Nephren- Ka communed with the Eater of Souls in Irem and brought the worship of the Shining Trapezohedron to Egypt."

Bond blinked, only half understanding her. The Russians were keeping pace behind them.

"Soris led the revolt against him with the help of Isis. Nephren- Ka buried himself with his priests and servants in a secret chamber. He sacrificed a hundred of his followers, enacting various rituals, and he and his priests carved out the future they had seen on the chamber walls."

"Fascinating," said Bond, as the police car pulled up to the brown stone train station and the Russian sedan parked across the street. There was a row of rattletrap taxicabs idling at the curb, the driver's in a knot on the sidewalk, smoking and talking animatedly.

"This is our stop. Keep hold of my hand. We're going to be moving rather quickly. Do you have a compact or something like that?"

"A compact? No, nothing like that." Of course she didn't.

"I have my notebook," she said hopefully, holding up a cracked black leather notebook wrapped in rubber bands.

"Give it to me," he said into her ear. "You've mistakenly left it behind, do you understand?"

In turn, he passed her a five-pound note.

"Give this to one of those cabbies. Tell them to drive to the first train crossing and wait for us there, and he'll have a fare to Luxor and a ten-pound tip."

"But the police..." she murmured.

He put her notebook in his pocket as the policeman opened the door and waved them out.

They stepped into the air. The exhaust of the cars was strong, intermixed with the smell of the train's diesel engines. The air was

a bit cooler with the growing dusk, but only a bit. One policeman remained in the car while the other took them both by the elbow and led them to the curb. When they reached the front of the station, Petra suddenly whirled, breaking the policeman's grasp.
"My notebook!" she exclaimed beautifully.
The policeman, confused, released Bond to grab a hold of her.
Bond strode purposefully back toward the car, calling back over his shoulder; "Don't worry, I'll get it."
He heard the tapping of the policeman's shoes on the street behind him. In front of him, the driver stepped out of the car, and across the street the Russian with the crewcut, wearing sunglasses now, got out of his sedan. Bond pulled open the back door of the police car and leaned far into the back, making a show of patting down the seat.
The first policeman had his hands on him, and dragged him back out, so that he dashed the back of his head on the roof.
The other policeman came around the bonnet, his gun drawn.
The first policeman hollered in his face as Bond held up the notebook, apologizing profusely. The policeman grabbed his arm and wrenched him around, fairly pulling him back to the front of the station, where Petra was standing on the curb looking concerned.
Bond noticed a taxicab groaning gears as it pulled away and spluttered off down the dusty street.
He handed her the notebook and she smiled.
"You'd forget your pretty little head if it wasn't fastened on," he admonished.
The Russians flanked the policeman, who stood with his arms folded watching them board the train.

Bond and Petra found a seat looking down on their escorts. The Russian offered a half salute and flung the butt of his cigarette off the platform as the train pulled away. Bond's last sight of the man was of the smoke billowing from his nose like from the muzzle of a bull on a cold day.
As soon as they were out of sight, they got to their feet and went to the end of the car, where a conductor was arguing loudly with an Egyptian couple, all three of them shouting to be heard over a screaming infant.
Bond stepped between them and handed the bedraggled couple their

tickets. "Excuse me," he said to the baffled conductor. "We've changed our minds."

With that, he wrenched open the car door and he and Petra stepped out into the smoky air. The door slammed shut behind them, and the conductor pressed his face to the window.

"I've never jumped from a train," said Petra, eyeing the moving ground dubiously.

"It's like falling off a bike," Bond yelled over the clashing of the cars. "Only faster."

And he leapt.

9. Getting to the Bottom of Things

The girl slept against Bond's shoulder the three and a half hours to Luxor, which suited him fine. The driver tried to talk to him in a hodge podge of French, English, and Arabic, but soon surrendered to his passenger's stoicism.
Bond spent the hours mulling over all that had happened, trying to connect it to a kidnapped Royal, and failing to see the connection D had sworn was there. Well, that wasn't entirely true. The connection was Fesche. It was the reason for the connection he couldn't surmise. Ancient temples, some kind of pharaonic cult, it was all the sort of mumbo jumbo D's ridiculous department would be investigating, but somehow it had crossed over into his world. He knew only a little more than the Russians did, which bothered him.
They reached Luxor a little before midnight, and Bond paid off the driver and used the telephone at the Winter Hotel to wrangle them a suite courtesy of the Transworld Consortium, and a cabin on board a cruise ship bound for Cairo early the next morning.
The voice on the other end of the line told him to expect a call in a half hour, so he led the sleepy girl upstairs where she collapsed on the luxuriant bed and commenced to snore almost mannishly.
Bond tipped the bellboy a considerable sum and asked him to find them both a worthwhile change of clothes and some food, promising it would be worth his trouble, then waited by the phone, smoking and watching her sleep. On the dot, the phone rang, and he picked it up quickly, but not quick enough.
Petra stirred lithely on the bed and blinked at him sleepily.
"Just a moment," he said into the receiver, clapping a hand
to it. "I'm sorry, it's the concierge," he said to her. "Why don't you go and shower? He's bringing up fresh clothes and dinner in a bit."
She rose from the bed without a word and plodded out of the room, yawning. Bond heard the bathroom door shut and the water gushed.
"Bond."
It was D himself on the other line. "Confound it, what was the delay?"
"Just getting rid of the bellboy, sir."
"Well? Do you have the doctors?"
"Doctor Bottoms is with me. Dr. Sadat won't be returning." There

was a pause on the other end.
"That's a pity. What happened?"
"Someone paid him a visit before I did."
"I was afraid of that."
"Yes. I thought perhaps you might be ready to tell me what's really going on here now, sir."
"You'll be flying back out of Luxor then in the morning?" Well, there was his answer. Bond frowned.
"No, we're moving onto Cairo. Doctor's orders. We should be there in two days."
"Cairo?" D was silent for a moment again, apparently taking in the words 'doctor's orders.' His next words sounded almost hungry, impatient. "Two days? Are you walking?"
"Actually we've come under the scrutiny of our eastern competitors. It seemed prudent to take a more circuitous route."
"Very well. Let me speak with Dr. Bottoms."
"She's indisposed at the moment, sir," Bond said, lighting another cigarette. "But I can pass her a message, if you like."
"What do you mean indisposed?"
"I'm afraid that's rather need to know, sir."
D made a strange noise in his office in London that the international call couldn't quite capture. Bond smiled to hear it.
"Listen here, Bond. It is imperative that–"
Bond heard the squeak of the water cutting out in the next room and crushed out his cigarette in the brass tray on the table. "We'll make contact again in Cairo, sir."
The bathroom door opened, and Petra emerged in a cloud of steam, garbed in a white terrycloth robe, her head swaddled in a tall bundle of towel, like some oracle emerging from her inner sanctum to hand down prophecy. The whiteness of the robe and the towel and the bright marble of the bathroom behind her contrasted with her sun kissed skin, which was smooth, brown and rich as sanded maple.
Bond set the phone on the cradle and unplugged it from the wall as she unwrapped the towel from her head and massaged her wet black hair. She leaned on the corner of the wall.
"Who was that?"
"Bellboy. Bringing the clothes and some food up. Hungry?"
"Starving. But we should check in with headquarters."
"I did while you were sleeping."

She slowly ceased drying her hair and hung her towel around her neck, looking at him with her huge eyes from the midst of her nest of springy hair. There was a gold chain with a small, glittering teardrop shaped pendant, which dipped into her cleavage. He hadn't noticed it before.

"You reported in? No one asked to speak to me?"

"I relayed to D your plan to head to the Cairo Museum to obtain the Seed. He said he approved, told me to follow your lead, and to expedite your mission. He was concerned about the Russians. Said we shouldn't make contact again till Cairo. Smoke?" he said, offering her his case.

"No," she said, shaking her head. "It killed my father."

He shrugged, and lit another.

"Lung cancer. It's a horrible way to die," she pressed.

"There are worse ways," said Bond dismissively.

"That's true," she admitted, sitting on the edge of the bed and drying her hair again.

Bond admired the finely formed leg that slid from the slit of her robe. There was a timely knock at the door, and he rose from the chair beside the table and went to it, peering through the peephole.

He lifted the chain and let the bellboy and his silver cart in.

There was a platter of fruit and two crackling brown paper parcels wrapped in twine.

"I hope this will be to your liking," said the bellboy, somewhat apologetically. "The kitchens are closed for the night, so I have only fruit. But my cousin is a tailor across the river, and I woke him for clothes."

"I'm sure they'll be fine," said Bond, paying him and showing him the door. Petra had already lifted the platter and was picking at a bunch of grapes.

"I'm famished," she said.

"You did well today," Bond said, watching her eat. "For an archaeologist, I mean."

"Actually I'm an investigative mythologist," she said.

"A what?"

"I'm an agent. So was Sadat. We both knew the risks going in."

"From Fesche and his Nephren-Ka fellows."

"The Majestic Order of The Great Dark One."

"That's a mouthful."
She murmured her agreement around a half a dozen grapes.
"So's that," he pointed out.
She smiled and put the back of her hand to her lips. "Sorry. I did say I was famished."
"It's alright."
"You know, you don't look like one of D's. You look like one of the boys from upstairs."
Bond shrugged, inwardly impressed with her acumen. "It takes all types, I guess. You don't look all that much like a bone picker either."
"Is that what you think I am? A bone picker?"
Bond smiled.
"What time is our flight in the morning?" she asked.
"No flight. We're taking a cruise. It'll be less conspicuous."
"It's nearly three days to Cairo by cruise from here!" she exclaimed, looking alarmed. "We can't afford to take that long."
"Why? Are we on a timetable?"
She looked aghast. "Certainly! The triple conjunction's less than a week away. If we don't have the Seed by then..."
"We'll have it by then," he said, inwardly cringing at her astrological talk. He was just beginning to like her. "You're the only one who knows where it is."
"But if Fesche finds it..."
"Is there any way he could? None of his lackeys lived to see where we went. We're effectively off the map for the time being as far as he's concerned."
She was quiet, thoughtful.
"You wanted me to tell you about Fesche," she said.
"Tomorrow," Bond yawned. "Finish eating, have a drink. The boy brought you some clothes in that parcel. I'm going to have a shower."
"But James!"
"Later," he said.

Later, he stepped from the bathroom in a towel, glad to be rid of the stink of the cab and the unavoidable dust.
She was standing before the full-length mirror. The boy had been considerably appreciative of her figure. She wore a cream-colored sort of wiggle sheath. It was unzipped, and the part plunged to the

small of her back. Her hair had dried, and she had brushed it. She was trying out various styles of wearing a black silk kerchief. It appeared she had an element of narcissism after all.

Bond admired her in the mirror, watched her eyes on him with satisfaction. "Lovely," he said.

Her lips parted, and the words came out a little huskier than perhaps she might have wished. "There was no sleepwear in that parcel."

Bond smiled and went to the bed, drawing back the cover. "I noticed that," he said nonchalantly.

She turned and watched him as he deposited his towel on the floor and slid between the sheets.

One of her bare feet twisted inward on the carpet, girlishly. "There's also only one bed," she said with a half-smile.

Bond fluffed his pillow.

"Be a dear and cut the light," he said, pulling the chain on the nightstand lamp.

She turned and crossed the room to the light switch.

By the time she reached it, the dress had slid from her right shoulder. Then the room was in darkness.

"We're both adults, Pet," he murmured.

"Yes we are, aren't we?" she purred.

He could barely make out her silhouette as she came back across the room to the foot of the bed.

"I promise to be a gentleman and stay on my side if you promise not to snore like a man," said Bond.

He felt her weight on the bed, heard the hiss as she slid across the covers.

When she brushed against his arm, he didn't feel the fabric of the dress any more.

"I don't snore," she said, her lips close to his ear, the breath hot.

Two promises were broken.

10. Fesche and Cheops

Dr. Abdelrahman Suphi stood on the top step of the Nilometer and held his breath as the last of the British tourists, a pasty, flabby woman in her seventies, paused and leaned against the ancient corridor wall while her dutiful grandson waited for her to catch her breath.
That was all the tourism on Elephantine Island needed, for one of the hotel guests to die of a heart attack on the steps leading up from the water.
The woman regained herself and with the help of her young assistant, rejoined the tour group, fanning herself with her brochure.
He smiled at her and hoped she would make it back to her room at least before she succumbed.
"This structure was used by the priests of the goddess Satet to measure the level of the Nile and predict the volume of water in the *Akhet*, the flood season, when the river overflows and covers the flood plain, depositing the rich black silt so necessary for a bountiful crop yield. The predictions of the priests helped determine the amount of taxes for the year. You can see the depth markings along the corridor wall," he said, pointing, and noting that only a few of the gawkers took pictures or even looked. They were gobbling over a pair of feluccas passing by, snapping photos, trying to replicate some kind of postcard. Why did he bother trying to instruct the ignorant?
"This particular Nilometer is one of the oldest in all Egypt, and is probably the one mentioned in the seventeenth book of Strabo's *Geographica*. Notice the Hindu and Roman numerals beside the hieroglyphs. This structure was last reconstructed probably around the time of Emperor Trajan. It was actually still in use up until the construction of the Dam."
The British had nicely upset the natural ebb and flow of the Nile with their progress, flooding ancient sites and making the Upper Nile impassable to traditional wildlife so that what few hippos and crocodiles still existed north of the cataract would be the last to be seen in Egypt.
"Elephantine Island," he continued, "known as Abu in ancient times, was sacred to the flood goddess Satet and her consort, the source god Khnum, whose temple we saw earlier. Khnum's caves, from which

he was said to control the Nile, are beneath our very feet."

A few of the fools looked down at the ground. One lifted his foot stupidly.

He clapped his hands together.

"And now, if you'll proceed up to the museum proper, you will see some of the artifacts found here on the island, including our mummified ram."

That got them chattering and cooing, and like geese they turned from the river and shuffled up the hill toward the museum, the old woman and her grandson huffing behind. Mummies always got them moving.

Dr. Suphi folded his arms and watched them, shaking his head. The British came and ransacked their history, spiriting away the treasures of their heritage, and then came to see their country and looked disappointed at their shabby little museums and empty temples.

He could hear his young assistant Hasef even now saying, "Remember your blood pressure, Cheops. They pay our salary after all."

Cheops, the Hellenized name of the fourteenth century Pharaoh Khufu, of which Suphi, or Suphis, was an alternative.

A little joke nickname he had among the local scholars.

He wiped his sweating forehead and looked out over the verdant shore at the boats lazing along the Nile, and admitted to himself that it was a more photogenic sight than the old stones that so intrigued him.

When he turned with a sigh, there was a very large man standing before him, twisting the cap closed on a silvery flask and replacing it in his coat pocket. He towered over Dr. Suphi, and wore a tailor made double-breasted evergreen suit and a dark red keffiyeh which hid his face, leaving only a pair of mirrored sunglasses which reflected his own comically startled and distorted expression.

"Excuse me," he said. "Did you have a question?"

"Oui," said the man in the evergreen suit, in a voice that was deep and guttural.

A Frenchman. Dr. Suphi spoke excellent French, and was please for the opportunity to exercise the skill. He enjoyed speaking French. It was a graceful language, compared to the broken bark of English he normally had to halt through all day.

"Something about the Nilometer?"

"No. About an object in your archives, recovered from the Low Dam digging."

The second person to take such an interest in the past few days. The last had been that lovely half-British archaeologist from UNESCO.

"Ah? One of our Nubian artifacts? You're a researcher, Mister...?"

"Fesche."

"Well I'm afraid if there's something you want to see you'll have to make an appointment. However, I should warn you ahead of time, most of the more interesting pieces were shipped up to the Cairo Museum long ago."

"I'm looking for a particular artifact. A black dodecahedron of indeterminate composition."

Dr. Suphi felt his expression stiffen, though he could not read the face of the man in the evergreen suit.

His father had been there when the dam workers had broken into the old tomb and found the artifact in question; the very same artifact the girl from UNESCO had been so excited about. It was an odd piece, a twelve-sided black object not of stone, but of some manner of metal. It hadn't been long in their collection before a man from the Cairo museum had taken it. He'd never actually seen it himself outside of photos. It was covered all over in warnings and curses, all pertaining to some sort of Osiran cult. His father had told him the thing had been curiously warm to the touch, and quite clean for an object that had lain in the earth for thousands of years.

"What a strange coincidence. An archaeologist from the British Museum working with UNESCO was just here inquiring about it. I didn't even realize it was known outside of Egyptian scholarly circles. Has someone at Oxford published a paper I'm not aware of?"

"Is it still here?" the Frenchman asked, and Dr. Suphi noticed the thick fingers of his overlarge, gloved hands, curled and uncurled at his sides, as though in anticipation of holding it.

"No, I'm afraid it was never here. Or at least, it hasn't been here since around 1913, the year after we opened. We housed it briefly, but it was taken to the Cairo Museum almost right after it was catalogued. I've no idea what's become of it."

"Did you tell Dr. Bottoms the same thing?"

"Yes, certainly. She'd spent all day looking through our photographic archives, comparing it and other pieces to her own notes. She copied our photos, but she left in quite a hurry after that. I phoned my colleague in Cairo to expect her." He paused, frowning to himself. "That's funny, Mr. Fesche. Did I mention her name?"

The Frenchman lashed out, dealing him a tremendous blow in the center of his chest with the palm of one hand. But that hand felt like a piece of stone, and all the wind blew from his lungs. He was flung from the step and experienced a horrible moment of weightlessness and dread before he crashed down on the stair. He felt the impact of the ancient stone as it snapped his spine, and then the world was a jumble and he felt almost nothing as the spun and turned and crashed down the ninety stone steps and came at last to an abrupt halt with a splash in the water at the bottom.

His view was a strange, bent angle, and the Nile was lapping at his cheek. He could see his right leg extended up the stairs. His ankle was badly skinned, and the bone was jutting beneath his sock. He could smell the Nile and taste blood.

The huge Frenchman was coming down the stairs, his heavy shoes thudding on the stone.

He moaned. Paralyzed, It was all he could do. He could not summon the strength to scream.

The Frenchman reached the bottom and pulled off one of his gloves. The left hand reached down and took hold of Dr. Suphi's face, the palm pressed over his lips, dislodging a cracked tooth, which he felt break off and drop into his blood-filled mouth.

Now the smell in his nose was not the Nile, but the pungent scent of the open ocean and fish, such as he had smelled in his youth on vacation on the Red Sea, splashing in the salt-heavy waters. There was no malleability to that hand. It was like being gripped by a piece of coral.

It turned forced his head to the left. There was nothing he could do to fight. The last thing he saw before his face dipped below the water was the green of his sleeve. Green, the color of death and rebirth, the skin of Osiris.

He gasped involuntarily and drew the Nile into his lungs.

11. "He Overstepped His Bounds"

Bond had slept very little for a number of reasons, and woke Petra before dawn.
They dressed and checked out, taking a hotel car to the pier where they breakfasted at a café and did some light shopping, awaiting the arrival of the slow-moving steamer that would take them to Cairo.
The steamer was a tall, three-decked sternwheeler with an all-Egyptian crew and a smart-looking wait staff of Nubians in white turbans and navy-blue galabias. Bond and Petra settled into their cabin before taking the air on the deck to watch the great temple of Luxor pass slowly by.
Bond kept his eye on the other passengers.
Petra was entirely enamored by the temple. "It's so beautiful. I know I must sound like a tourist, but it is. And it sings to something in my blood, I think."
She smiled up at Bond, and laid her head on his chest.
He ran a finger down her smooth cheek, traced her neckline, and found the golden pendant he had noticed earlier. It had markings and two slender protrusions like horns on the tapered top. These were encased in blue-green faience. He held it between his fingers and the sun glinted off it.
"It was my mother's," she said, touching his fingers holding it. "It's an Aper amulet. Some say it means preparedness for travelers. That's why it looks like a traveler's sack."
"These look more like snakes," Bond said, peering at it closer.
"Asps *were* a sign of royalty in old Egypt," she said, "but my mother always taught me they were blue lotus buds. Nefertum, the child Ra, was born of a blue lotus that rose from the primal waters. And Atum, the finisher god, the first to emerge from chaos, from whose flesh the world was made and who will one day return to the dark waters from which he sprang, arrived in the bud of a blue lotus."
"Why don't you tell me about Fesche now?" he said casually.
"Fesch. I don't really know much about him other than his name. He discovered the key to activating the Mindbreaker."
"Mindbreaker?"
She pulled away from him and looked at him, narrowing her eyes.
"Did D tell you anything at all? The Mindbreaker is a prehistoric device. A weapon. Fesche learned about. We don't know

specifically where. Probably through the Majestic Order of the Great Dark One."

"What use would Fesche or anyone else have for a weapon over 2,000 years old?" Bond interrupted. "What is it? A particularly sharp arrowhead?"

"Don't discount the achievements of the ancients, James. Haven't you ever heard of the Antikythera mechanism? Sponge divers found it in the wreck of a Roman ship off the coast of a Greek island in 1900. It dates back to at least 100 BC, and is probably the earliest known analog computer, a device not replicated in complexity for a thousand years. And how do you suppose the Sajama Lines in Bolivia were etched? Tens of thousands of perfectly straight lines over kilometers of rugged terrain 3,000 years ago? Besides, we're talking about prehistory. The Mindbreaker is a remnant of technology that preceded the construction of the pyramids by an untold number of millennia, more advanced than our own. It was said to have the power to drive entire populaces insane. The hieroglyphs at Philae say that Nephren-Ka obtained it from Nyarlathotep himself, and employed it against his own people before he was defeated. Soris had the Mindbreaker transported far from Egypt, and the priests of Isis took the key and embedded it inside a black dodecahedron – the Seed of the Black Pharaoh. Then they buried it."

Bond let go of her and leaned over the rail, watching the water. This was all a damned wild goose chase. Why had he been given this assignment? Did D have some irresistible political pull due to his father's contributions to the Service or a friendship with some Royal? Had M been obliged to humor him while coordinating the actual mission to retrieve the Princess? 008's laconic assignment seemed more and more likely to be the real mission. Why had M chosen 008 over him? Had he slipped so far in M's estimation that he was delegated to babysitting this lot of quacks? And yet that didn't explain Trixie Treat's ties to this Fesche, or Fesche's link to the kidnapping, or Anwar having the same distinctive tattoo as these Majestic Order of The Great Dark One loons.

She sidled up next to him, clasping her hands over the water. The breeze stirred her hair. She was ignorant of his secret judgment, the poor thing. It was all ridiculous. He did his best to remain composed. "And this... triple conjunction you mentioned?"

"All I know is the window for activating the Mindbreaker closes at midnight, May the ninth. The end of the third conjunction. I don't know the details, but whatever it is, there won't be another opportunity for another sixteen years after that."

"Oh, you're joking. Petra... you don't really believe this, do you? My God."

She turned to him.

"You're not a member of O at all are you, James? You're exactly what I thought you were. One of those 00's from upstairs."

Bond looked at her, denying nothing.

Her eyes grew half-lidded.

"I saw the phone unplugged this morning. What did D tell you to do? Why didn't you let me speak with him?"

"D approves of you heading to Cairo to get this trinket you're after. I wanted to know what this was all about, that's all."

"Is that why you slept with me?"

Bond said nothing. It was only partially the reason, but she wouldn't want to hear that. However there was nothing he could say now to curtail her anger.

"I see. And now that you know?" she continued.

He chuckled. "I wish I didn't."

"Because you don't believe any of it."

"Who in their right mind would?"

"James, do you really think there could be an entire subsection of the intelligence service dedicated to... to what? Fantasy? You think O is populated with lunatics? You think I'm deluded?"

"All I know is I'm chasing around the sand after some antique gewgaw when there are more important things I could be doing."

"Such as what?" she fairly shouted, her large eyes beginning to shine.

What did it matter, belaboring the issue? He rubbed his eyes tiredly. When he opened them again, she was gone from the rail.

He spent the daylight in the shaded bar, drinking bourbon until he was loathe to rise.

At some point there was a commotion on the starboard side and the bartender rushed to see what was the matter, offering Bond a brief and unwelcome respite in his drinking.

When he returned, the dark faced bartender smiled a crooked, too-wide grin.

"Hippos, sahib! A rare sight north of the cataracts these days." Bond stared.

"Because of the dam," the bartender went on. "Don't you wish to see them?"

In answer, Bond tapped his empty glass.

They cleared the floor behind him come sundown, and the boisterous, sweaty entertainment director announced the arrival of a rich skinned, rubber spined Nawar *ghãziya*, who began to whirl and gyrate about the clapping tourists, her castanets chattering, as a mizmar trio broke into a thudding, skirling tune Bond felt somewhere between his upper thigh and solar plexus.

The thrumming of the tabla sent the belly dancer's ample hips shuddering left and right like alternately recoiling machine guns, and her superbly precise movements played her tinkling costume like an accompanying instrument. Apparently the restrictions on bare midriffs were unenforceable on the river at night, for Bond got a long and appreciative look at the dancer's stunning abdomen which undulated like an ocean swell, the sparkling jewel in her navel riding the course of her movements like a tiny storm-tossed vessel.

She danced close by him in turn, and her smile was the smile of a skilled artiste, evident also in her dark eyes. She was no cheap club dancer, long deadened to the empty catcalls of impotent drunks. She enjoyed her performance and the adoration she gleaned from it. She whisked her wiry black hair across his face and hurtled across the room to another table, leaving him with the lingering scent of jasmine.

His thoughts went naturally to Petra stewing alone in their cabin. Damn it all. Damn her and her poncy D for their preposterous beliefs, and damn M for throwing him in with them. For the umpteenth time he questioned his purpose, then knocked back a martini to cap off the day's drinking, paid out, and walked unsteadily out of the bar.

He navigated the decks slowly and deliberately, like a sailor on a tilting deck, though the progression of the steamer was steady and uneventful. He took one last look over the side at the dark, churning waters, and was surprised to see an empty powerboat tethered on the starboard side. Something nagged his gut, churning the ill-advised mixture he had been concocting all day. He had his PPK, and he rushed up ladder and aft to their cabin. He tried the door slowly and found it locked.

He sighed. Perhaps the boat belonged to the dancer and her manager. It was just the alcohol eroding his instincts.

He rapped on the door. "Petra," he managed.

"James!" came her cry in answer, and it was very nearly a shriek.

He ripped his pistol clear and kicked in the door.

In the cozy cabin he saw her flat on her back on the bunk in a silken nightgown she had purchased in a shop on the shore that morning.

Pinning her to the bed was the man in the scarlet keffiyeh and the evergreen suit, fairly filling up the room, like a bull gorilla.

Mr. Fesche.

One gloved hand held her notebook, the other was pressed to her chest, the fingers spread, the middle touching her chin.

Fesche looked over, but if he was surprised, Bond couldn't tell. He was expressionless in the headwrap and mirrored sunglasses, like an Arabian Invisible Man.

"Stand up, Fesche," Bond ordered. "Slowly."

Fesche pressed down on Petra's chest.

She began to wheeze.

Bond fired. The report was an ear-ringing roar in the close cabin, and he saw the bullet rupture the dark green cloth of the big man's shoulder. He didn't want him dead. He wanted the Princess.

But the bullet didn't even rock the giant back against the wall.

Instead Fesche rose from the cot and charged him.

Bond fired twice more. Killing shots now. It couldn't be helped. The right lens of his attacker's sunglasses exploded. The keffiyeh tore, and a third bullet struck him below the chin. A tight spread, all things considered. But the giant collided with him, and it was like being struck by a speeding lorry. Bond gasped as he was carried out into the hall and smashed clean through the opposite cabin door, losing his gun.

He groaned on his back as Fesche stooped over and seizing him by the shirtfront, reeled him into a crushing embrace.

God, Fesche's arms felt like he was wearing plate armor under his coat. There was no malleability to his flesh.

Inches from Fesche's face now, he saw the man's blue eye glaring at him from the ruins of his shattered lens, apparently, by some freak of chance, unharmed by his bullet.

Bond wormed one hand up and clawed desperately at Fesche's face, yanking the torn head wrap from his face.

What lie beneath was abject horror.

Fesche was hideously deformed. His pale skin was mottled with patches of black, as though in the latter stages of some necrosis. Those black patches were in turn crowded with strange, tight clusters of pink tumors, like patches of jungle pushing through an unlikely snowfield. One spread of sores completely encrusted his eye, and when Bond raked his hand down, seeking to gouge the eye, he groaned as he scraped his own fingertips bloody. The growths were not bulbous pustules ready to burst, but sharp and calcified, like sea coral. The hair on Fesche's head was not hair, but bristling spines, as of a sea urchin.

Indeed, exposed, his grotesque flesh seemed to exude a noxious sea smell, like old fish in the sun.

The stench assailed Bond's nostrils and swiftly plunged into his already churning stomach. He managed to raise his leg and lower his pinned hand enough to free the small knife from his ankle sheath. He tossed it up to his free hand and jabbed the point between the bony brow and cheek into the soft part of Fesche's left eye.

That got the giant to stumble back, releasing Bond and clutching at the wound instinctively.

Bond hooked his leg behind Fesche's and clutching his sleeve, used his ungainly backwards momentum to swing him down the corridor, caroming the bigger man to the fore.

"James!" Petra called, and slid his gun along the deck. Bond snatched it, and fired twice. Both hit, and as before, both did nothing. Fesche regained himself and closed again.

Bond met him, ducking under another grab and throwing him across his hip as before. It was like fighting a particularly clumsy bear. Fesche was immensely strong and tough, but appeared to possess no formal martial training. Unfortunately no counter blow Bond attempted had any other effect other than to force Bond to come away with his hand or elbow singing. Fesche's flesh must have been covered all over with that strange, hard growth.

Bond slipped past him, leading him toward the deck rail, and Fesche followed like an enraged brute, swinging ponderous blows that dented the walls but failed to connect.

He spied an emergency fire axe and smashed the glass, pulled it out, and chopped at Fesche like a tree. The axe should have cleaved him from the shoulder to the middle of his chest, but it bounced off, shuddering in his hands as if he'd struck a boulder. Bond turned the axe sideways to block a downward blow, and Fesche's ham fist snapped the thick axe handle in two. Bond dropped the pieces and backpedaled out of the corridor into open air, feigning fear, perhaps an easier deception than he liked to admit.

He gave Fesche a target he couldn't resist, then slipped his lunge expertly so that he thudded against the outer rail. Bond swung around and clambered on his broad back, using the remnants of his keffiyeh like a garrote and driving his knees into the man's hard back. "Where's the Princess? Where?" Bond demanded.

His position was precarious. It was a gamble, but he needed Fesche alive. Fesche however, had no such compunctions towards Bond.

The big man reared back and threw himself forward, flinging Bond over the edge of the rail.

Bond released the keffiyeh and grabbed madly at the railing, missed, and managed to grip the lip of the deck itself.

Then he was dangling above the dark, churning river, with the monstrous Fesche looking down on him once more.

There were shouts. The crewmen rallying to respond to the shooting. The stern wheel ceased its revolution and the steamer drifted. Bond heard the frightened cries of the passengers, others angrily demanding to know why the engine had stopped, the captain ordering the gun locker open. Fesche might have smiled. It was impossible to tell in that atrocious face if his twisted leer was static or at all under his command. The bleeding ruin of his left eye socket had not improved his appearance. He reached into his coat pocket and produced a silvery flask that caught the moonlight. He twisted the cap and took a pull of whatever it was, unconcerned by the eminent arrival of interlopers.

Then he leaned far over the rail to extricate Bond's fingers.

All of a sudden he was soaring over Bond's head with a surprised oath. He splashed heavily into the Nile.

Petra's face appeared, a welcome replacement for Fesche's. She reached down with both hands to pull him up.

"Someone's gone overboard!" someone else shouted somewhere down below.

A searchlight winked on and slashed out into the night. There was the sound of horrible groaning, unlike anything Bond had ever heard, followed by the sound of Fesche screaming.

The light streaked towards the source, and illuminated a bloat of glistening river hippos, perhaps a half dozen. The light glinted off their shiny humps, and also shone on their gaping maws, displaying immense teeth that were tangled with shreds of evergreen cloth. Apparently hippos forgot their vegetarianism when unexpectedly roused from sleep.

A woman down below shrieked.

Bond held Petra close. She shivered against him. He fought down his own trembling.

"James! James!" she gasped.

Footsteps in the corridor, and a couple of Nubians bearing electric torches appeared and shined the lights in Bond's face for the benefit of a pistol bearing officer.

"Sir! Madame! Are you alright? What's happened?"

"He overstepped his bounds," said Bond, gesturing over the rail.

12. The Tricks of Treat

"How do you suppose he found us?" Petra asked.
"I don't know," Bond admitted. He badly needed a drink. "Maybe they had men checking the hotel registries."
It was laughable to him, puzzling out the how of his finding them, considering what had happened.
"Look, James," she said, as Bond sat down on the cot. "I found this on the deck."
She set the silver flask Bond had seen Fesche drink from on the nightstand, then turned and rummaged in her bag.
The flask was old and scratched, and a coat of arms, the colors dulled by age and use, was embossed on the side. It depicted a golden eagle on a blue shield, straddling a letter F. The name FAESCHE in an old, gothic script. Curious, he picked up the flask and twisted open the cap.
"It's filled with sea water," he remarked, grimacing.
She had a bandage roll, and a small bottle of Bactine. She proceeded to clean and tape his bleeding fingertips.
He laid his head back as she worked, and closed his eyes, trying to make sense of what he had seen. He had shot Fesche three times, and there was no blood anywhere in the cabin. Only chips of pink coral and the pancaked 7.65 mm slug. The man had broken an axe handle with his fist. Bond had seen such things in Japan, accomplished by disciplined, highly trained men. Fesche hadn't fought like one of them. He was just obscenely strong.
They'd told the captain that Bond had found a man in the cabin with Petra when he came to retire, and that though he had fired at the man, he had missed. In the struggle, Petra had pushed him over the side. The captain had confined them to their cabin for the duration of the cruise.
"James, you mentioned a 'princess' when you were fighting Fesche."
He shrugged. He didn't see a point in not being forthright with her now.
"The Queen's daughter was kidnapped from her boarding school two nights ago by a man matching Fesche's description. The other kidnapper was shot by her bodyguard. The kidnapper had an inverted ankh tattooed on the back of his hand. D told me that Fesche was an associate of Trixie Treat."

"Your mission is to find the Princess, then?"

"My mission was to bring you and Sadat in. That's all."

"But D didn't really tell you anything about our assignment. Mine and Sadat's. He got you to agree to it by dangling the kidnapper in front of you."

"He didn't even tell me his name."

"Everything I know of Fesche, Sadat and I heard from D," she confirmed. Need to know. Even for her.

"I had no choice, really," said Bond. "It was either take the assignment or resign."

"You were prepared to resign."

He looked at her. "I shot him three times. I *hit* him, Petra."

She nodded. "There's more to Mr. Fesche than we knew."

"The goddamned bullet is lying right there!" he shouted, holding up the flat 7.65mm slug. It looked like it had hit the hull of a tank.

"It's alright to be afraid, James. The world is a bigger and darker place tonight than it was only a few hours ago."

"Petra, what is all this? How could. . . ?"

She leaned in and kissed him. It was the kind of thing he would've done to silence an over-querulous woman. It made him smile, almost laugh. Fesche was dead, anyway. The hippos, at least, had done him in.

Hadn't they?

"I want you to take this," she said, pressing something into his hand. It was cold in his palm, and rough.

Some bit of pyramidal black rock, like iron ore, etched with a miniscule circular symbol.

"It's a lodestone," he said. She put her hand in his and opened her palm. A second stone of the same ferrous substance, but cubical and cut with a hollow pyramid, rested in her palm. As she released it, Bond's jumped from his hand and clacked into the space shaped for it. The two fit together almost seamlessly.

Nothing magic about it, they were magnetized. She separated them and returned one to his hand.

"What is it for?" he sighed, though he didn't care to ask.

"If we're separated for any reason, we'll be able to find each other," she said.

Bond gritted his teeth and stuffed the stone in his pocket. He gripped

her arms tightly. "Listen here," he hissed. He wanted to shake the ridiculousness from her. He wanted to curse her. He wanted to slap sense into her.
Instead he got to his feet, pulling her along. "Pack your things. We're getting off this boat."
"How?"
"We're going to take that motorboat. We shouldn't be far from Qena. We'll go ashore there."
"And then?"
"I don't know," he said, stuffing Fesche's flask into his pocket. "Maybe we'll take the bloody train."
It would work well. The Russians at least, wouldn't be expecting them to get back on the train.
"You shouldn't have given away our tickets."
He glared at her.
She was smiling.

They boarded the night train at the Oena station. Petra dozed in her seat, her head against the window, while Bond took a pair of Benzedrine tablets to stay awake.
The train pulled into Cairo a little over an hour later at ten 'o clock, and they found a payphone. He expected Petra to report in to D, but to his surprise, she produced a number scrawled on a torn bit of brochure he recognized from their bungalow as being one of the Aswan Museum brochures.
"Who are you calling?"
"Dr. Suphi at the Aswan Museum gave me the number of the Chief Archivist at the Cairo Museum. He said he would phone ahead and let his colleague know to receive me and extend every courtesy no matter what the hour."
"How hospitable will he be when you propose to take one of the artifacts from his collection back to England?"
"D will make it happen. If he doesn't, I have you," she said with a shrug, and then turned away as the last coin clinked home and the phone began to ring.
Bond lit a cigarette and waited, watching the passersby, looking for anyone taking a particular interest in them.
He half-listened to her conversation, but it was all in Arabic. Could he trust her, he wondered? How *had* Fesche found them on the

cruise? He had perused every inch of her for an inverted ankh and found nothing. That of course, meant nothing.

If M was correct, and a resurgent S.P.E.C.T.R.E. was some- how involved with this cult, they would hardly brand a deep cover operative with their clubhouse sign, no matter how fanatical.

She was certainly more than a mere ditch digger collecting old pottery, but she had told him that herself.

Petra hung up the phone.

"He's going to see us in an hour." He tossed his glowing butt and moved to the phone.

"What are you doing?"

"Reporting in," said Bond, watching her face.

"Now?"

"Won't take a moment." Was she nervous?

He dialed the memorized number and soon had the operator for Transworld Consortium on the line. In another thirty seconds, D himself answered.

"Bond! Are you in Cairo?"

"Yes."

"Do you have it?"

"We're going to get it. Dr. Bottoms has made the arrangements."

"Is she there?"

"Yes."

"Let me speak to her." He held the receiver out. She took it.

"Yes, sir," she said. And the same, a few times more. One 'no sir,' and a 'Fesche' and an 'on the boat,' ending with 'hippos.'

"We think so, sir. Yes."

She passed the phone back to him.

"Bond," said D "You must exercise extreme caution. I'm chartering a private flight to take you Heathrow. It's going to wait on standby at the Cairo airport, so after you've attained it, go directly there. Take no chances. The Seed must leave Cairo tonight, do you understand?"

"I understand."

"And don't write Fesche off."

"What?"

"You heard me."

"When I see you again, *sir*. I hope you'll dump all this 'need to know' bollocks. Because it appears there's a great deal that I need to know."

"When you arrive."

Bond hung up the phone and hailed a taxi to the museum.

"Are you alright?" she asked him as the cabby weaved through honking traffic, taking them on a brisk tour of Cairo traffic. "You look pale."

"I'm fine," he said tersely, slipping another Benzedrine. What the hell did D mean, don't write Fesche off? The man had been pulled to pieces by hippos.

The lights of the traffic and the streets became a neon blur, and every squeal of tires and bleat of horn penetrated deep into his skull.

The cabby let them off in Tahrir Square and they crossed to the garden in front of the grand red stone edifice of the Museum. The garden was dim, and littered with the tips of obelisks, pharaonic statues, and dark stone sphinxes, each bathed in a bank of light from a lamp on the floor, casting them in impressive contrast. Shadowy figures conversed in the shade of the palm trees, only visible by the pinpoint orange glow of their cigarettes. Bond peered at them as they passed, but none took any interest. Tourists snapped photos with the statuary, or in front of the lily pad pond.

Petra stopped in front of the white stone stair and looked about.

"He told us to wait here at the main entrance," she told Bond.

Bond didn't like being exposed, he drew her to a bench, and they joined the shadows, some of them old men conversing, some
of them young lovers whispering in the shelter of the dark.

He lit a cigarette himself, and waited. That was when he saw her.

She clacked by them with purpose, a blonde woman, tastefully dressed in a black topcoat and pants, knee high boots and a black kerchief, the effect of which rendered her skin extremely pale, the red lipstick exceptionally vivid.

There was no mistaking Trixie Treat.

She crossed the garden with no backwards glance, headed purposefully for the street. She hadn't seen them.

Where had she come from? Why was she in the vicinity of the museum? She wasn't waiting for them, else why was she leaving? Had she headed them off somehow and acquired the Seed already?

Bond rose abruptly from the bench. "Petra, I have to leave for a bit."

"What?"

"Stay here. I'll return in a little while."

There was of course, no telling that. He left her before she could offer more protest. He left her whispering his name urgently.

He slipped behind the statues as he tailed her, but it was to no purpose. She never looked back. She was totally unaware of him.

She reached the big thoroughfare, Meret Basha, and went to the corner, then turned and lifted her pale hand for a taxi.

Bond watched one pull over, and whistled sharply for his own.

He nearly lost her when the light changed, but lucked out in getting a wily old Nasr driver who spoke enough English to know it would mean a hefty tip if he managed to keep up with the cab in front, and was willing to break a few traffic laws if it meant turning in early for the night.

They drove south for a few blocks, executed a sharp left onto Kasr Al Nile, and then turned east, deeper into downtown, where the sidewalks crowded with young people beneath the old French neoclassical buildings, bustling in and out of shops and nightclubs, and the intrepid old driver had to vie with Rolls Royces as well as Fiats to keep pace with its brother Nasr ahead.

This had been the European district prior to 1954, and home to Egypt's elite, though by the looks of the street denizens, the neighborhood was slowly being reclaimed by the commoners.

Treat's car pulled over and discharged her at Talaat Harb Square, recently re-Christened from Midan Suliman Pasha as part of the President's reforms. Bond leapt out of his cab a block behind, pushing through the crowd to catch her.

She paused on the corner and produced a pack of cigarettes. Bond saw his opportunity and moved in, digging out his oxidized Ronson. He stepped in front of her as she put the cigarette to her lips, and reached out, lighting it.

She looked up at him, the flash of the lighter revealing her face. She was a lovely thing, high cheekbones, smoky eyes trapped within a web of long dark lashes. She smiled felinely as she inhaled. If she recognized him, she showed no sign.

"Ta," she said, and held out another of her cigarettes to him.

It had a black tip, like the one she was smoking.

He took one, put it to his lips, and lit it.

It was sweet smelling, good tasting. Some local blend. He'd tasted it before, but he couldn't quite place the brand.

"Nice to meet a fellow Briton," Bond said.

"We haven't met yet," said Treat, arching one eyebrow flirtatiously, her eyes passing over his form. "I was about to pop into a café for some Turkish coffee. Would you care to join me?"

"Lead the way," said Bond. He hated Turkish coffee.

They came to a narrow, glass fronted café down the avenue, the walls hung with Egyptian flags and framed, autographed photos of Omar Shariff, Stephan Rosti, Shoukry Sarhan, and Faten Hamama. The patronage was sparse however, and the blue robed waiter moved at his own pace among the few occupied tables, a wrinkled cigarette dangling nonchalantly from his pouting lips. Swarthy diners smoked and sipped, rustled yellowed newspapers, or scraped and slurped at bowls of green molokhia.

They sat at a table near the door, watching the people pass by through the glass. They said nothing till the waiter had taken their orders. She ordered for both of them, in Arabic. When the coffee came, Bond had ground the cigarette out.

He watched her drink. He had an odd feeling. Like his earlier recollection about their having seen each other at a conference was incorrect. How had he been able to pick her out of a crowd so easily? Well, because he had studied D's photos of course.

But no, it wasn't that. There was a mole beneath her left breast. He was sure of it. But how did he know that?

"What brings you to Cairo?"

"Purely pleasure," said Bond, composing himself and sipping the bitter, unfiltered brew.

"Oh? You're a tourist?"

"Not really. I'm fortunate to have a personal and professional interest in Egyptian antiquities."

"Have you been to the Museum yet?"

"It's on my itinerary," Bond said. "Pardon me, but don't I know you from somewhere?"

"Don't you think you'd remember me if you did?" she said, with a playful smile and mock indignation.

"Perhaps we have some mutual acquaintances."

"This feels like baiting," she laughed lightly. "Name someone."

"Marius Domingue," said Bond.

She raised her eyebrows and made a show of ruminating. "I don't believe so. Try again."

Bond reached into his pocket and produced Fesche's flask. He set it on the table between them, the crest and name prominent.

"Fesche."

"If you have this," she said, taking the flask and turning it over in her hands, "then you must know the reason why he's late in meeting me."

"He got too close to a group of wild hippos, I'm afraid."

"Are you, James? Afraid?" she asked, sipping her coffee, unconcerned. "You will be. Very soon now, I should think."

"I didn't realize we were on a first name basis, Ms. Treat," said Bond, retrieving the flask and sliding it back into his jacket pocket, making sure she saw the Walther.

"You're going to make me cry. After all we've been through. You mean to say you don't remember how we met?"

Something in her tone agitated him. "Why don't you tell me how you and Mr. Fesche met?"

"If you wish. Two years ago a team of Soviet engineers pulled him out of a flooded antechamber while digging the foundation of the Aswan Dam. He was brought to me in Leningrad, to the very same building where you and I were acquainted. Do you remember, James? Oh we had such times there. When you came to me you thought you were a Japanese fisherman, of all things. I rebuilt you, then I broke you down, and sent you back to M. You must believe that last part wasn't my idea. I was sorry to see you go."

"What. . . ?" he began, but found he couldn't form the words. A building in Leningrad. Grey. Grey walls, grey floors. Everything grey, except for Trixie in her smart uniform with the blue epaulets. The bed in the center of the grey room with its red silk sheets.

"But my superiors wanted a weapon. They wanted to see if you would kill your old master, the Admiral. But you failed. Who turned you away from me? Was it Sir James Molony? Of course it was. M wouldn't have trusted his favorite with anyone less. He had you shipped off to The Park for a long, relaxing stay. How long did your recuperation take, James? It only took a month for me to break you."

Bond blinked rapidly. His eyes were swimming. Something in the coffee? No. He had seen the waiter pour it in both their cups from the same pot. Why was he remembering her lying in bed in a grey room, the KGB uniform jacket hanging from the back of a steel chair? Why did he recall rolling in those red silk sheets, Treat tossing that spun gold hair across his chest? Why was he remembering a bank of Russian doctors standing at the foot of the bed, watching dispassionately, scribbling in their notepads. That strange, sweet smell hanging in the room.

"But back to Fesche," said Treat. "He told me the Osirans had planted him in the desert in 1799 to prevent him from recovering the Seed of The Black Pharaoh. But now you've found it, haven't you? You and your brown girl. You're both so very clever."

1799? What?

She slid one cool hand over his. Her touch was electric. He felt the sensation of his skin prickling, like the shockwave from an explosion, where the epicenter was her fingertips.

"Oh James, how I've missed you," she whispered, switching it on again. "Do you remember how it was? How we were together? It could be like that again. Shall I take you back? You must say please, you know. That's all. Just say please, and I'll do it."

Bond gritted his teeth. He was pouring sweat. It took a maximum effort to pull his hand out of her grip, but when he did, it was like he'd been holding it to a hot stove. Relief flooded all through him and he sagged in the chair.

"Where is it, James? Where is the Black Dodecahedron?" she reached out and took his trembling hand again. One warm fingertip traced a line of fire along his wrist, as though exciting the blood vessels in his artery. "You'll tell me, won't you?"

"At the Museum. . . in the Archives," he heard himself say, as though from far away. "Petra. . . meeting the archivist in. . . in an hour."

He gripped his trapped hand by the wrist and tried to pull it free. Trixie held on tightly with both hands. Bond gasped.

"And how are you getting it out of Cairo?"

"Private jet. Waiting at the. . ."

"At the airport, of course," she finished for him.

She leaned forward and kissed him. He almost screamed. When she withdrew, he fell back hard into the chair, quivering, every muscle contracting. Her touch was worse than any torture. It had filled him with a tremendous, uncontrollable desire, yet somehow prevented him from even thinking of acting on it as well.

She smiled and raised a hand, snapping her fingers.

Two of the other diners stood up and went to the windows, pulling down the shades. The waiter turned the door sign and locked the entrance.

"Take him to the car," she said. "Don't worry, the Black Lotus will keep him facile as a puppy."

The two men nodded and leaned forward. One pulled his PPK from its holster. He tried to fight, but couldn't seem to command his muscles. Black Lotus? Why did that seem familiar? It was in the cigarette she'd given him. Of that at least, he was certain, but he couldn't say why.

As they grabbed hold of his arms, he saw a cufflink on one man's jacket. It was a Maure; the black silhouetted head of a Moor with a red bandanna on a white field, the symbol of Corsica, yes. But most especially, the symbol of the Unione Corse.

"*Dosvedanya*, James," said Treat, rising from her chair as they pulled him to his feet and dragged him toward the back of the café.

13. A Skorpion's Sting

Everything was distorted.
The walls of the café ran like wax and then began to shift and spin. The waiter seemed to float to the back door, and when he opened it, the dark alley behind yawned like the whirling void of eternity.
Bond groaned as the things on either side of him, no more men but shambling, dripping pillars of silver light and rainbow hued petroleum sludge drew him inexorably toward that hungry mouth.
In there was madness and more, retribution. Goldfinger, Oddjob, Dr. No, Red Grant, Klebb, Gaillia, Drax, Scaramanga, countless others, they were all in that hole, waiting where he'd put them. Waiting for him to join them at last in the tortures he had consigned them to. They were orbiting around a black star hunched at their epicenter like a dark spider. Blofeld.
God, Tracy was there in his clutches, bloated and rotten in her wedding dress, only the slow leak of ichor from the bullet holes keeping her from bursting like a balloon.
It was horrible.
Too horrible.
Yes, much too horrible.
The drug. The Black Lotus. He knew, deep in the rational part of his brain that was drowning in nightmares, that this was all a hallucination.
The chugging metal monster that opened its jaws to devour him wasn't what it appeared to be. Why would such a creature have an Egyptian license plate situated on its hind end? This was the dragon of Crab Key all over again. He fought down the urge to scream as he was flung down its throat. When he closed his eyes as tight as he could, the vision didn't change. Another reason he knew it wasn't real.
But then everything did change. He was in the back of the Lancia and Tracy was in the driver's seat. He saw himself, a queer feeling, to see the back of one's own head. He was leaning left, thumbing an unseen car past. He heard the engine of the red Maserati he knew was behind them roar in answer.
No! No! No! Not this! Not here!
He jammed his shaking fists in his pockets, scrambling to find the standard issue purgative in the lip balm tube.

Instead his fingers closed around something sharp that pricked his thumb. It was that lodestone Petra had given him.

It was better than a purgative. The horror melted away from his eyes like honey, and the thing crawling into the backseat after him wasn't a viscous, glowing blob, but the waiter from the café, Bond's gun in his hand. The waiter shut the door behind him, and said in French, as much as Bond could parse out from what Tracy had taught him, "I think he's coming down. Should I kill him here?"

"That's not possible," answered the driver from the front seat, twisting to look into the back.

Bond groaned and shivered.

"Don't kill him here," urged the third man, as he got into the passenger's seat and slammed the door shut behind him. "Look at him. He's a mess. Let's go."

Bond continued to shake and groan. The drug wasn't entirely gone. It was there on the edge of his vision, a flooding room threatening to overcome him again.

The sedan started up.

Bond couldn't see where they were going.

They were not on the Autobahn. They were not on the way to Kitzbuhel, winding between the white-capped peaks. They were not, he told himself. She was not here. She was in the ground.

They drove for a bit, turning, pausing at traffic lights which bathed the back seat in shifting hues which he forced himself to accept were real. The waiter's gaze wandered out the window.

Bond kicked his wrist sharply. The gun fell to the seat between them. He sat up abruptly.

The waiter bent to retrieve the pistol and Bond dealt his exposed throat a blow with the edge of his hand that sent him flopping back against the seat, eyes bugging, gasping hoarsely and clutching to repair the irreparable damage under his chin.

The driver cursed.

The third man turned in the seat, a gun in his hand.

Bond snatched up his PPK and blew the gunman's brains across the windscreen.

The driver wrenched the wheel, squealing the tires. The engine groaned and car horns sounded their disapproval of his antics.

Bond jabbed the muzzle of his gun into the back of the driver's seat and fired three times.

The car jumped up onto the sidewalk and Bond was nearly thrown into the front seat when the bonnet crumpled against something unmovable with a jolt of finality.
Bond didn't have to open the door. Some helpful passerby rushed up to help and eased him out. Others were trying to pull the dead men free. A woman screamed at the sight of all the blood in the night. No one saw him drop his gun into his coat pocket.
Bond staggered into the crowd, even the tepid Cairo night air freezing against his sweaty skin. He shrugged off the helping hands of several good Samaritans and then he heard someone call his name; "James!"
"Tracy?" he murmured, turning.
It was Petra. She took him by the shoulders, and he leaned heavily against her, embraced her, shaking the notion she was his dead wife from his fogged head.
She guided him through the crowds. They were the only two not going toward the scene of the accident, and were quickly lost.
The sound of the sirens never sounded close.
"Are you alright?" she gasped, when they finally stopped, and he sat down hard on a bench while she held his sweating face in her hands and pried open each of his eyes.
"Treat. It was Treat. She slipped me something."
"Black Lotus," she said, wrinkling her nose. "I was able to lend you some of my own resistance through the lodestone, but it's not enough. Here, drink this," she said, tipping a small vial of something bitter and stinking to his lips.
As soon as the acrid stuff slid down his throat, he was heaving and retching between his knees. It was the purgative from his own pocket.
"Better?" she asked. He nodded.
"Did you get the Seed?"
"I haven't seen the Archivist yet. I sensed you were in trouble and left to find you."
"Treat knows. I told her. I told her everything," he said, spitting one last gob of poison into the dark and then lurching to his feet.
He took her by the hand, and though he loped like some stalking monstrosity, pulled her on, orienting himself quickly.
They were a block down from the museum. They re-crossed the street to the park, and by the time they were back at the front door, he was

confident he was thinking clearly again.

The front door was still locked, but there were lights on inside now. Petra made as if to knock and he stopped her, shaking his head.

They quietly crept to the right of the door, to the gift shop entrance. Here Bond took out his PPK and lightly cracked the glass door with the butt-end, then poked the shard onto the floor.

He started to reach in, but Petra whispered; "Let me."

Her arm was more slender, and she snaked in and unlocked the door. They crept in among the dark shelves, and at the threshold to the museum's rotunda, they found the night watchman lying in a pool of spreading blood, garroted.

Bond motioned for her to be still and listened until he heard the sounds of shoes, two or three pairs, echoing on the floor of the central atrium, which was lit.

There was a stair to their right, and Bond motioned for her to follow, as quiet as could be. They went to the stair and Bond was impressed with her stealth. He looked down and noticed she had taken off her shoes.

They ascended in the dark and then, crouched low, returned to the light of the atrium via the surrounding first floor balcony. They were just another shadow among the unlit display cases of papyrus scrolls and canopic jars. Below them spread the large, well-lit atrium with its wealth of treasures, basalt sphinxes, pyramidal capstones, and enough stone sarcophagi to fill a mausoleum.

Four dark haired men in suits walked the exhibits, chatting lowly in a language he didn't understand, but which had a hint of Italian. Corsican? Decidedly not on staff.

More of Treat's Unione Corse on loan from Marius Domingue.

The garrote was definitely their style.

"Where are the archives?" Bond whispered.

"Back behind those colossuses," Petra said, nodding to the immense married couple seated on a granite throne at the far end. "Off of Administration."

Bond nodded and motioned for her to stay put, then slid along the east wing until the colossal statues were directly below him. He was looking for stairs down when a sound a librarian might have mistaken for a dropped tome resounded through the place.

Then somewhere down below a heavy door squealed open and slammed shut, and the murderous heels of Treat came clicking into the atrium.

Bond cursed inwardly as he caught sight of her passing into the hall underneath.

The four men turned and walked toward her.

Bond vaulted the balcony rail and dropped lightly down onto the left shoulder of the seated pharaoh, ducking behind the flap of his headdress, and crouching there in shadow.

Treat had a packing crate the size of a toaster in her hands. "The guards?" she asked as she came to the retinue.

"All dead," said one of the men, in Greek. She kept walking, and they fell in behind her.

The Archivist was dead too. She had probably gone straightaway to the rendezvous and claimed to be Petra. If Dr. Suphi had provided the man with a recommendation solely by phone, the Archivist had had no notion of what she looked like. Treat had probably gone in under false pretense, got the Seed easy as pie, and left the poor devil bleeding out over a workbench. He aimed at her back from the dark. He had seconds before she was out of range of the stubby pistol. She couldn't leave.

And yet in the last instant something adjusted his aim. His PPK crashed and the gunman to her left staggered, spun, and fell conveniently into an open sarcophagus.

The others scattered, producing weapons, one of them an EPK machine gun, which began to chatter in his direction.

Bond dropped nimbly onto the throne between his two gigantic benefactors, slid to the floor, and dove behind a black statue as bullets raked the tiles behind him.

He couldn't see where Treat had taken cover. Would he be able to kill her if he spotted her? What had troubled him in that moment? Shooting a woman to death in the back, or shooting her in particular?

There was no opportunity to mull over their previous exchange.

The Corsicans alternated fire. They'd had some training, probably during the war, but Bond was relentless.

Contrary to their experience, he didn't cower beneath their suppressive fire, but systematically moved from cover to cover, advancing on their line, shooting as he came, sparingly, no bullet wasted.

He winged the machine gunner, and the man broke into a panicked run. Bond shot him dead center and he fell writhing for the bullet in his back, smashing face first into a display case in the middle of the hall. Chips of millennial granite exploded from the block in front of him, but he clambered unexpectedly over the cover and caught the third man reloading. Only one left, and Trixie Treat.

Had the thunder of their guns in the cavernous atrium masked the deadly clicking of her heels? He hadn't even spotted her. Was she hunkered down behind some sphinx with a bullet for him?

The last of the Unione Corse men tried to ape him and rushed out of cover. Bond coolly sent him skidding across the polished white floor on his back, a smear of bright blood in his wake.

He crept closer.

"James watch out!"

The cry from Petra still in the shadows up above was too vague to be helpful. He looked all around, then rolled across the floor in surprise as he spotted Treat leaning around a basalt obelisk with a nickel plated Skorpion; an ostentatious, womanly thing. Vain. But a womanly pistol was no less deadly. The Skorpion erupted in her hand, and he narrowly avoided its sting. Bullets blew apart an ancient bas relief behind him as he flattened himself against a mummy case.

Empty brass skittered across the floor and bounced off the noble noses of two-thousand-year-old personages.

She clicked away, cradling the crate in the crook of her arm like a baby, but as he peeked out, the Skorpion burped at him again and he withdrew. He took a sharp breath and crossed the room. She raked a path behind him, bullets smashing glass and chipping stone.

She had reached the entrance to the outer rotunda. She knew she was nearly home free, and in her eagerness, spun on her heel and ran for it. Bond rose and leveled his pistol.

It should have been an easy kill. He had her bobbing golden head sighted. But his hand began to tremble, faced with no alternative target as before. He couldn't pull the trigger. He'd never experienced the sensation. It was not hesitancy borne from some noble notion. His finger was locked. He couldn't physically squeeze.

She click clacked across the rotunda, nearing the front door.

Petra rushed out of the wings, a brass rope stand poised over her shoulder like a cricket bat.

Trixie Treat saw her coming and got off a burst, but the heavy stand came across and struck her hard enough to put her down.

The crate crashed to the floor. Bond was already running.

By the time he reached them, Petra had kicked the Skorpion down the hall and was leaning on her makeshift club, panting.

Bond saw blood running down her hand. He went to her, but she shrugged him off. "Get the Seed!" she hissed.

Bond scooped up the crate in one arm and drew Petra to her feet with the other. He paused as, on the floor, Trixie Treat stirred, and her blue eyes fluttered open. The left blinked back the blood trickling into it from her hairline. She looked up at him, into his eyes.

He tried to raise his gun to dispatch her, but he couldn't lift his arm. She smiled at him.

He whirled away, hobbling for the front door as her laughter echoed in the rotunda, and in his ears.

14. A Flight Delayed

Out into the night and across the front yard.
Were there more of them? Bond checked all around, but no one rushed at them out of the shadows.
Police sirens wailed in the night, bound for the Museum. Someone had heard the cacophonous gunfire and reported it.
When they reached the street, Bond saw a well-dressed Egyptian in his twenties leaning on the hood of a maroon Bizzarrini Strada, smoking and chatting up a girl much too young for him.
Apparently he was enticing her with the promise of a ride in the brand-new coupe. He was dangling the keys before her as though she were a kitten, and she was smiling girlishly, hands clasped behind her back like a child who could not entirely trust their own hands in a candy store as she twisted back and forth.
Bond came between them and snatched the keys from the boy's hand and helped Petra to the low-slung passenger door.
The man leapt to his feet, cursing boisterously, but Bond showed him the pistol and he went off with the screaming girl into the dark museum yard, casting distressed, lingering looks back at his car as Bond got behind the wheel. Don't worry, he wanted to say. Just a quick shot to the airport and the police will have it back safe and sound.
He gunned the 327 V8 engine and slipped out into traffic as Petra sank into the mustard leather seat beside him.
"Are you alright?" he asked.
She nodded, but clutched her left arm tightly, and her eyes fluttered as though she were sleepy. The owner would bemoan the state of his interior when he got his precious auto back.
"I need directions to the airport."
She shook herself awake and began to direct him, avenue by avenue until they had left the congestion of downtown behind, and they were buzzing east down El Orouba Ave. Bond allowed himself the indulgence of 385 horsepower, smoothly shifting into fourth gear as the nighttime traffic thinned and the road became a lovely, sparsely inhabited straightaway.
Petra had torn a strip of her clothing and was wrapping her arm tightly.
"You're sure you're alright?"
"It's only a cut. You should have killed her," she admonished bitterly.

"Yes," Bond agreed.
"Why didn't you?"
"It wasn't chivalry, that I can tell you."
"You knew her from somewhere?"
"I'm not sure," Bond said, irritated and not ready to pursue this line yet. "What about the Seed?"
She pried open the crate with her fingers, and flicked on the interior light. Bond winced at the glare, but saw the thing they'd been after revealed.
It was a strange, multifaceted object about the size of a football, made of a black basalt-like material similar to the temple on Philae. He noticed each side appeared to bear a hieroglyph of some sort etched into the stone.
"That's it?"
"That's it," Petra affirmed, closing the crate again and resting her head on the seat back.
She closed her eyes.
Thirty minutes later they merged gently onto Kobri Al Matar, and passed into Heliopolis. The headlights of a dark colored saloon, a Quattroporte, slashed them, illuminating the interior briefly as they sped by. The car, a Tipo 107, swung in behind them.
It was the first car Bond had seen in kilometers, and he immediately tensed as it roared to keep up pace with them.
He eased the accelerator to the floor, but after falling back a bit, the Maserati came up close behind. Someone late for a departing flight? The dark rear window slid down and Bond saw the glint of the muzzle and stomped the brake as it flared to life, spitting lead that pierced the left front quarter of the aluminum bonnet and blinded the Strada's left headlight. Petra gasped and was flung forward, smacking her head on the dash.
The Maserati squealed to a stop and Bond kicked the accelerator again, roaring past, knocking Petra back into the seat as machine gun fire traced the rear quarter panel.
They blew out of the city outskirts, flying toward the airport at 150 kph.
200.
Bullets tacked like flying gravel on the back of the Strada, and the rear window blew into a silver web spun by the round black void in the center. Petra kept her head almost to her knees, gripping the door

handle and bracing herself on the dash with white knuckled fingers. Evidently she didn't want to see the catastrophe coming.

210.

A pistol joined the machine gun, and Bond sank into the low seat, wincing when a slug careened off the roof on the driver's side.

220 and the saloon began to slip behind, but the car was shuddering, the wheel alive and fighting in his fists like the reins of a galloping bull. Smoke began to seep from under the bonnet. The headlight wasn't the only thing their pursuers had clipped.

He eased up, let the other car gain, swerved left and right, crossing the center line again and again, matching its predatory movements to keep it from sliding up alongside them and delivering a pirate's broadside.

Steel and rubber hurtled through the night, death demanding to be sated in harsh, incessant, supersonic pops.

The Maserati drew close enough to tap their rear with its front bumper. It was almost enough to send them spinning, flipping off the road.

Bond held on, and forced the Strada on as much as he could. The car was dancing a fine line. He could feel the heat of the motor on his knees. Smoke was pouring out now, smudging the windscreen.

One of the rear tires blew, pierced by a bullet. Bond wrenched the steering wheel to the right to compensate. They had been in the oncoming lane, pushing 230 kph.

It was blind luck that returned them to their proper lane as the big red Bedford stacked with lumber pulled off the service road and loomed into view.

The unseen driver bleated a furious warning.

The Quattroporte responded with a shriek of its tires, but too late.

The Maserati smashed into the side of the lorry, hard enough for the load to tilt and spill clattering across the road. In the rearview mirror, Bond saw one of the gunmen still hanging out the window pinwheel through the air and smack limply into the Bedford's passenger door before they rocketed past, the horrific crash shrinking quickly into the dark, hungrily swallowed, the ever-present devourer glutted at last, pouncing upon the twisted steel carrion like a lion breathless from the chase. Petra slowly lifted her head, wide-eyed, terrified.

"They caught their flight," Bond said grimly. "Let's not miss ours."

They abandoned the smoking, bullet riddled Strada at the curb to the bewildered protests of a skycap, and walked briskly into the terminal, straightening themselves out as best they could. Bond put his coat over Petra's shoulders to hide her bloodied arm.

It wasn't long before Bond spied the Egyptian man in the flight crew uniform with the sign that read Transworld Consortium.

Bond dug out his business card and showed it to the man.

"Mr. Bond, Dr. Bottoms," said the man. "You appear to be a bit the worse for wear."

"We'll be fine once we're in the air," Bond assured him.

They walked down to the private service hall and out onto the dark tarmac where a new Model 23 Learjet waited.

As soon as they were aboard and in their seats, the crewman closed the hatch and retired with a tip of his cap to the cockpit. A few moments later they felt the rumble of the engines firing up, heard their high-pitched whine. The jet began to taxi.

Bond sank tiredly into the seat as Petra secured the crate containing the Seed next to her, buckling it in like a child before she even secured herself.

He checked his Rolex.

"Five and a half hours to London," he announced, patting his pockets, and finally producing his cigarettes.

"Oh James, you're not going to smoke in the cabin are you?" Petra whined tiredly.

He wanted tobacco badly, but by the look of her, she was as strained by the incident on the road as he had been by his encounter with Trixie Treat. She would be deep asleep in an hour, once her adrenal levels normalized. He could smoke later. He slipped the pack into his shirt pocket, annoyed.

"Petra my dear, my lungs are the least of your worries. Here," he said, leaning across the table, "let me take a look at that arm."

"That's your life, is it?" Petra ventured quietly as he began

to unwind the blood-soaked rag pulled tight around her upper arm.

"Two auto wrecks in the span of a few hours, with a gun fight in between. And how many dead?"

"Maybe not as many as would be if Treat had gotten hold of the Seed," Bond said with a shrug. It was a placating statement.

There was a first aid kit in a compartment in the hull. He took it out and replaced her makeshift tourniquet with gauze.

"That's true," she said. "So you've accepted the threat the Mindbreaker poses now?"

He looked into her lovely large eyes, knowing their estimation of him was in the balance.

Bond had dreaded that question. He hadn't had much time to mull over everything, but he had come to the decision that nothing Fesche had done could not be explained. He knew from experience that there were certain narcotics a man could be administered that would increase both his strength and his pain tolerance exponentially. He hadn't got a look under the man's suit. Perhaps he'd worn some kind of tough body armor. That was within reason. As to his appearance, what of that? Some sort of advanced condition. A hardening and mortifying of the flesh, probably. He would have himself checked out after tangling with the dirty beast.

And as for all this Mindbreaker and Seed business, it was all very well for lunatics like D and Treat to be up in arms over this fantastic conspiracy. And Petra, she had been drawn into it by personalities more commanding than her own. She would not be the first woman he'd ever encountered to do so. Once D had his ancient Egyptian bijouterie, he would report to M that he had encountered Fesche but failed to apprehend him. He'd want another crack at Treat though. If the Princess was still alive, then she was with the Unione Corse. He would go to M with that information as soon as they were back at headquarters. And if M wouldn't let him go out again, then the hell with it. He'd resign.

It was as he leaned across to cut the gauze, aware his prolonged pause was as damning a response to her query that any lie he could have cooked up could ever be, that he happened to look through the narrow space between the wood paneling into the cockpit, where the plane's exterior lights were illuminating the long runway.

The crewman they'd met in the terminal, who was the copilot, was on the radio, requesting clearance from the control tower.

A chill went up Bond's back.

A lone figure was running straight at the plane from out of the darkness, his eyes glistening like an animal caught in torchlight.

"My God!" exclaimed the pilot. "What's that lunatic doing?" That lunatic with a face like something from a lurid horror show, that figure overlarge and broad, leapt straight at the idle plane, the tatters of an evergreen suit flapping behind him. He sprang onto the very nose, and propelled himself straight at the cabin's windscreen.

"Get down!" Bond yelled, pulling Petra from her seat as the glass exploded inward and the pilot and co-pilot shrieked in terror and surprise.

The combat in the cockpit was brief and bloody. Bond saw Fesche grip the pilot by the nape of this neck and smash him face first into the controls as the copilot screamed into his headset.

The plane lurched and shot forward, knocking Bond back into his seat. He unbuckled and struggled out of his seat, pulling Petra from hers.

"Wait!" she said. "The Seed!"

She was fiddling with the crate's restraints.

In the cockpit, Fesche had fallen to one knee, but was righting himself. Through the shrieking wind blowing through the broken windscreen, he could see the runway diminishing as the Learjet rolled forward at takeoff speed. If the copilot didn't take control and ascend, they would reach the end of the runway in less than a minute.

Bond pulled her away from the crate with a curse and dragged her toward the hatch.

"No James! No! We can't leave it! My God!"

He dealt her a hard blow with the back of his hand that made her sag against him. Then he hoisted her over his shoulder and went to the door unimpeded except by the wind.

The copilot's distressed cries to the tower were cut short as Fesche ripped him free of his chair and drove his head against the rear wall of the cockpit.

Fesche turned to squeeze out into the cabin proper. His murderous, wild eye met Bond's, then flitted to the crate still strapped in Petra's seat, then came back to him.

What now, James? His mind screamed. *Have you ever punched through the windscreen of a cockpit on your precious Benzedrine? Ever heard of a man on Phencyclidine fighting his way clear of a group of hippos? And beneath that torn suit, there was no body armor. So what stopped the bullets, James?*

The tower control was hollering at the dead crew to cease their progression down the runway in Arabic and broken English. Bond gripped the hatch door and tensed as Fesche stepped into the cabin. Unbelievably, the madmen moved past him and went for the crate, sparing him only a twisted sneer and the stench of fish.

Bond wrenched the hatch open and braced himself as the screaming air blew in anew and the bottom stair tumbled down and began to scrape and spark on the rushing tarmac below.

Bond hugged Petra to him like an infant. There was a good chance they'd hit the wing, or dash their skulls open on the ground or the fuselage, or be crushed by the rolling landing gear or drawn into the engine. But even those odds were preferable to the plane colliding with the barricade at the end of the runway in the next few seconds. That was a hundred percent. Bond leapt and tucked in his knees, making them both as small as possible. He knew a crushing impact was coming, and when it did, his brain did the bouncing in his skull, and all the air blew out of him. They hit the tarmac rolling, finally coming to a stop with Bond flat on his back and the unconscious Petra on top of him.

He got one look of the jet smashing through the barrier at the end of the runway, of the wings shearing off. Then there was a bright, cacophonous explosion and a wave of stifling heat. The stench of jet fuel filled his nostrils and his eyes rolled up on him.

15. A War of Lunatics

Bond waited for an eternity in D's office down in the bowels of O Section. Upon his discharge from hospital (thankfully, a London hospital, he found upon awakening), he had been spirited straight here, not even given the option of reporting to M.

A matter of utmost importance, they'd said. And yet here he sat, going on thirty minutes.

He'd come away with a mild concussion and a bottle of ache-numbing paracetamol, a few scrapes, and some significant bruises. Fortunately, nothing broken.

Of Petra, he'd had no word.

He was lighting his third Senior Service of the morning when the door opened and D strode in, another black dossier tucked beneath his arm, or perhaps the same one as before.

"You really mucked things up, 007," he said without preamble or delicacy. He dropped the dossier on his desk, fished in his pocket, and brought out Feshce's flask.

"Except for this," he said. "This allowed us to positively identify Fesche at last. Jean Fesche. A lesser known son of Franz Faesche, the father of Cardinal Joseph Faesche, uncle to Napoleon Bonaparte. This explains his appointment to the Commision des Sciences des Arts."

Bond stared blankly, rubbing his head, and drawing on his cigarette. "You've lost me, sir."

"The Commision was the scientific arm of the Emperor's 1798 expedition into Egypt. It consisted of scientists, artists, cartographers, all attached to invading army to study and catalog- "

"I mean to say," Bond interrupted, "you're saying Fesche is a descendant of Napoleon?"

"A contemporary. He was in fact, the Emperor's uncle. Jean Fesche gained his reputation as an archaeologist studying the remnants of ancient Phoenicians and Roman settlements in his native Corsica. Perhaps he first heard of the Seed of The Black Pharaoh there, from something he uncovered."

Bond had been rubbing his temples the entire time. "You're joking."

"Dammit, Bond!" D exclaimed, slamming the flat of his hand on the desk. "When are you going to come to terms with what your own eyes have seen? You've dealt with Fesche first hand. You know more than I what he is. When Napoleon's expedition reached Philae, Fesche disappeared. He struck out to find the Seed on his own and didn't return."

"Until the Soviets dug him up while building the new Dam," Bond finished, pursing his lips. That was the nonsense Treat had told him. "Yes, well he's a black smear on the end of a Cairo runway now."

"No he isn't."

Bond lowered his hands. "What are you talking about?"

"Two bodies of the crew were pulled from the wreckage of the Learjet. Both have been positively identified as the crew. No other remains were found. Fesche survived. And he has the Seed now. And we only have two days to recover it."

"That's impossible. I saw the plane explode before I blacked out."

"I don't know what Fesche is now. I can only surmise, from what Dr. Bottoms has told me."

"Where is Petra?" Bond asked.

"Still under observation and troubling her caregivers about rejoining you," said D, disapprovingly. "If she's released, she'll be along."

Bond smiled thinly. At least she was alright.

"What was I saying?" D asked, distracted.

"Fesche, sir."

"Fesche. He has made a pact with a very dark power. Perhaps the same entity that granted Nephren-Ka his power. Nyarlathotep, the Crawling Chaos."

D swiveled in his chair, pushing across the room to his library shelf, and leaning forward to squint at the spines.

"Or, Nyarlathotep has brokered his pact with something else. The Old Ones are oft-times deucedly difficult to pin down."

"The Old Ones?"

"Before the universe as we know it came into being, the Outer Gods swam in primordial matter. The Nuclear Chaos, Azathoth. Yog-Sothoth. Shub-Niggurath. Ubbo-Sathla. Others."

Were these names or concepts? Bond didn't know.

D ran his hand along the spines, doubled back, found what he wanted, and slid a thick leather covered tome out with a hiss. "I don't know your religious beliefs, Bond," he said, scooting back to his desk. "I doubt, given your duties, you even hold any. But what I'm telling you is not fancy, or mythology. It's the pitiful scraps of a terrible knowledge men have slowly pieced together over his woefully brief time on this earth. Billions of years ago, before man was ever a notion, this planet was a battleground for alien beings. Its hemispheres were divided among creatures of immense power and intellect. Not so great as the Outer Gods perhaps, but certainly godlike to us. There first came a race of beings we'll simply call the Elder Things. These beings were the first to colonize the earth, and it may be from their machinations that humanity inadvertently evolved, though our creation was certainly not any deliberate end they worked towards."

Paging through the book, he came at last to what he sought, and spun the book so that it faced Bond across the desk. It was a reprint of some old woodcut such as Bond had seen in the British Museum. It depicted a scene of native worship. Hunched figures prostrating themselves before a strange idol of an enthroned, humanoid figure with a dreadful octopus-like head and sweeping wings. Strange. Stranger than any of the animal headed gods he had seen on the crumbling walls of Old Egypt.

"About three hundred and eighty million years ago," D said, "the first of the Great Old Ones arrived. This was Great Cthulhu and his Star Spawn, whose servants, the Deep Ones, warred with the Elder Things and their allies for domination under the command of his marshals, Dagon and Hydra. This was the origin of the Shatterer Of Minds, or what we call the Mindbreaker."

Bond peered closer at the woodcut. The congregants he had assumed to be human were either garbed in elaborate fish-men costumes, or they were truly some weird amalgam of man and amphibian, with wide, piranha toothed mouths and bulging, frog-like eyes, webbed fingers and gilled, misshapen necks. D opened the dossier, and fanned a trio of photos across the desk beside the book. They were all blown up photographs of the Black Dodecahedron. There was a white card next to the artifact bearing a number and an Arabic label.

"Thanks to Dr. Bottoms' copies of the photographs of the Black Dodecahedron from the museum at Philae, I was able to study most of the glyphs on the facets of the Seed. I'm missing some information of course, but they are a warning as well as instructions. The Mindbreaker was not a device at all, but a being called Ikla-Bafthgul, biogenetically engineered by the Star Spawn to oppose the Elder Things. When the war between Cthulhu and the Elder Things ended, Ikla-Bafthgul was rendered inert and imprisoned as part of their treaty. Mothballed, if you prefer. The Dodecahedron doesn't specify how this was done, but perhaps it was accomplished in the same way the Old Ones themselves were eventually imprisoned; locked in the depths of the earth or in other dimensions, or lost in strange cul-de-sac of space-time, by a force or to a purpose we don't yet understand. They're terribly powerful, and though they sleep, they still affect those who are susceptible through some process we can't quantify, possibly telepathic. The Mindbreaker is immortal, or perhaps just extremely long lived, but dormant. Both weapon and beast."

"And this," said Bond, glancing at the Dodecahedron. "Is a smelling salt?"

"Think of it as a combination locked attaché containing a firing key."

Bond had been gripping the arms of the chair throughout D's unbroken narrative, not out of anger, he was surprised to find, but because somehow, he knew these things were not delusions. The book he had shown Bond was quite old.

But did antiquity make them any less delusional? Like Petra, was he falling victim to them? Maybe his exposure to all this old madness, the resurfacing of suppressed memories about Trixie Treat, the unbelievable encounters with Fesche, all were conspiring to drive him mad. Maybe it was sanity he was holding onto and not the arms of a chair.

"I'm not telling you these things to incense you, 007," said D, pulling back. "I'm telling you because you need to know, if you're to proceed further on this mission. Just as I needed to know if you could face Beatrix Treat again and not revert to your previous suggestive state."

Bond swallowed and glared at D "You knew who she was."

"Yes."

"Did M?"

"Certainly. She was the Soviets' top brainwasher, and she knew our own techniques from the inside. It made her perfectly suited to break you after you were apprehended. Sir James Molony got the *how* it was done out of you. They put you in an adjoining cell to hers, led you to believe she was a captive like you. She gained your trust. They allowed you to engineer a nearly impossible rescue. The sort of thing you've earned your reputation doing, I should think. Then when you were free, she got further into your head, using a series of bizarre tantric and sado-sexual techniques she developed herself. When you were re-captured. . . "

"That's enough," said Bond, getting to his feet. "I've heard enough."

"Do you remember what she did to you?"

He remembered some of it. She had got into his head, as D had said. In a remote cabin where he'd been led to believe they had escaped to safety, she had betrayed him, returned him to Leningrad, then broken him down and rebuilt him. His memories of her were conflicted. She was a damsel in distress and a lusty whore and a cruel dominatrix all at once. He could picture her as three separate individuals, even different in appearance. But he knew they were all the same vile bitch.

She had rearranged his mind and sent him back to London to assassinate M Like a puppet with a new hand up its back.

"Bond," said D "There's something else you should know. It was apparent to M that you were not yourself when you returned. Everyone advised him to put you immediately in a deep dungeon somewhere and forget about you. He refused. Even after you took the shot, he refused to let you go. When I came to him with this assignment, well, there's never been any love between O and 00. But when he learned Treat was involved, he signed the orders readily. He wanted to warn you about her. I thought it better you find out yourself."

Bond squeezed his teeth together behind his lips. The old man hadn't given up on him. He was giving him an opportunity for revenge. Just as he had with Blofeld.

"I have heard you described as a misogynist," said D "But in perusing your record, it seems you deal with men much more harshly than with women, and your fondness for the latter has inevitably led to your most remarkable failures."

Bond bristled. The dandy (perhaps that was what D stood for) was astute, if lacking in manners.

"What about the Princess?"

"That's where our timetable accelerates. The Dodecahedron says that the Osiran cult that defeated Nephren-Ka encased the Seed inside. They were just men, 007. They should have buried it out in the desert and killed every man who knew where it was, but faced with the temptation of its power, they left themselves an out. A just-in-case.

The Seed can only be released from the Black Dodecahedron by the blood of one of a royal house, shed during the triple conjunction. Treat is going to sacrifice the Princess in a day's time to unlock the Seed and wake the Mindbreaker."

"For what purpose?"

"Certainly if it does what the legends say, drives men mad, it's an incredible weapon. But Treat is not of a mind to reform S.P.E.C.T.R.E. She is a fanatic. A worshipper of the Old Ones; a very select portion of humanity that pursues its own destruction as fervently as a moth to a candlelight. There's an ancient saying Bond that the Old Ones can only return to this reality when the stars are right. But when you've been in this business as long as I have, as long as my father was, you come to understand that the stars are quite often right when viewed from various angles. Maybe each Old One awaits a different set of astrological circumstances. The fight to keep them at bay is never ending. It taxes the heart and the mind, as Dr. Bottoms can attest."

Of that, Bond was sure. Of that and nothing else, except perhaps that somewhere the Princess Royal was being held at the whim of lunatics, and in two days' time, she would die.

Perhaps this was a new war, he had found himself in. A war of lunatics.

"Maybe the Mindbreaker is a step towards rousing some greater menace," D mused.

"What's next, sir?"

"I was hoping you'd say that, 007. Unfortunately there's been no sign of Fesche or Treat since last night. We don't know where the Mindbreaker or the Princess actually are."

"Corsica seems a likely place to look, sir," Bond said. "At the café in Cairo, Treat's men were Unione Corse. Marius Domingue should be our next line of inquiry."

"The Unione Corse is out of my area of expertise. How difficult would it be to get to Domingue?"

"Very," said Bond, thoughtfully. "But I know someone who might help, if he can be found. I'll need a phone."

D pulled open his desk drawer and produced a telephone. "Marseilles," Bond said to the Service operator when her voice came on the line. "Appareils Electriques Draco."

After a few minutes, a tinny voice answered in clipped French.

"I want to arrange a meeting with Marc-Ange," Bond replied in kind.

"There is no one by such name here," said the voice, detecting his accent and switching to an irritated, halting English.

"Tell him it's James Bond. Tell him to name the place and the hour, but to make it soon. I'll hold."

After another cigarette had burned out, the Frenchman clicked back on. "He will arrange to meet you where you first met, at sunrise tomorrow."

"I'll be there," said Bond, and hung up, and then, to D, he said; "I'll need a seat on the next flight to Dieppe."

D took the phone and lifted the receiver. The door to the office opened.

"Two seats," said Petra, standing in the doorway, a slash of white tape above her eye.

Bond smiled.

"And a car. Something fast."

16. Herkos Odonton

Despite the coolness of the pre-dawn air, Bond had the driver's window of the burgundy saloon open so his smoking would not disturb Petra overly. Already a bevy of wrinkled butts lay in a heap beside the car. He couldn't count how many. More than he was supposed to be indulging in.
It was a new model Bentley S3 Continental Drop Head Coupe they'd given him, and he'd barely resisted the temptation to lower the roof and let the chilly wind roar over them on the road to Royale-les-Eaux.
They had passed the dark churchyard where Vesper Lynd lay moldering, and he pulled in at the sleepy filling station for petrol while Petra went inside and bought a bottle of Eau Royale. He ruminated on how the first and last loves of his life were all tied to this seaside village, and wondered where Petra Bottoms fit in, and if, in the shadow of immemorial gods and monsters, any of it really mattered anyway. Then they were buzzing up the road to the agreed upon meeting place across the river.
"Will your contact show?" Petra asked.
He had thought she had dozed off. But no of course, if she had, her snoring would have rattled the windows.
"He'll be here."
"Have you slept?" she asked.
"I'll sleep when I need to."
"Don't be afraid, James," she said, for what seemed like the thousandth time. "It's a very great burden to take on, I know."
She did know. She had been at the forefront of O's battle against... what? Something greater than S.P.E.C.T.R.E. and S.ME.R.S.H., certainly. Suddenly he felt as though he'd wasted his life.
"How did a girl like you ever get into all this?"
"My mother and father were awakened to it. Their shelves were crowded with books on the Old Ones and their servants. There was never any choice for me really. My parents abhorred ignorance. *'Ignorance is the night of the mind, but a night without moon and star.'* My father used to say that. I always thought he'd made it up himself, but it was Confucius. I used to wonder how they could love, how they could produce a child in a universe as bleak and hopeless as this one seemed to be."
Bond looked at her expectantly.

She rested her head on his shoulder and smiled up at him. "I asked my mother once. She said; 'we humans come into
the world alone, and cleave to each other for a time, and then
depart alone again. We find meaning in each other. Whatever the origins of our existence, whatever its nature, we are not mere mistakes born of chance if we do not believe ourselves to be. Faith drives the world. The faith of the followers of the Old Ones drives them to destroy it. The faith of we who oppose them preserves it. Nothing else.'"

"Faith," said Bond, dubiously, but in a dreamy mood and near dozing at the sound of her voice. "Not love?"

"Love is faith in one another."

The sun was eroding the dark of the east, and like a forward observer, the headlights of the big, corrugated aluminum truck slashed between the dunes and shone upon them for a moment before the vehicle hissed to a stop and sat idling, heaving diesel smoke into the lightening sky.

It was the same truck as before, a little the worse for wear. Patches of rust showed on the side.

Bond snuck another pill and opened the door of the Bentley. He ground out his latest cigarette as Petra stepped from the opposite side.

He walked over to the truck as a man in a dark suit stepped out of the cab.

No one he recognized, but the man motioned for them to proceed to the rear and they did as he fell in behind. A lot of space under his right arm. A left-handed shooter.

There was the number plate. 'Marseille-Rhone. M Draco. Appareils fiectriques. 397694.' The same as before? Probably. Even his memory wasn't that good.

The ramp opened and they went into room beyond, past the stacks of cardboard boxes stamped with electronic equipment brand names, and to the aluminum door that led to the forward compartment.

The dark man stepped between them and rapped on the door, murmuring something.

There was a muted reply, and he opened it. They stepped into the luxuriant office beyond.

The same desk, the same comfortable chair, but not the same man seated there.

Marc-Ange Draco had aged since the last time James Bond had seen him, which had been at Tracy's funeral. The walnut like face was grim, the neatly trimmed hair a little greyer, the *joie de vivre* that had so enamored James Bond on their first meeting quenched. He had gotten old somehow, and had the overall look of a man waiting to die. He wore a shabby dark blue suit that was a little behind in terms of fashion for a head of the Unione Corse, and his mustache was untrimmed, his fingernails a little uneven.

He did not rise with a broad smile as he had when they had been uncertain enemies and Bond had greeted him with a thrown knife. He barely raised his eyebrows as Bond walked in and put his hands on the back of the chair across the desk.

"Hullo James," said Marc-Ange. "It has been some time." Bond's eyes wandered to the space behind Marc-Ange's head, where on the wall had once hung the calendar he had hurled a knife into. There was no calendar there now, and the mark, if it still existed, was covered by the only wedding photograph he had ever seen of that fateful New Year's Day. It was candid. Probably shot by one of Marc-Ange's men or the Consul General's wife. They were standing in the drawing room, the Consul General pronouncing them man and wife as they looked on. He wondered macabrely and perhaps a bit dramatically, which of them the hole in the wall rested beneath. It felt like he could sense the mark of the knife cutting him as he tried not to look irritably at his own smiling face, and at Tracy's, her lovely head inclined to his chest, the hand with the golden band inset with two diamond clasping hands poised on his arm. She was so lovely, so unaware that it would be the last photograph ever taken of her alive. Why hadn't Marc-Ange taken that damn thing down, knowing he was coming?

Marc-Ange mistook his eye line, and turned toward the filing cabinet also behind him.

"I do not keep this so well stocked anymore. I do not drink as much as I used to."

"No Marc-Ange, it's alright. I'm not in the mood."

The old man paused and turned, he thought, gratefully back to the desk.

"Not in the mood? This must be important indeed. More export business, James?"

Petra had sidled up alongside him now.

Marc-Ange's eyes flashed at her, and for a fraction, the old deviltry returned, and he smiled.

"Sit down, my dear, sit down. We are still gentlemen here. Even if we are not drinking, I would not refuse a lady. Shall I get you something?"

"No thank you," Petra demurred.

"It's probably for the best. I drank all the best stuff long ago." He shrugged, then his dark eyes went from Petra to Bond. "Oh God, James. You are not here to ask my blessing are you?"

Petra put the back of her hand to her mouth and cleared her throat.

"No," Bond smirked.

"You were my son for all of an hour. Do not think you need my approval, for you have it. At any time. It's for the best. It is not good, James, for a man to bury his love in the ground and forget to live."

"You speak from experience?"

"Yes, and fluently." He looked at Petra, and his eyes glazed. "You will forgive a maudlin old man, my dear. I have lost mother and wife, daughter, and granddaughter. And now I have nothing."

Bond gritted his teeth and went to the file cabinet, wrenching it open.

"I thought you weren't in the mood?" Marc-Ange muttered.

"Now my mood's changed. God, you were right. You did drink all the good stuff."

There was nothing but clinking bottles of warm Kronenbourg, hardly worth it. He took out one and slammed the top off on the edge of the file cabinet, and put it down before Marc-Ange.

"I told you I don't drink any more. I don't even know how old this stuff is," he protested.

"Perhaps it'll poison you and you'll drop dead like you want," said Bond, popping the top off another and slamming the cabinet closed.

"James!" Petra exclaimed in admonishment.

"I'm sorry dear, did you want one?"

"Why do you speak to me like this, James?" Marc-Ange whined miserably.

"You're still a head of the Unione Corse," said Bond, coming around the desk. "Don't pretend you're some heartbroken old hound. The heroin trade is booming. Driving the Americans up the wall, as they say."

"I am a chief in name only," said Marc-Ange, fiddling with the beer bottle as Bond drank his, bitter and skunky. "I have no heirs. I have not truly governed the Corse in a year."

"Who did you hand the reins to for safekeeping then? Was it Marius Domingue?"

This roused the old man, and he spat on the floor.

"That night-fighter! That Judas! He tries, James. Oh, he tries to make himself more than he is. An orphaned lapdog of. . . "

"Of S.P.E.C.T.R.E."

"S.P.E.C.T.R.E., yes. When there was such a thing. He diverted much that was rightfully mine to his secret pursuits with that organization. And when it was gone, when you buried that filthy bastard animal and his bitch-whore whom I will not trouble my sweet Teresa's soul by naming, he returned to us, his so-called brothers in the Corse, hat in hand, begging forgiveness for the transgressions I had learned of, oh but not so forthcoming about the many he thought I did not know. He is a skulking rat, biding his time. He thinks I do not know of his aspirations."

"I want to speak with him," said Bond. "Alone."

Marc-Ange's eyes lit for the second time, and he absent-mindedly sipped his awful beer, cringing at the taste.

"How can you drink this swill?" he exclaimed, setting it down on his desk.

"How soon can you arrange a meeting?" Bond pressed.

"Will you kill him?"

"Do you want him dead?"

Marc-Ange considered, then shrugged.

"It is of little consequence to me. If, in the course of your discussion he ceases to be, I would shed no tears. It is his clan I would like to see buried. Ideally, I would like to see it given to your American counterparts. The whole country, it seems, is pumping heroin into their veins, and now the CIA is no longer willing to do business with the rest of the Corse. They need another great seizure to appease the mothers of the addicts and I would like the attention off of my operations. The Americans need a scapegoat to tear apart like the jackals they are."

Bond smiled. There was still fire in the old man, and shrewdness. Dominque annoyed him, and was cutting in on his business, possibly surpassing him. Due to some intricate tradition of the Corse perhaps, the old man could not eliminate him and remain in good standing. But if his operations were to be broken up by foreign intervention, what could anyone say?

"I believe he uses the Trinicellu to move his product to and from the airports at Bastia and Calvi. A hundred pounds of unrefined heroin every other week, dispersed through couriers on the passenger cars. It should be passing through Ponte-Leccia on its way to Calvi tomorrow."

"But why not turn him in yourself?" Petra asked.

"Herkos odonton," said Marc-Ange, with a devilish smile.

"Herkos odonton," Bond repeated, and clinked his bottle with Mar-Ange's. "Keep it behind the teeth. It would be dishonorable to simply turn him over to the authorities."

"But aren't you the authorities too?" Petra asked, bewildered.

"Authority? Hah! James was very nearly family," he said, and to Bond's chagrin, flung his thumb over his shoulder at the wedding picture. He could feel Petra's eyes on it. "And you my dear? How rude of me. Why did we not introduce ourselves?"

It was settled. All Marc-Ange had needed to spur him on was alcohol, talk of love lost, honor, rivalry, and a pretty girl to flirt with. By the time it was all said and done, he was still not the man who had offered him a million pounds to 'save' his daughter, not the man who had led the assault on Piz Gloria, but the ghost of that great man was haunting his wasted shell now, kicking up the dust and rattling chains.

Marc-Ange picked up his phone and in a matter of moments, he had made arrangements for Bond and Petra to fly into Bastia within the hour. Domingue had a chauffeur. The tire of his car would suffer a puncture, and the chauffeur would take the car into a local shop for a replacement, only he would be replaced. Bond would have all the time alone he wanted with Domingue when he drove him to church in the morning.

Bond and Petra would follow the trailer truck back to Dieppe where Marc-Ange's private plane would be waiting. In Dieppe, Bond would place a call to the CIA, to make arrangements to uphold his end of the bargain. Marc-Ange left his desk and escorted them to the ramp, to the apparent surprise of the guard.

"I will have the bar on the plane better stocked," he promised.

"You'd better," said Bond in parting, and shook the old man's hand.

Marc-Ange gripped it, and did not immediately release. Bond feared for a moment the man would draw him into an embrace and stiffened. He had once taken pleasure in Marc-Ange's fatherly attentions. Now they were unwelcome. Neither of them were now what they had been then.

"You should have come to see me sooner, James," he said.

"Yes, I suppose so," Bond said, burying the guilt he felt. This was the father of a dead daughter, the woman Bond had sworn with a ring and Marc-Ange's blessing to protect. He could scarcely look him in the eye. In the end, Tracy's ghost stood between them, and Marc-Ange released Bond's hand.

He and Petra returned to the Bentley and followed the truck as it pulled back onto the main road.

"That worked out better than I expected," he remarked lightly, and then saw that Petra's face was streaming tears.

She turned toward the window.

"Oh James," she said. "I'm so sorry. I didn't know. Your wife. . . "

"She's dead, Pet," said Bond.

And he said nothing more until they reached Lieppe. The drive seemed quite longer than before.

17. Seven, Double Oh Seven

Marius Domingue had been a stocky man during the fat years in which he had served the organization called S.P.E.C.T.R.E., but those days were behind him. Being the head of an upwards-climbing narcotics clan in the Unione Corse should perhaps have engendered in him a more salubrious appearance, but his weight had dropped significantly in the past month. His face seemed drawn with constant concern, and he had begun regularly attending church, something he had never been known to do in the past.

His subordinates were optimistic. They saw the stress on their capo as being a natural side effect of the recent increase in CIA attention, itself an expected tribulation that went hand in hand with an ever-expanding success in the heroine trade. The capo was expanding into new markets, brokering new deals in Egypt, if the recent diversion of manpower to Cairo was to be correctly interpreted. As Domingue became more of a player, his gray hairs of course increased. It meant more money for everyone involved. That was the capo's job, and everyone accepted it, though it was a shame to see their patriarch's previously robust appearance take such a drastic turn.

He was haggard most days, bordering on unkempt. He had to be reminded to bathe. He paced his rooms long into the night, and ordered all the house lights inside and out be kept lit until he fell into restless sleep. Everyone agreed he would come out at the other end of it, however. He was young yet, and hadn't he taken on God as an advisor at last, after such a previously long sojourn among atheistic foreign conspirators? This was good. Marius Domingue must put God first in his life, and ask His blessing in business. Marius Domingue must come back into the fold of the Unione Corse. Lucciana was a fiercely Catholic commune in a staunchly God-fearing mountain precinct. It was little over a hundred years ago that they had gone to outright war with the neighboring village of Borgo when a dead ass native to that parish had been left to rot in the road one Easter weekend, earning the displeasure of the local sexton when its noisome appearance despoiled the sanctity of the holy procession. The Borgoans of course, had denied ownership of the dead animal, and the two towns of armed and angry villagers had taken turns carrying the carcass back and forth and depositing it on the steps of each other's respective chapels, the Luccianans going so far as to bear the swollen ass onto the roof of the Borgo house of worship and there impale it on the steeple, leaving it to disintegrate. The Borgoan podestà had at last admitted culpability by ordering the ragged and stinking carcass down and buried, satisfying the outraged Luccianans, many of whom had been Domingues themselves, though not before the D107 between the two villages was lined with a new crop of roadside tombs.

So when Marius Domingue stepped from his door that morning after a mostly untouched breakfast and sagged into the back of his waiting Jaguar Mark X, none of his bodyguards thought anything amiss. He was off to the chapel, as was his recent custom, and in fact, these, Luccianan guns who had served the Domingue family of old, quite approved. For six days now he had been regularly attending the morning mass, some said, undergoing his own private Novena.

They opened the wrought iron gate at the end of the private drive to his bright villa and waved to the chauffer as the car rumbled down through the dust onto the pavement of the D107. So routine had his attendance become, the guards at the gate turned their backs and never noticed the car turn right and head down the mountain instead of the customary left towards the local chapel.

Marius Domingue, in the back of his own car, did notice, however. When he leaned forward to ask of his driver Pasquale if he had missed the turn, he saw a stranger's blue eyes look back at him in the rearview mirror, and reached for the SIG P210 under his left arm.

The brakes of the Mark X screeched and he was flung forward so hard he nearly tumbled into the front seat. As it was, he found the barrel of a stubby pistol pressed against his hairline.

"Two fingers," said the driver, in British accented English.

Not CIA then. Who? One of Trixie Treat's cult? No, he was too fair, too cold and composed. The eyes of her men brimmed and raged with barely contained madness. SIS? Interpol?

He complied, and dropped his gun on the front seat.

The driver pulled the car over to the side of the road, got out, and opened his door. He was tucking the P210 in the pocket of his black chauffeur's trousers. The double-breasted tunic was partly unbuttoned, one flap hanging casually, and the gun in his hand was a Walther. He cast his cap off spinning into the bushes.

"Why don't you sit up front with me, Number Seven?"

Marius Domingue stiffened to hear his old S.P.E.C.T.R.E.

designation, but at the same time, was grateful to know for certain this false chauffeur was not one of Treat's henchmen.

He acquiesced, and slid into the passenger's seat. The driver got back in, and soon they were bumping along down the mountain through the woods and fields, past the pink and white stone family tombs, past groves of waving asphodel and aloe, the engine of the Jaguar scattering blackbirds picking at a dead squirrel in the road.

"Who are you?" he asked.

"James Bond," said the driver.

"Oh thank God," he murmured.

Bond took his eyes from the winding descent long enough to assess that Marius Domingue looked more than a little less sure than the man who had been photographed in the café with Trixie Treat a month ago. His eyes were bloodshot, as though he hadn't slept much, and stubble encroached upon his face. His collar was wrinkled, his tie drawn.

"I understand you've been talking to God a great deal lately, Marius. Is there something weighing upon your conscience? I'm not a priest, but perhaps I can arrange for the special intercession you've been seeking." Domingue stared out the window and rubbed his eyes.

"God, you want to talk about heroin at a time like this," he said, chuckling. "Is that really all you want, Mr. Bond? Are you still stamping out the last vestiges of S.P.E.C.T.R.E. because of what Blofeld did to you?"

"I'm only a little interested in heroin, Mr. Domingue," said Bond. "I'm more inclined to hear about what you and Number Thirteen have been cooking up."

"My God, if you only knew," he laughed, a little too boisterously. He laid his forehead against the glass, as if to cool it. "If you knew, you would drive us both off this mountain. And I would thank you for it."

"The day is young. Having second thoughts about Mindbreaker, are you?"

Domingue turned. His eyes were wild on him, bugging in their sockets.

"You know? No," he said, shaking his head and looking back out the window again. "No, I know you Secret Service types. You're just fishing with something you overheard. There's no time for you to stop it, even if you could."

"The only fish I'm looking to catch is one that wears a dark green suit and a red head wrap."

Domingue shook his head, but Bond could see he was listening.

"I'm willing to believe you didn't know what you were getting into, Marius. Trixie came to you with a way to rebuild S.P.E.C.T.R.E., or maybe just a way to keep the CIA out of your operations and bring the other Unione Corse clans to heel. Judging from your recent successes, maybe she helped you in some way to gain your trust. She told you about a weapon that could be directed to drive people insane on a mass scale. She probably said she was developing it herself, and given her background with the Soviets and S.P.E.C.T.R.E., you believed her. So you gave her the manpower and the funding she said she needed. You even facilitated the kidnapping of Princess Anne. Maybe she told you the ransom she and her friend Fesche intended to get from the royals would give them the funds to complete the project. Except you found out what she was really up to. Did you keep tabs on her through your men?"

"If you know all this," said Domingue quietly, "then tell me what I learned."

Bond swallowed. This was the moment of truth then, wasn't it? Maybe Domingue would laugh in his face and call him a lunatic. Maybe he needed to hear that.

"It's not a weapon. It's alive. Fesche has been trying to wake it up since Napoleon's time. The blood of Princess Anne and the Black Dodecahedron are what they needed to do it. Well now they've got both. I've got the why, the when, and the how. I need you to tell me where."

It was as though Domingue had been holding it all in.

He practically vomited his next words. They burst out in a half-wail, and tears spilled down his face.

"My God, you *do* know! I don't know where! Somewhere in Calvi! Oh God, oh my God. Had I know, had I only known! My man wasn't able to learn where."

"They found out he was reporting to you and killed him?"

"No! No, they didn't care that I knew by that point. He wrote me all he had learned in a letter and mailed it to me. About Fesche, about the cult, about everything. Then he shot himself. I thought he'd gone mad. This was a month ago."

"So you met with Trixie again, in Bastia."
"Yes. She told me everything. About the Old Ones, about the Black Pharoah, the Dodecahedron and the Seed within it."
"Why did you believe her?"
"She brought Fesche along. One does not meet him and come away a skeptic, does one, Mr. Bond?" He was sweating badly, and his hands were trembling. "Please, do you have a cigarette?"
"Later," said Bond. "Why do you think the Mindbreaker is somewhere in Calvi?"
"She showed me things too, under the influence of this damned Black Lotus," he spat the last, and furiously tore something from his pocket.
Bond almost killed him, but then a wrinkled packet of cigarettes like the ones Trixie had given him in Cairo fell onto the dash. He could smell them. Black Lotus, she'd called them.
Domingue pulled his own hair and pressed his hands to his temples as though he could squeeze the unwanted knowledge from his brain. "My man told me he had seen Ikla-Bafthgul with his own eyes. He was there when they uncovered it, in the basement of some old stone cliff side house. He saw it. Described it in the letter. God. Even that was enough. I burned it after I read it. The letter was postmarked in Calvi. I can't sleep, thinking about it. I can't keep down food, knowing I helped her. I've started going to Mass. Praying for intercession. But what am I praying to Bond? Is there anyone even listening? Am I fool?"
"How many cliff side houses are there in Calvi?" Bond said, ignoring him. The man was becoming unhinged. "There must be something else you remember."
"There are ruins all along the coast, some dating back to before Nelson's invasion, to the Romans and the Phoenicians. You're out of time, Bond. You'll never find it. And even if you do, how can you hope to stop it? How can anyone?"
The last was a desperate, spluttering plea. His eyes were leaking mad tears.
"What's Trixie's plan for it?"
"Her plan?" Marius Domingue laughed again. "What plan? Destruction! That's the only plan the Old Ones have."
"Why didn't you stop her, if you're such a devout Catholic again?"
"I tried, but it was too late. Fesche killed the two assassins I sent.

He's as unstoppable as his masters. It's coming, Bond. Very soon now."

Without warning, as they passed a particularly sheer and precarious bend in the descent, he gripped his door handle and wrenched. There was no escape that way, only a suicidal plunge.

Bond hit the lock button and stymied the attempt. He stopped the car on the lonely, high bend.

Domingue laid his forehead against the glass and wept, heaving like an overgrown child.

"Oh God, Bond. Let me die. Or kill me. I don't want to be here when it wakes up. I don't want to see what's coming."

"There's just one last thing, Marius. The heroin. The truth is, I *am* more than just a little interested in that too. How do I recognize your couriers on the train to Calvi?"

Marius Domingue stared, and began to laugh a little too exuberantly. "The heroin?"

Bond didn't smile.

He cocked the hammer of the Walther.

"It could go very slow for you, Marius. There's plenty of petrol in the tank. We could drive around for hours."

Domingue stared at the gun, blinking rapidly, breath huffing out now. "We use tie colors. Every other week it's different. This week it's red."

"Red ties. How many couriers and which train?"

Marius shook his head, flecking the window with sweat like a dog in from the rain.

"Two. One at Furiani, the other at Ponte-Leccia. The third train of the day."

Bond lowered the hammer on the automatic and put it in his holster. "Very well. Thanks for the information. You're free to go, Marius."

He thumbed the driver's side button, unlocking the passenger door.

Marius Domingue stared at Bond, then reached for the door handle again.

When it opened, he began to laugh. "Adieu, Bond!"

The man stepped out and leapt into space. He laughed the entire way down the side of the cliff, until his amusement was cut short by the heavy sound of his impact on the rocks.

Bond reached across the passenger's seat and pulled the door shut. He took out his cigarette case and lit one, his eyes going to the crumpled pack Marius had left on the dashboard. It bore a stylized black blossom on the cover and brand name Liao. He took the pack, slipped it into his pocket.

Fifteen minutes later he was pulling into the Chemins de Fer de la Corse station at Bastia. He stripped out of his chauffeur's costume and changed into a dark blue suit he had stowed in the trunk.

Inside the station, he found Petra waiting on a bench with a one-armed, one-legged man who grinned at his entrance, and raised a steel hook in greeting. His straw hair was a little white at the edges, like a crop of wheat caught in a freak early frost.

"Hello, James. Mathis sends his regards." René Mathis. Head of the Deuxième Bureau.

"Hello, Felix. I didn't expect to see you here," Bond replied, smiling broadly to see his old friend.

"Likewise," said Felix Leiter, the winsome Texan and ex-CIA man who had been through the ringer with Bond more than a few times. He rose like a man with two good legs and pumped Bond's hand with his own. "We had another of your men down here the past week, helping us out on the Marseilles side. Fella named Ibaka. When I got the call you were coming in, I was worried something had happened to him."

Bill Ibaka. So this had been his assignment. Nothing to do with the Princess at all.

"Not that I'm aware of. We're here on an unrelated matter that just happened to cross into your back garden."

"The way things fall into your lap, James, I wish you'd stay. We could have the whole Connection busted up in a week."

Bond shrugged. "And cut your man hours? You'd never be able to afford retirement that way, Felix."

Felix gestured to Petra. "I'll say this, your lady agents just get more charming every year."

"You're too kind, Mr. Leiter," said Petra.

"Felix. Watch out for this one, honey," said Felix. "Now what about our pigeons?"

"The couriers are on the third scheduled train."

"There's five a day," said Felix. "We've got thirty minutes to the third train. Nice timing. What about descriptions?"

"They wear color-coded ties, rotated on a bi-weekly basis. This time, they'll be wearing red. There are two, each with about fifty pounds strapped to them. One gets on at Furiani, the other at Ponte-Leccia. They'll probably have plane tickets on them, and once they hear about their capo, they'll be more than willing to talk about their American contacts, I'm sure."

"Why, what's happened to Marius?" Felix asked.

"He's stepped out. Indefinitely." Felix nodded.

"Coming along on the train? For old time's sake? You can't beat the scenery."

"You know I can't resist watching you work, Felix. But I'm afraid Pet and I will just be along for the ride this go 'round. We have an important appointment to keep in Calvi."

Felix nodded.

"We'll have a chopper waiting at the next stop past Ponte- Luccia to extradite. Let's see... that'd be... Petralba. I'll get my men ready," he said, and limped off to a conspicuous group of Americans and Frenchmen smoking in the corner of the station.

"Pet, get on the phone to D. We're looking for an old coastal house. Stone. Anything that might be tied to Treat or Fesche. Check public records, deeds, anything."

Bond looked up at the timetables on the board over the ticket window. "He has about two hours and forty-five minutes to come up with something."

She clicked off to the phones.

Bond reached into his pocket for a cigarette, and found the wrinkled pack of Liao cigarettes he had taken from Marius' car. He also had Fesche's flask of seawater.

On a whim, he opened the flask, took out one of the black tipped cigarettes, and began to sprinkle the strange dark weed into it.

He noticed a small brown skinned boy holding his mother's hand in line at the ticket counter, apparently puzzled by what he was doing.

"Just giving it a little extra kick," Bond remarked with a wink.

18. U Trinighellu

The Trinicellu or 'little train' was a metre gauge autorail, just two old boxy yellow and red Renault ABH8's that slipped from the Bastia station, heavy diesel engines chugging along at a little over 70kph (the ride rough enough for the little train to earn its nickname, 'the boneshaker') and hissed to a stop eight minutes later at the Furiani platform.

They saw the courier standing right outside the window as the train pulled up, a man in a bright red tie and a dark suit, checking his watch habitually. The look of a stocky businessman, but the thinness of the face gave away the extra fifty pounds bulking up his person.

Felix had brought along four agents, two CIA and two of the Deuxième Bureau. They marked the courier as he sat down, but no one made a move to grab him.

"Isn't that the man there with the red tie?" Petra whispered to Bond. Felix, who sat behind them, leaned forward.

"No point nabbing him now, honey. It's another hour to Ponte-Leccia when his friend gets on. So long as he doesn't get off, we can enjoy the ride. You're headed to Calvi? That's the end of the line. Ever been there before, James?"

"No."

"Nice place to retire. Find a good woman, a nice beachfront house, watch the kids play in the sand."

Bond looked at him. What was he getting at? Best to beat him to the punch.

"You sound old, Felix. Maybe you should go through the real estate listings once this is over."

"On the contrary," he said, brandishing his steel hook with a click. "Most of me's still brand new."

"I thought you'd gotten a private detective's license. Why do you keep returning the Company's phone calls?"

"Cheating husbands and arson cases don't have the same bite."

Bond nearly remarked that neither did sharks, but held his tongue. He liked Felix a great deal. What would his old comrade at arms say if he knew what the Service had put him up to? Running down cultists and saving Princesses from human sacrifice? It was the sort of thing Felix probably read on the toilet. He found himself wishing he could tell him. Just so there was someone with whom he had a real rapport to suss this out with.

There was something there with Petra, of course. But it wasn't the same. These things were of Petra's world, not his. He was out of his element. He kept talking to Felix. Kept himself in the moment. Because if he left that moment of normalcy for even an instant, if he allowed his mind to slip into contemplation about his strange mission, he might leap off a cliff as Marius Domingue had and die laughing. Felix was a Texan, and could talk as long as there was an unblocked ear. Beside Bond, Petra grew restless. She had been aloof since finding out about Tracy. There was something she meant to say, something it was probably best for her not to say. She was chomping at the bit to get it out, of course.

But Felix kept talking, reminiscing in a low tone about Goldfinger, Quarrel, Pus-Feller, and Jamaica, and going off on tangents comparing the beaches of Kingston and Calvi again. He really was giving serious thought to permanent retirement, Bond realized. Well why shouldn't he? The CIA had cost him his gun hand and his livelihood. That line about cheating husbands and insurance fraud, was that what being a one-handed private detective was all about? How close had Bond come to the same fate? There but for the grace of God. He understood why Felix kept coming back.

But could Bond come back again after this? The missions were getting harder. And now, knowing that there were entire portions of his life he had forgotten about. What else had he forgotten? Trixie had made a crack about him thinking he was a Japanese fisherman when the Soviets brought him to her. He didn't remember anything about Japan after Blofeld's castle had exploded.

And the Old Ones... prehistoric beings that could survive the ages. What the hell was that about? He wanted a drink.

He was stirred from his thoughts by their arrival at Ponte-Leccia.

Another man in a red tie rose from the bench on the open platform and shuffled onto the train as many of the passengers exited.

Felix checked his watch and nodded to one of his men, who got up from his seat as the doors closed, pretended to read the timetables, and then sat down across the aisle from the second courier. Both drug mules had two men on them now.

As the train pulled away from the station, Felix patted Bond's shoulder. "Seven minutes, James. Best to say our adieus."

"Take care of yourself, Felix," said Bond. "And tell René hello for me."

"Nice to meet you, Pet Bottoms," he said to Petra, and winked so only Bond could see.

James Bond smiled as the driver announced Petralba and Felix Leiter lurched up the aisle.

The train came to yet another small town nestled in the green hills, and as it came to a stop, the CIA and Deuxième men nearest the couriers leaned forward and whispered in their ears, each removing something from their jackets that made the two men stiffen and rise. The other two agents rose, and all four men ushered the couriers back onto the lonely platform.

Felix paused in the doorway and gave Bond a quick, lazy salute with his hook.

The other half dozen passengers in their car didn't even look up as he stepped out and the doors closed behind him.

"Who is René?" Petra asked. "Another of your girls?"

"Yes and the ugliest one you could imagine," said Bond with a chuckle. "Much uglier than you."

She propped her elbow on the seat and pushed back her hair as she leaned on the heel of her hand, fixing him with those lovely brown eyes. The cut on her scalp was scabbed over, just a tiny dark line near her hairline now. She had even covered it in makeup just for him.

"Do you ever think about retiring, James?"

"I did retire once. It didn't work out."

"You mean your wife. I'm sorry."

He had given her that. They had an hour to Calvi. Might as well get this out of the way. She had probably asked Felix all about Tracy already, but just the same, she said; "What was she like?"

"Oh, feisty. Beautiful. Spoiled. Damaged. Like me I suppose. That's why we got on so well."

He watched the countryside roll by behind Petra's head like a man running down a row of pastorals. The train was slowing as they came to a rural crossing.

"Would you ever do it again?" He bit his lip.

"No, Pet. Not ever. I'm sorry." She lowered her eyes.

"You have your reasons, I suppose. So what will you do then, when you do get too old to go traipsing about with your gun and your kisses?"

"Then, my dear, I shall look you up, and we'll feed pigeons from a bench in Regent's Park and complain about how the London drizzle makes our bones ache."

She smiled and looked out the window.

"I suppose D will have you too busy brushing up on monsters at the library for you to sit on a bench with me," Bond went on.

She looked at him.

"James," she said, laying a hand on his. "Now that you know what I know, would you rather you didn't? Do you wish you'd never met me?"

"My dear, I shouldn't trade knowing you for the crown jewels."

"But the Old Ones?"

He badly wanted that drink now.

"Maybe some things are better off not knowing," said Bond quietly.

"What about you?"

"No, James. I wouldn't go back to sleep for anything. I want to spend as much of the time I have left wide awake."

He looked over her shoulder as the train crawled across the country road. Two cars waited patiently, but as Bond watched, a slew of Motobécane cycles growled up from behind the touring traffic, slipping up both shoulders of the road. The riders, six in all, were dressed in black leathers and helmets, made further uniform by riding goggles. All of them were armed with MAT-49 submachine guns, which they brought to bear in unison.

"Down!" Bond yelled, and pulled Petra to the floor as the six machine guns opened fire, raking the side of the train car with 9mm parabellum, blowing out all the windows and bathing them in glass.

The other passengers danced in their seats wildly. Bond saw the old man across the aisle from them still holding his newspaper as if struggling to read it while it shredded in his quivering hands. Only the stream of bullets held him aright.

The fire was continuous. With 32 round magazines, the assailants maintained a steady, deadly hail of lead, and drowned out any screams that might have occurred. The bullets pecked at the sides of the train, but 9mm parabellums weren't going to pierce the heavy steel sides of the old monster auto rail, and they were safe on the floor, though slashed by glass.

When at last the gunfire ceased, there was no sound but the idling of the motorcycles and the long note of a depressed car horn through the now open windows, like the wail of the car mourning its dead driver. One of the motorists on the road must have attempted to intervene or escape. Then came the metallic staccato of magazines refreshing, bolts being drawn back.

The train was still moving, but had not increased in speed. Bond drew his PPK as he heard boots crunching hurriedly.

Right above their heads, a leather-gloved hand gripped the frame of the shattered window, and one heavy boot mounted the edge.

Bond saw the barrel of the machine gun, still trailing smoke, and then the helmeted head of the owner as he peered over.

He put a bullet through the septum of the gunman, caught the falling machine gun, and shoved Petra roughly aside, getting to his feet, broken glass sliding off his shoulders.

The other assassins stood astride their bikes in the road, waiting to see what their comrade would report.

Bond opened up on them from the ruined window as the train pulled slowly past.

Two fell from their bikes and the others leapt for cover behind the cars. The machine gun clicked dry, and Bond let it fall, then pulled the quivering Petra to her feet and made for the front car. They clashed through to the forward car and found a scene of carnage much like the one they had left. Three dead passengers here, and the engineer slumped against his controls.

Bond went to the operator's chair and pulled the dead man unceremoniously to the glass-littered floor. One look at the controls showed him the throttle and the brakes, vacuum and air both.

Motorcycle engines revved behind them. Shouts. He pulled Petra into the cab.

"Open the throttle wide. Brake for the turns so we don't derail."

She was shaken and bleeding from a half dozen cuts, but nodded. "How do I brake?"

He showed her the mechanism, then turned to head back into the car.

"Where are you going?"

"To repel boarders," he said. "Keep your head down. There's nothing to run into."

She crouched by the panel, and he left her there.

The motorcycles were off road now, and gaining on the train like a pack of hungry wolves panting exhaust fumes and flecking their prey with slavering bullets. There were double the number Bond had counted. They were flanking the train.

He got down low beneath the gunfire. Their pattern was predictable, but that didn't make it any less challenging to counteract. A heavy burst of gunfire to keep his head down, and then one of them would get up alongside the train and leap for the broken windows. Bond shot the first two that tried this, but more bikes had apparently joined the others from the opposite side of the train, and he couldn't cover both cars.

A group got aboard the rear car, and Bond crouched behind a seat and traded shots with any who tried to gain the front. Here he had the advantage, as the door between cars was a natural bottleneck. But while he could drop them dead in that doorway, he still had to keep an eye out for any coming through the windows.

The train was speeding along now, and the bikes were buzzing at breakneck velocity to keep up. The bodies of four bikers propped open the door to the next car now.

The train flew past the stop at L'Île-Rousse, the commuters scattering as the bikers drove up and along the platform.

Bond was out of bullets. He crept forward, making for a dead man's MAT-49, when another came stumbling in over the bodies from the rear car. Bond batted the machine gun aside with the edge of his hand and drove his knuckles beneath the man's chin. He was choking to death when the bullets from one of his fellows behind tore into him. Bond pushed the corpse into the rear car, ducking behind him like a riot shield, and drove him into the gunner. The second man fell backwards, and Bond drove his heel into his chest with such force he yelped, and his machine gun popped into the air.

The three remaining motorcyclists brought their guns to bear, but not before Bond caught the MAT-49 in mid-air and sprayed them with the remainder of the clip. One fell out the window.

He dropped the empty submachine gun and picked up another as the last two assailants racing alongside the train accelerated toward the engineer's cab.

Bond ran back to the front car and directed chattering fire at the biker on the right, blowing his petrol tank from between his legs. The man made a desperate lunge and caught the side of the car, dropping his machine gun in the attempt.

Bond ignored him and raced to the front.

The biker on the left had his submachine gun extended to fill the engineer's cab with bullets.

It was then that they rounded the bend and a tunnel came up suddenly.

The biker smashed headlong into the side of the tunnel, and they were doused in darkness, the interior lighting having been blown to pieces.

The other man had managed to swing his legs into the train and avoid his comrade's fate, and he leapt blindly at Bond.

The fight was quick and furious in the dark. Bond lost the MAT-49 and felt the point of a knife trace his side. They grappled, broke each other's holds, traded several fast, hard blows of fists and feet, and Bond got a hold of the knife somehow in the dark. By the time the train exited the other side of the tunnel and light flooded the car again, the man was sagging to his knees, hugging Bond's leg, the knife jammed in his belly.

From the cab, Petra gasped.

Bond gripped the man's shoulders and eased him to the floor. "Who the hell sent you?"

The man gurgled something in Corsican. Bond caught the words Domingue and 'capo.' These were Corse men, bent on avenging their capo.

"But who sent you? Was it Fesche? Treat?"

"Treat," the man gasped. "Treat."

Bond went to the front of the train to take control, leaving the man to curl up and die. So they were all Corse. Domingues' men. But how had Trixie Treat known he had killed Marius?

"How could she have known? I hate to think Marc-Ange..."

"She knew because of your connection to each other," said Petra. "That's probably how Fesche knew where to find us in Egypt. She knows you're coming."

"Well I wish the hell it went both ways so I knew where to go."

"James," said Petra, thoughtfully, "maybe it does."

19. A Minute to Pray, A Second to Scry

When the bullet-riddled autorail came growling into the station at Calvi with two cars full of the dead, it was met with screams and gasps from all but one on the platform.
Bill Ibaka was the first to meet Bond and Petra as they staggered out of the cab. He was dressed in all leathers and a merino sweatshirt, with driving gloves and a pair of dark sunglasses. He ushered them quickly through the press of aghast onlookers to a waiting bright red Alfa Romeo Guilia SS, an ostentatious thing Bill had always favored.
"You two certainly know how to make an entrance," Ibaka said, as he shifted the car into gear and the twin cam engine sent them flying out of the parking lot with a sound like the roar of a 4-cylinder mechanical dragon.
Bond thought about asking Ibaka the wisdom of attempting to evade the local police in a blazing red sports car, but merely gripped the dashboard as 008 executed impossibly sharp turns down narrow alleyways and zigged and zagged south through town until they were burning down D81B heading for the coast.
"Why can't we just explain who we are? The police will cooperate won't they?" Petra asked.
"Not a chance, luv," said Ibaka. "Part of the problem with busting up the heroin trade in Corsica is it's impossible to tell which coppers are in which clan's pocket. Marius Domingue was a French Resistance member in Marseille. He personally eliminated several notorious members of the Carlingue in Paris, so even the Deuxième tend to give him a wide berth. Word is out that you scuppered him, James, and his men are after you. I suppose that explains the state of your carriage?"
"The Corse, yes," growled Bond. "Set on us by Trixie Treat. And for the record, I didn't kill Domingue. He did himself in."
"Just the same, I wouldn't plan a holiday in Corsica any time soon."
"Not that I'm complaining, but what are you doing here, Bill? Felix told me you were in Marseilles."
"I was," said Ibaka, "and enjoying the company of a certain mademoiselle whose papa has his fingers in some very large and very nasty pies on the French end of things. But I was pulled out and ordered on a flight to Calvi to hand deliver a package to the two of

you when you stepped off the train. Like some damned postman."
He reached over and popped open the glovebox. A small, paper wrapped package fell into Bond's lap. There was a telegram taped to it.
"Your eyes only," said Ibaka, weaving through traffic.

OH SEVEN, SIX NINE.
Bond stopped reading and twisted round to address Petra. "Your agent number is Sixty-Nine?"
"Yes, what of it?" Petra asked, completely innocent. Bond shook his head and went back to reading;
NEGATIVE RESULT ON NARROWING DOWN TREAT LOCATION FROM DESCRIPTION. STOP. FAESCHE FAMILY AN OLD ONE WITH NUMEROUS HOLDINGS ON ISLAND. STOP. SUGGEST YOU TRY AJACCIO BIRTHPLACE OF CARDINAL JOSEPH FESCHE. STOP. PALAIS FESCH-MUSEE DES BEAUX-ARTS HAS A COLLECTION BEQUEATHED BY FAMILY. STOP. HAVE INCLUDED SPECIAL EQUIPMENT VIA Q-O BRANCH TO AID YOU. STOP. NEED NOT REMIND YOU OF DEADLINE. STOP. URGENT YOU REPLY WITH PLAN OF ACTION. STOP. IF UNABLE TO REPLY SECURELY USE PROVIDED PEN. STOP.
-DARKHEART
Bond smiled thinly at the sign off. Like M and his MAILED-FIST, D favored a dramatic cypher moniker as well.
Bond tore off the paper. Inside was a plain cardboard box.
In the box was a handful of smooth star-shaped soap stones of various sizes, etched with strange symbols, the same as on D's jet black ring, he noticed, and a heavy bronze medallion bearing a crude image of what looked like a six legged woodpecker poised on a thorny tree bough. There was an object wrapped in black velvet too, which Bond unraveled. He grimaced when he found a small, black, mummified hand inside.
He rifled through the clinking junk, perplexed, and found at the bottom, a calligraphy pen. He examined the pen, as it was a bit heavier than it should have been, passing the box of trinkets and passed the box and the message back to Petra.
"The rest is for you, my dear."
Use the provided pen, the message had said. He unscrewed the tip

and a device slid out which he recognized. A radio transmitter. He slid it back in and replaced the tip.

In the backseat, Petra caught her breath.

"Father Christmas bring you something special, my dear?"

"Star Stones of Mnar," said Petra breathlessly. "And a Hand of Glory."

"What?" said Ibaka, half-grinning and glancing up in the rearview mirror. "Like a criminal's hand?"

Bond looked at Ibaka sideways.

"My gran told me a story about them. She said the left hand of a hanged man opens doors."

"This must have belonged to a diminutive felon," Petra mused, turning the putrid thing over and examining it. "It looks like the hand of a dwarf."

Ibaka's face fell, Bond noticed, when he saw her hold the thing up.

"Well, it's the spy's version," said Bond dryly. "For portability."

Next she took the bronze medallion out of the box and turned it over in her hands reverently. "And the Seal of N'gah."

"Delightful," said Bond.

"Don't feel left out, James," said Ibaka, frowning at Bond. "There are a couple magazines of your 7.62mm in the glovebox."

"What are your orders, Bill?" asked Bond, as he retrieved the ammunition.

Ibaka was staring strangely at Petra in the rearview.

"I'm to get you to safety," said Ibaka, "then I'm to transmit your reply to HQ with expedience."

"Hence the driving. You have a sending station?"

"No. There's a submarine out there," Ibaka said, nodding to the ocean now bordering the right side of the road. "HMS Ranger."

Bond bit his lip. Ranger was an experimental submarine, about five years ahead of what the Soviets and Americans currently had. A nuclear-powered ballistic missile platform the Navy had been fielding in foreign waters as an intelligence gatherer, so far undetected. She had a cruise missile payload currently, but the idea was to fit her with nuclear warheads from the Polaris program. She also had a cypher machine onboard.

"Pet," said Bond. "How long will your solution take?"

"Not more than twenty minutes," she answered. "But I need some supplies, and a quiet space to work."

"Can you lend us a half hour of your time, Bill? No questions asked?"
"My bird in Marseilles will wait," Bill said. "Where are we going?"

After a perplexing shopping trip at a local market that gleaned a box of candles and a bag of salt, their next stop was a seaside motel.
It was nearly eight o'clock by that time, and Petra wasted no time in setting her plan for severing the hypothetical mental connection between Bond and Treat, to James Bond's chagrin.
William Ibaka had hardly shut the door to the bungalow behind him when she was rolling up the rug and tearing open the sack of salt. She kicked off her shoes and began to funnel the salt through her hands, describing a wide circle on the floor.
"What the hell is all this then, 007?" Bill asked, lighting his pipe.
"Don't ask questions you don't want to know the answer to, Bill," said Bond, taking off his coat and hanging it on a chair.
"Why don't you wait outside?" Petra suggested as she completed the circle and began to scratch a complex emblem in the circle with a bit of chalk. "We're in the general vicinity of Treat and once you disappear from her perception, she might send someone to the last place she felt you." She paused in her work, went to the box, took out one of the polished Star Stones and tossed it Ibaka.
He caught it, held it up to the light and puffed rich smelling tobacco, but said nothing.
"It might protect you," she said. "In case."
"Sure, sure," said Ibaka, dropping it in his pocket, his hand already on the knob. "Cheers, James."
Bond wondered if Ibaka would ever say another word to him after this mission. When he turned back to Petra, she had completed her design. It was the emblem from D's ring, and the Star Stones, as she'd called them.
"What is that design? What does it mean?"
"The Elder Sign," she said. "It has some power against certain Old Ones and their servants."
The stones themselves she placed in the five points of the chalk star, and she set a lit candle on top of each one.
"Take off your clothes and step into the circle," she commanded.
"The hell with that," said Bond.
"For the ritual to work, we must both be sky-clad," she said, unbuttoning her blouse.

Bond shrugged. Well, that was a different matter, wasn't it?

"Don't think of it as magic," she said. "It's actually a long forgotten science."

"Certainly," he said, admiring her figure as she finished removing everything aside from her mother's amulet.

"Manmade fabrics disrupt the passage of etheric currents through the body's energy nodes."

"Undoubtedly," said Bond, pulling off his last stitch.

"Oh shut up and sit down," she said. "As soon as the ritual begins, you'll be cut off from her scrying. It'll be like reversing a two-way mirror. I'll be able to find her, but she won't be able to see you. When it's over, the connection will be broken entirely."

Bond thought back to his initial meeting with D. His pointed questions about his Soviet brainwashing.

"Do you suppose D was aware of this connection to begin with?" Bond asked.

"I don't know, James. But you must believe he didn't tell me if he was."

She took the package of Liao cigarettes from his pocket. He had left one in there. She lit it and began to wave it about the room, proceeding clockwise around him. The sweet scent of the black tipped cigarette hung in the air.

"Is that stuff safe?"

"In a small, secondary dose like this, yes."

When she had completed the circle, she went into it and knelt in the center, facing him. It was a sensuous affair. The smell of the drug gave him a pleasant, warm sensation, made him more readily accept the absurdity of it all. They touched bare knees, and she began to move her hands in strange patterns, murmuring. He heard various odd sounding names, a few vaguely familiar.

"I've heard some of these names in my Aunt Charmain's bible study as a boy. I thought you said there was no God."

"I didn't say that. There are many gods. The one your Aunt Charmain prayed to just isn't what you think He is. Now stop interrupting."

She continued to chant and move her hands in slow patterns, and finally touched his shoulders, and ran her fingers in deliberate patterns down his chest.

He reached out and took her wrists.

"Don't tell me your mother taught you this."

"Of course she did."
He winced slightly.
"Is this tantric magic?"
"No."
"Because I've heard of parties like this, but never been."
"Don't be juvenile, James. This is quite serious."
Her eyes passed over him over and she smiled.
"However, I see there's nothing wrong with the flow of your sacral chakra, at any rate."
She was a wondrous kook. Then suddenly she was gone.
And it was Trixie Treat kneeling in her place, lustrous golden hair falling over her bare shoulders, a wry smile on her lips. So dangerously beautiful. There was the mole beneath her left breast.
The hotel room was gone too.
They were in the center of the silk-sheeted bed in the building in Leningrad. She fooled him into thinking she was a prisoner like him. But there was something else.
He blinked and she changed again.
And this time she was Tracy. Smiling, warm, as she only was with him, her self-destructive intentions laid to rest at last, but still there in the benthic depths of her blue eyes.
"We have all the time in the world, James. All the time in the world."
He kissed her, ardently. Grasped her head between his hands, wanting her to be real. He could smell her hair. That scent of Guerlain's 'Ode' that made his heart ache.
"Tracy," he murmured. "Oh God. Tracy, darling." He drew her closer.
She pushed away.
"That's enough for now, James. Remember, you have to ask nicely."
She was Trixie Treat again, mocking. The bank of spectacled Soviet doctors behind her, grinning to each other, the impotent lechers.
That was how she'd gotten into his head. Somehow, the Black Lotus, the Liao, the way she'd done her hair, even the carefully selected scent. How had she gotten that? It had all confused him into thinking she was Tracy.
"You bitch!" he roared, and clamped his hands around her throat.
She gasped, blue eyes bulging. Like Tracy's, but not. Not pained, but sadistic. Then she was Tracy again. He squeezed harder, digging in his thumbs now. It wasn't Tracy. It wasn't. Then it was

a lovely almond-eyed Japanese girl, waves of long black hair shimmering.

"Taro-san!" she gasped. And then, when she opened her mouth to scream, it was a baby's cry that sent chills up Bond's spine and arms. He released her.

Or rather, he released Petra, who rocked back on her heels coughing, then fell forward on her hands and knees.

"Pet! I'm sorry! I..."

Then there was man's scream from outside the door.

Bond jumped to his feet and left the circle, swiping his Walther from the table, flinging the holster aside, and wrenching open the door.

He ran out naked into the night, heedless of the hotel lights, of the expressions of shock from the guests opening their doors and poking their heads out.

"Bill?"

"Here, James! Here!"

Bond rushed toward the sound of Ibaka's voice, and found him trembling, his hammerless snub-nose Centennial drawn and pointing apparently at the dead night clerk lying in the corner.

Yet he hadn't heard a shot.

Bill Ibaka was wide eyed, his dark skin covered in sweat. "Did you see it?" he whispered, when Bond came up beside him.

The clerk was propped in the corner, arms and legs outspread, as if he had fallen or been pushed into the angle.

He was covered in a viscous, syrupy slime that appeared blue as laundry detergent splashed in a wide pattern on the pavement. There was no blood, but the man's belly had been ripped completely open and the organs apparently torn free and absconded with.

"He asked for a light. We were talking. I noticed smoke billowing out of the corner behind him all of a sudden. Thought there was a fire. And then... I saw something."

Ibaka stepped forward, slipping slightly in the blue slime, and put the palm of his hand to the wall.

"No. There's nothing. I thought I saw... like, a dog or..." He chuckled nervously, something Bond had never seen Ibaka do.

Then he looked sharply over his shoulder, into the darkness, at the onlookers. "We've got to get the hell out of here."

Bond nodded in agreement, puzzled at the clerk's demise.

The police would be here inquiring.

"And for God's sake Bond, where are your trousers?"
They returned to the room and found Petra already dressed and extinguishing the candles, retrieving the star shaped stones, and shoving them in her jacket pockets.
"Get the car," Bond said to Ibaka, and he nodded and left, his revolver still in hand, Bond noted.
He got his clothes and dressed. "Are you alright?" he asked her.
She nodded vigorously, though he saw the purpling streaks about her slender neck.
"I'm sorry."
"It's alright. You didn't know what you were doing."
"I knew what I was doing, just not who I was doing it to."
"What happened to Bill?"
"I don't know. Something… someone killed the clerk."
"Something? Did he see what did it?"
"I don't know. The man's been gutted. Something… he's covered in some sort of blue slime."
Petra froze, wide-eyed.
"Blue slime? Was the clerk badly mutilated?"
"Never mind that. What about all this? Did it work?"
"I know where they are," Petra affirmed. "The Princess is with them."
"Let's go, then."
He snatched his coat off the chair and shouldered into it, stuffing his gun into its holster.
The red Guilia SS squealed to a stop in front of the door and revved its engine.

20. The House of Whispers

Bill was stuffing Benzedrine into his mouth when they got in the car, and he threw the Alpha Romeo into reverse and sped out of the parking lot into the gathering darkness.
"What did you see, Bill?" Petra asked, as Bond rummaged in the glove box, producing a Corsican road atlas. "Was it like a sort of skinless dog?"
"How did you know that, girl?" Bill exclaimed, looking back at her with popping eyes.
"It was a Hound of Tindalos," she announced. "Treat must have summoned it. The Elder Sign protected you."
"Magic?" Bond murmured, unfolding the map.
"I told, you it's not magic, it's ancient geometric science. The hounds originate in an angular dimension. They require sharp angles to penetrate into our curved plane of existence. The Elder Sign, it's a kind of catchall ward against such beings, a Swiss Army knife of talismans. The five-pointed star within a double circle asserts the power of the closed curve over five seventy-two-degree angles, traps them within. It's what saved your life, Bill." Bill hit the brakes and swung the speeding car onto the shoulder.
He reached into his pocket and pulled out the Star Stone and
slapped it on the dashboard. "Well you can bloody well keep it, luv!" He threw open the driver's side door and stomped out into the headlights.
Bond glared back at her.
"That's enough," he snapped. "You said you'd figured out where they are. Show me on this map. Then I'll have a talk with him."
"Give me a pen," said Petra.

Moments later Bond was standing beside Bill Ibaka on the side of the lonely road, watching the sun blaze as it sunk into the west, into the sea. The surf crashed on the shore a few hundred yards out. This particular slice of northwest Corsica was strange; a place where the abundant stone was carved by wind and the sea into fantastic, alien shapes. It magnified the strangeness of everything he had been through recently, and for a moment he got the sinking sensation he had stepped out of the car into one of these foreign dimensions Petra spoke of.

"What the hell are you into this time, James?" Ibaka asked in a quiet voice. "I thought maybe, lack of sleep had caught up with me or I'd been hit with some kind of hallucinogen. I wasn't, was I?"

The sea wind had dried the sheen of sweat on his face, but his whole body posture showed he was still out of kilter. What had he really seen?

"Don't worry about it, Bill. It's nothing. Queen and country, right? Listen, I've got to borrow your car. And I need something else from you."

"What?"

"If I drop you at the next town, how fast can you get back to the *Ranger*?"

"Thirty minutes or so."

He spread the map out on the hood of the car, and Bill looked over his shoulder, settling, glad to be doing something other than dwelling on whatever he had witnessed.

"Right here. See it?" Bond said, tapping a tapering point on the coast south of La Revellata he had marked with a pen from the glove box. "Punta Bianca. There's a great old stone house. An old sanitarium or something high on the bluff. With a little luck, the boys should be able to spot it. I need the *Ranger* positioned off the coast, in range and ready to let fly when I trigger this," he said, producing the calligraphy pen with the hidden beacon. "If you don't get a signal by 23:50, I want it leveled anyway."

Ibaka looked at Bond. An attack on foreign soil without even the meager excuse of a flubbed missile test in international waters was as serious as business came. The sub would have to launch its strike and get the hell out of there as fast as possible or risk not only an international incident, but the exposure of Her Majesty's secret prototype.

"Something heavy's happening. What's up, James?"

"Need to know, 008. And I need to know if I can count on you."

"Sure, sure," said Ibaka. "To the last round."

Bond folded up the map and handed it to him. He put it in his inside jacket pocket, and they returned to the car.

They let Ibaka out at a petrol station in the first town they came across and then made a beeline for Revellata. It was full on night now. Nine 'o clock and under three hours to spare.

"Tell me about this place," Bond said as he drove.

"D could never have found it," said Petra. "In the old days it was built as a lunatic asylum. That's why it's so remote."

"To keep people's consciences clear," Bond murmured, turning up a winding old road long forgotten, checking the map to make sure it was the right one.

The vast seat was right ahead of them now, a churning lightness beneath the black sky. A storm was picking up.

"It was built on top of the place where the Mindbreaker lays buried. Whatever power drove it or called it to this world, it was supposed to splash down in the sea, but it fell short. Remember how I told you the Old Ones speak to humanity in dreams? Sometimes people who are attuned are able to hear them even when awake."

"You mean madmen," said Bond.

"Oh James, what it must have been like for those poor souls, to hear it speaking to them. The asylum was a failure. No one got better who went to it. They got worse. Jean Fesche grew up there. He was illegitimate; the son of Franz Faesche by a prostitute. His mother worked on the staff at the asylum, and eventually became an inmate herself. Jean Fesche was acknowledged later in life, and put through school in Bastia, but his connection to his elder brother the Cardinal was downplayed. He grew up in that house, and the Mindbreaker called him. He dug up the cellar. He found it. He. . . joined with it. It infected him like a venereal disease. It made him heartier so he could find the key to freeing it."

"You got all that from Trixie Treat? I'm surprised Fesche is so forthcoming. He didn't seem like the talkative type."

"They're lovers," said Petra quietly, closing her eyes as thought to blot out some unsightly vision. "I've seen it. She wants the immortality it gave Fesche. She thinks it will make her into something the Old Ones will spare. She thinks she and Fesche will be a kind of lord and lady over whatever land Cthulhu leaves behind when he rises."

"Cthulhu."

"Ikla-Bafthgul's cry will summon the Deep Ones to it. It will render all who hear it insane, ripe for submitting to the will of Dagon and Hydra. The Deep Ones will come out of the sea in force and copulate with us, spawning new Deep Ones, bolstering Dagon's forces. Then Ikla-Bafthgul will be brought into the depths, to Dagon and Hydra themselves, the marshals of Cthulhu, in the city of Kifra'ka-N'la. Beneath the waves, its cry will awaken Cthulhu himself, and he'll lead his followers in an invasion to retake the surface."

Bond shook his head. Too fantastic and too terrible, if true, to think about. Focus on the mission at hand.

"The Princess is alive?"

"She's kept in the cellar near it," Petra confirmed. "They can't shed her blood to open the Black Dodecahedron until midnight tonight."

"How many cultists?"

"Two dozen members of The Majestic Order of The Great Dark One. They've gathered from all over the world to see this come to fruition."

Men and presumably women with the upside-down ankh tattoos. How many of them were fighters? You couldn't tell with fanatics. A better question was how many of them would fight if their mad goal was threatened?

They came to another branch in the road. This led to a precarious unpaved drive that went up the stony hill. Over that hill, if any of this could be believed, there should be the house, invisible from the road. Well, the drive had to lead somewhere. He turned down it.

"What about a way in?" he mused aloud.

"Treat can't see us now. She's flying blind. She doesn't know we're coming."

"Of course she knows. What else would we be doing? She'll double the guard," said Bond.

"There might be a way for one of us to slip in unseen," said Petra. "If the other is captured."

She reached into her pocket and brought out bronze seal D had sent them.

"I know an incantation from the Book of Eibon. It's supposed to render a bearer of the Seal of N'gah invisible. But it only works for one."

Bond scratched his chin. Invisibility spells now. Could they wager their lives on such mumbo jumbo? Maybe she could slip in with a bit of distraction though. They were ten minutes from the spot now, if her little ritual had worked. He pulled the car over.

"You know the layout by sight," said Bond.

"I do. But James, it should be you."

"I'm sure I can't pronounce anything from the book of what- ever it is. I'll flub it and wind up a toad or something. Besides, I'm no good

if I have to bumble around trying to find the cellar stairs. You can get in and find your way easily, right?"
"They'll kill you on sight!"
"I don't think so, Pet. Trixie's like a cat with a sparrow. She'll want to toy with me a bit first before she bites my head off."
He reached in his coat pocket and brought out Marius Domingue's P210.
"Take this," said Bond, handing the pistol over.
She opened the door and got out into the windy dark, the bronze talisman in one hand, the gun in the other. The night sea breeze blew her hair about her face.
"Should be a twenty-minute jog down the road. Just follow it."
"You're just going to drive up?"
"Why not?" he said, with a flippant air. "I'm expected, after all."
Petra leaned in and kissed him through the window, and pressed one of the Star Stone Elder Sign things into his hand.
"I'm going to leave the keys under the passenger's seat," Bond said, as though he were instructing his wife on some mundane arrangement concerning the groceries.
She nodded.
"Be careful, James."
He left her glowing red in the taillights of the SS. Then she was swallowed up by the dark.
He continued down the drive, rounded the jutting stone hill and was rewarded by the sight of an old stone house, two stories tall, with moss climbing up the side and rows of dark windows, some of them broken. The edifice was poised on the very edge of a sheer drop down into the sea.
Parked on the broad, unkempt lawn were several expensive looking cars, the only sign that the old house was inhabited at all, until the headlights of the SS swept across the weathered front door and two swarthy men in dark suits, stepped forward, eyes gleaming like yellow beads.
Bond cut the engine, set the keys under the passenger's seat, and stepped out of the car.
The two men approached warily. They wore fezzes, and both had one hand under their jackets. Not quite professionals, these two.
"Terribly sorry," said Bond. "I got a turned around back there. I wonder if you might help me."

The men looked at each other. No, these were base amateurs. Bond supposed he could have them both down and stuffed in the boot of the Alfa Romeo in about nine seconds. But that wasn't the plan. If they went missing and a relief guard came before Petra made it inside, she'd be worse off.

"I'm trying to find Trixie Treat," he said.

Now the guns came clear of the jackets. Still close enough to take from them, but Bond slowly raised his hands.

A few moments later he was in the drafty house, sitting in a chair listening to the wind whisper through the broken windows.

One of the guards stood over him with his pistol drawn. The contents of Bond's pockets had been laid on a weather beaten old table. His pistol, silencer, watch, his ammunition, his knife, his wallet, the Star Stone, and Fesche's flask. The transmitter pen was still inside his shirt pocket.

The other guard had gone for an adult, and returned presently with Trixie Treat.

Her hair was down, and she wore an open sided gown made entirely of fishing nets, bound at the waist by a golden belt, the clasp of which was a large octopus-like head with a face full of golden rope tentacles that stretched almost to the tops of her bare feet.

"Hello Trixie. I like your dress."

"James," she purred. "Where is your little wog girl?"

Bond's face fell and he glowered at her, practiced.

"Your blue beastie out of the corner did for her at the hotel."

"How did you stop it from killing you?"

She turned to the table and answered her own question.

"I see. A Star Stone of Mnar." She picked it up, looked it over as she went to the window, and tossed it out like a Frisbee. It went soaring out over the cliff. "I'm impressed, James. I didn't think you went in for that sort of thing."

"I don't, really."

"Then why are you here? To save your homely little Princess? To hear the song of the Mindbreaker for yourself? Or something else?"

"Something else," said Bond, swallowing hard, quivering a bit.

Trixie smiled like a contented tigress atop her kill while he put on his best worshipful look.

"Was that all that was keeping you so standoffish? And now without your little trinket, are you mine again?"

She giggled lightly.

"Wait outside," she said to the two cultists. Then she repeated it in Arabic.

They looked confused, and she glared at them until they went outside the room and pulled the creaky door shut behind them.

She twirled the end of her golden hair playfully and sauntered across the room toward him, letting her ample curves sway, catching hold of one of the long golden ropes hanging from her belt and swinging it round in a circle.

"Tell me what it is, James. Do you have something you'd like to ask me at last?"

"I do," Bond whispered, nodding as she came to stand between his open knees.

He clamped his hands around her throat, for real this time, and grinned to see her shocked eyes bulge in her reddening face as he squeezed blood into her cheeks.

"How are you going to scream for help, Trixie?"

He got to his feet and wrenched her about, forcing her toward the cracked glass window. The door burst open, and the two guards rushed in and tackled him, as he had known they would. He didn't mind the blows from fists and pistol butts so much, as long as he could hear Trixie Treat gasping for breath and whimpering in the corner.

"Get him to his feet," came a deep voice from the doorway. Bond was pulled to his feet, blinking blood from his eyes. Fesche stood in the doorway. No need for obfuscation now.

The keffiyeh, the sunglasses, they were gone and he stood in all his horrible glory. He had foregone his usual suit too, and was dressed similar to Trixie, in a fishing net tunic and octopus head belt. Beneath this sparse garment the extent of his mutation was clear. Ninety percent of his body was encrusted with barnacles and green mucous. Starfish clustered to his chest, and budding anemones sprouted up and down his legs alongside quivering urchins. He was quite inhuman.

Bond chuckled at the sight of him.

"You look like the catch of the day in that get up."

"Stand up you silly bitch," Fesche said to Treat, ignoring Bond.

"Just what were you expecting to happen? One last tumble with him before you shed your humanity?"

Trixie Treat rose slowly to her feet.

"He shouldn't have been able to do that," she muttered by way of an excuse.

"Go and take the Princess down to the cellar."

Bond couldn't check his watch, but he estimated that twenty minutes had passed. Bill Ibaka was back on the *Ranger* and Petra, hopefully, was somewhere in the house.

Trixie moved to obey, then, apparently on impulse, reached out and slashed Bond down the cheek with her nails.

She was about to go to the door when her eyes fell on his disheveled shirt, and she plucked the pen from his shirt pocket.

"I told you imbeciles to take everything off his person."

"It's just a pen," one of the guards said.

"Just a pen! Idiot, he's James Bond!"

She unscrewed the pen and let the transmitter fall into her hand. She showed it to Fesche with an air of triumph.

"What is it?"

"A standard issue radio transmitter. It would have brought more of them. It hasn't been triggered."

She handed it to Fesche.

He closed his fist around it, and when he opened it again, it was nothing but bits of twisted and broken metal in his palm. He shook it contemptuously to the floor. Bond worked his jaw. That put things on a more insistent timetable. No stopping the attack now. The best he could hope for was that Petra had managed to get the Princess out. Fesche grabbed Treat around her slim waist and pulled her in close, slavering over her mouth with his repulsive lips.

Bond grimaced as they parted, and Fesche sent her out of the room with a smack to her round bottom with the back of his hand.

"Well, Mr. Bond," said Fesche, turning to him when she exited. "Shall we make it an eye for an eye?"

"The night's young," Bond said.

"*Au contraire*. It is very late. And there will never be another dawn. Not for you, and not for anyone else."

"Why, Fesche? Why would a man ever commit himself to this, knowing what will happen?"

Fesche strolled to the table and looked disinterested at the items spread out there, until he came to the knife. His hand hovered over it, then picked up the flask.

"I thought this was lost. Why did you keep it?"

"My superiors figured out who you were by the crest, Jean Fesche."

"My father gave me this, on the day he acknowledged me. Gave me an allowance. Wrote me a letter of introduction to the school of my choice. Changed our surname, just a bit, to differentiate me from my brother the Cardinal and, I should think, from himself. Funny how a simple thing like that made all the difference to him and to me. That was when my mother died, in 1783. Do you know the Old Ones, James Bond?"

He shook the flask, heard the slosh of liquid inside. Bond fought down his anticipation. "I've been briefed."

Fesche twisted the cap off and drank. First a sip, then a deeper swallow. When he had finished tipping it back, he sighed contentedly, as though he had just tasted a particularly fine vintage Bordeaux.

"You don't know enough. If you did, you wouldn't ask me why. The persistence of inevitability. Man is like a gull's feather on the tide. It cannot resist the pull. The Old Ones, Ikla-Bafthgul, Nyarlathotep, they are eternal, and oh, so very patient. Their schemes stretch across millennia, certainly outlasting the brevity of my own existence. They have spoken to me since I was in my cradle. I knew the whispers of this house before I knew my own father's voice. When I left for school, and studied the old Roman ruins of Mantium, I learned of St. Devota. She was a Christian woman, born in Mariana. You know it as Lucciana, I believe. She was part of the staff of a senator named Eutychius. This was during the Diocletian persecutions. A prefect named Barbarus, who secretly followed Nyarlathotep, learned of her. She was devout and chaste, the sort of morsel certain Old Ones savor. He tried to secure her for a ritual sacrifice, but Eutychius intervened. The senator was poisoned, and she was taken anyway. Her mouth was smashed with a hammer and she was dragged to death over stones and through brambles, gagging on her broken teeth, her pulped lips, so that her suffering would stir the slumber of the long lost Ikla-Bafthgul and lead Barbarus and his followers here to its resting place. Divination by torture. Three Christians stole her body from the cult however, before her entrails could be read, and sailed with it to Monaco, fighting off the hosts of Father Dagon the entire way.

The Church, my brother the Cardinal, they venerated her as a martyr. Built a chapel to her. But it was not the tale of some pitiful virgin's destruction that spoke to me. It was the words of Barbarus, which I found in a hole in a cave in the Mariana hills. Those words echoed the dreams I had had in my childhood, and I knew them to be true. The testimony of Barbarus, high priest of the Majestic Order Of The Great Dark One, led me to the true faith, which is not unproven faith at all, but the only worthy truth of this universe; that were are infinitesimal in importance, that the Old Ones ruled existence, and must do so again, as sure as the tide returns to shore. So I took up the quest of Barbarus, to awaken Ikla-Bafthgul and bring the return of Cthulhu. I had no choice, really. Persistent inevitability."

Fesche looked faraway then, at the wall, but through it. Beyond it. Through time, perhaps.

"My mother worked here as a cleaning woman when I was a child. An honest trade. Good work for a former whore. Ikla-Bafthgul would whisper to me, with the tongues of the inmates, day and night. They became his mouthpiece, and the mouthpiece of others, who taught me much about the Outer Dark, led me to my vocation. Even in that black, dank tomb in Egypt, where there was no sleep, no rest, I heard the Old Ones. Long, dark years with nothing but their hissing speech for company. They directed me to this point in time, at last. The stars of Ikla-Bafthgul are right. The Shatterer of Minds will awaken tonight, and I will have the peace of total oblivion at last. The Call of Cthulhu is nigh. *Ph'nglui mglw'nafh Cthulhu R'lyeh wgah'nagl fhtagn.*"

"*Ph'nglui mglw'nafh Cthulhu R'lyeh wgah'nagl fhtagn,*" the two guards intoned.

Fesche leaned on the table, then stumbled.

"I hear them. I hear them still! They promised me they would stop!"

Bond smiled. The Black Lotus had taken effect.

Without warning, Fesche lunged at one of the guards and clamped his hands on either side of his head.

"Shut your mouth!" he roared into the man's fearful face.

With one shrug of effort, Fesche crushed the man's head like an overlarge grape. It burst in his hands, causing a geyser of blood to spatter the ceiling.

As the other guard stumbled backwards, Bond struck him in the chin with his elbow, dove for the table, and came up with his knife, which he flung across the room, depositing it in the surprised guard's throat.

Fesche spun and faced Bond, pressing his bloody hands to his own ears now.

"Quiet! Quiet! Quiet!" he screamed. Then he charged.

Bond knew he couldn't match that bull strength. He sidestepped and threw a leg at the giant's feet.

Fesche stumbled over Bond's outstretched leg and fell forward, smashing through the window, taking most of the frame with him, and disappeared into the night, tumbling end over end down the sheer cliff face, a hundred feet below, presumably to the surf and rocks at the bottom.

The saltwater flask with its seasoning of ground Black Lotus lay discarded on the floor. Bond kicked it out into space.

"Last round's on me, old boy."

He went to the table, gathered up his things, screwed his silencer onto his PPK, and moved out into the hall.

21. Saltash Luck

Anne had found herself a storybook princess at last.

Here she was, confined in a picturesque stone house, she knew not where, overlooking a majestic seaside cliff right outside her corner window. Even the ground floor afforded a fantastic view of the sea. Her captors treated her kindly enough, especially the beautiful blonde woman, Beatrix, who said she too had been kidnapped by the wogs and was being impressed to act as her personal translator.

Evidently, Beatrix said, she was being held until England capitulated on some radical Middle Eastern matter Anne didn't fully understand.

Beatrix assured her she would be fine, that the Prime Minister was cooperating at the behest of her mother, and that they expected good word would come authorizing her release by midnight tonight.

'They' of course, was that ugly brute of a man, Fesche, who had flown her out of England on an autogyro to, well, she wasn't precisely sure where she was now. Certainly nowhere in the Middle East, and that assuaged any fear she might have had as surely as Beatrix. She was still in some mostly civilized country, apparently on the Mediterranean. Sardinia, perhaps, Ibiza, or Corsica.

She suspected it was the latter, as through her door, she heard more than a few conversations in Corsican French, which she could pick up a bit of, thanks to her Romantic fluency.

Among all her jailers she had glimpsed, Fesche was the one who truly frightened her. He was like an ogre out of a fairytale. Hulking, deformed, and stinking of his namesake.

It was the last night of her captivity, and she was almost sorry to see it end. It had been frightful at first, but the past few days had turned out to be something of an exciting holiday. There was a good deal of bustle about the house. Had been, all day. She heard many voices outside her door, probably negotiators hammering out the final details of her release with her captors. She hoped she might be able to keep correspondence with Beatrix. She seemed like a nice lady.

Anne was folding the spare set of clothes she had been given and wondering when Beatrix would come around to bring her a valise to put them in, when her door unlocked and opened and a strange, pretty brown woman she had never seen before about the place stepped in, putting something small and black in her pocket.

"Princess Anne," said the woman, taking a rather large and clunky looking medallion off her graceful neck. "I need you to put this on."
"What? Who are you?"
"My name is Petra. I'm a special agent of the service. They've sent me to rescue you," she whispered, closing the door behind her.
Anne was stymied.
"Why, whatever for? I'm to be released tonight."
"Not in the way you think," Petra said.

The young girl, princess though she was, stood gawking at Petra like a confounded gazelle. She had been in the midst of folding her clothes, the poor, daft thing.
"Is this some kind of trick?" she said.
Petra went to her side.
"No, your highness. These people mean you no good and this house is going to be targeted by the Navy within the hour, so we have to make our way out. Please put this on," she said, holding out the Seal of N'gah.
The girl still looked confused, her face pinching even more. Petra had heard the girl was homely, and no doubt she was, but looking at her with a woman's eyes, she also saw the swan in the duckling.
"Why, whatever for?" the Princess said, even as she ducked beneath the chain and allowed Petra to place it over her head. "What is this?"
"Just a bit of costume jewelry," Petra said, thinking quickly. "But there's a radio beacon inside, in case we get separated."
She muttered the activating incantation over it.
"Oh it tickled just then!" the Princess exclaimed, touching the medallion.
Petra took the P210 from her jacket and switched off the safety.
"We're going to move very quickly now, straight for the front door. Understand?"
At the sight of the pistol, the girl's eyes widened, and she nodded quietly.
"Put your hand on my shoulder." She did so.
Petra moved to exit into the hallway, prepared to shoot anyone they saw, when her lodestone began to tremble in her pocket.
James.
It had trembled like that when she had left the Cairo Museum to find him, and she had found him in the car wreck. He was in danger.

She checked her watch. 2245. They had a full hour until the missile strike.

"Come on," she said to the girl, and slid out into the hall.

There was no one to be seen. The halls were deserted.

They crept down the hall, still seeing no one. They must all be gathered in the cellar, preparing for the ceremony.

Except for James. The lodestone shook, telling her he was still upstairs somewhere. What was he doing up there?

She looked at the Princess. The girl's eyes were big as anything, but she wasn't afraid. More excited. The Seal of N'gah would keep her invisible to anyone. It wasn't a proper invisibility spell so much as it was a perception deflector. As long as the wearer didn't interact with anyone, they could pass completely unseen, even to those who might actively be seeking them. She was safer without Petra next to her.

The foyer and the front door was in sight. So was the staircase leading to the second floor. Petra knew there were no guards outside.

"Princess," she whispered. "Can you drive a car?"

"I've taken lessons. Major Stuart, our driver, lets me back in and out of the garage."

"That's fine. Through that front door, you'll see a line of cars. There's a bright red sports car towards the back. An Alfa Romeo. It's unlocked. If you get inside, you'll feel the keys to start her up under the passenger's seat. I want you to go to the car, and duck down inside. Wait ten minutes. If I don't come out for you, drive inland until you reach the main paved road. Take it left and keep going until you reach a town. Do you understand?"

"But what if someone sees me?"

"No one will. I promise. As long as you don't speak to anyone, you'll be fine."

"But where are you going?"

"There's another agent. He's still upstairs. He may be in trouble. I have to bring him out, if I can. Can you do this?"

The Princess nodded slowly.

"Fast as you can, girl. Go! I'll see you in ten minutes." The Princess moved down the hall toward the foyer.

Petra turned and crept up the stairs.

Princess Anne felt exhilarated as she slid along the wall like a film spy. She even slipped off her shoes and crept along on the balls of her feet as she had been taught to do in Girl Guides when stalking an animal.

She was quite proud of herself, and had nearly reached the front door when a door off the foyer creaked open. Anne caught her breath and flattened herself against the wall. She breathed a heavy sigh when she saw who it was.

It was her friend Beatrix. "Oh Beatrix!" she exclaimed.

Beatrix halted in the doorway and looked confused. Her eyes seemed to pass right over Anne once or twice.

"Beatrix, here!" she hissed, stepping out of the shadows. Beatrix looked shocked to see her, but swiftly recovered. "Princess! There you are!"

"Beatrix!" Anne said, taking her by the hands in her excitement. "Come with me! There's a car outside. We can get away tonight."

"How did you get out of your room?"

Anne noticed then that Beatrix was dressed very strangely indeed, in a shockingly revealing garment.

"Why are you dressed like that?"

"Princess. Who let you out?"

"Oh a lady spy! Can you believe it? She says these wogs mean us no good. She's gone upstairs after the other spy and she's going to meet me in ten minutes. Come with me, Beatrix. Can you drive a car?"

She started to lead her to the front door, but stopped short when Beatrix didn't budge. Then she saw the two dark men in the shadow of the door behind Beatrix.

"Come with me, Princess." She turned to the two men. "You two, find the intruders. Kill them."

Princess Anne gasped as Beatrix stepped aside for the two men, who drew deadly looking pistols and moved toward the stairs.

She tried to pull away from Beatrix, but was dragged toward the doorway.

22. Last Call

Bond was moving to the stair when he saw Petra reach the top, Marius' pistol in her hand.
She spied him too, and smiled.
He scowled and moved closer to her. "What the hell are you doing here? Where's the Princess?"
"Waiting in the car. I sensed you were in danger."
"I'm always in danger. Let's go!" He gripped her by the elbow and spun her around.
"Where's Fesche?"
"With his namesakes for now," said Bond, taking the stairs two at a time.
Two guards appeared at the bottom of the stairs and looked up in surprise. Bond shot them both before they had time to raise their guns, his PPK eliciting no more than a pair of clinks. They stumbled back, rolled down the steps, and tumbled in a tangled heap on the floor.
Bond and Petra stepped over them and moved into the foyer. They reached the front door and strode purposefully out, down the porch steps, out onto the dark lawn.
Swishing through the grass, they passed between the parked cars and reached the Alfa Romeo. Bond opened the door. He checked the front and back seats, even popped the boot. There was no one in the car. He glared at Petra, then at his watch. Forty-five minutes till the house was destroyed. Except now the Princess was inside. Bond reloaded his pistol.
"You haven't listened to a damned thing I've said so far, so I don't suppose there would be any point in telling you to stay with the car."
She shrugged in answer.
He stalked back toward the house with her in tow. They strode into the foyer.
A man in fishnet robes was stooped over the two dead guards at the bottom of the stairs, examining them. He looked up as they entered, and Bond left him draped over them.
"Which way to the cellar stairs?"
"This way," Petra said, taking the lead.
She led him down the left-hand corridor, and there was no real need for further directions. There was a low murmur coming from a closed door nearby, the sound of chanting.

Bond pushed past her and went to the door. Locked. He tested it. It was stronger than the others, newly fit in. There didn't appear to be a lock.

"Barred," he guessed.

"Let me," said Petra, and she took the shriveled little black hand from out of her coat pocket. She turned it palm upward and place it in the center of the door, then swept it up as if it were lifting the unseen bar.

Bond heard a clatter from behind and the door swung inward easily.

Behind it, there was a dimly lit stone stair.

Bond went first into the cellar. It was a short walk to the bottom, but the cellar itself was not the end, only the beginning of their descent. From Fesche's story, he had expected a simple hole in the bottom of the cellar floor. But the excavation below them must have taken years and sizable manpower to dig.

The original cellar floor was gone.

In its place was a wide, wall-to-wall pit with an ancient scaffold set into the alternating walls, so the descent was a spiral affair. It looked like the dig proceeded down the length of the cliff on which the house was perched, and the smell of the sea itself wafted up to them and played water patterns in the light on the ceiling.

Far down below, some two dozen men and women in fishnet robes like the ones Fesche and Trixie had been wearing congregated around a dark hole in the bottom of the pit. Suspended above the hole was the Princess, swaddled from her toes to her head in white linen. Her sobs echoed through the cavernous space, punctuating the alien intonations of the ceremony.

"Ph'nglui mglw'nafh Cthulhu R'lyeh wgah'nagl fhtagn."

The same chant Fesche and the guards had intoned.

"It's begun," Petra whispered.

Standing at the edge of the dark well was Trixie Treat. She had a white-bladed, curved ritual dagger in one hand, and she was leading the chanting, gently spinning the Princess around with her free hand. They couldn't cut the rope and hope to haul her up from here. It would take too long, and she would likely fall into the black shaft below.

Bond began hopping down the rickety old scaffold. It was precarious, but there was no time. They had less than forty-five minutes to descend, free the girl and get back up before they were burned and buried alive.

Petra followed more carefully. Soon Bond had left her behind.

As he got deeper into the pit, he saw that the black well in the center of the floor over which the crying girl was suspended rose and fell with seawater. They were below the level of the sea here, and Bond saw crude sluices had been constructed to divert and redirect the tidal waters that sloshed in through apertures in the rock.

As the poor girl spun on the rope, she would swing back and forth between the gathered congregants, and they would take turns pushing her back and forth. It was torture. How long had she been hanging there? Her face was red from crying and the rushing blood. She was a slip of a thing, not even halfway through school. She was heaving, losing consciousness, the blood vessels breaking in her head. She might not even live another forty minutes this way.

Something in the sight of it, the madly attired cultists enraptured in their ceremony, even smiling as they batted the girl back and forth, Trixie Treat, the container for much of his recent outrage egging them on with flourishes of her dagger, and the suffering of the girl herself, all conspired to drive Bond toward rash action. He whipped out his knife and put it in between his teeth.

He was at the lowest part of the scaffold, just a ladder above the floor, and he leapt across the space, straight at the girl as she was swinging closer.

He grabbed hold of her ankles and swung, praying the rope wouldn't break. His momentum carried them both over the tidal well and across to a surprised cultist, whom Bond kicked full in the face with both feet.

As he swung back the other way he took hold of his knife and began to frantically saw at the rope.

One of the cultists reached out and gripped his ankle to stop the momentum, but was pulled forward and fell headfirst screaming into the deep well. He bounced off the black rock sides and sank into the foam. Curiously, his body did not resurface.

Bond sliced through the last bit of frayed rope as they reached the extreme end of their backswing, and they fell. He quickly positioned himself under the Princess so that he landed first, breaking her fall on top of him. It knocked all the wind from him, and before he could recover, half a dozen hands dragged her off of him and pulled him to his feet.

Trixie stood before him. The curved dagger in her hand was of

Egyptian styling, with a silver handle covered in hieroglyphs and a sharp ivory blade with scrimshaw pictograms all along the surface, in some swirling motif.
"Hello again, James."
Bond scanned to his right. The cultists held the swooning girl upright. She looked terrified at him, pleading. Her head was swaddled in linens too, so that only her face was exposed. Her arms and legs were tightly bound.
He struggled. The cultists held his arms spread and tight.
"Bring him closer," she told her followers.
He was dragged to the edge of the well, and she stood next to him and grabbed him by the back of the hair, forcing him to crane his neck and look.
The shaft filling and emptying of swirling seat water appeared to be carved, but if it was the work of a sculptor it was a masterwork, impossibly intricate. Overall it gave the impression of a great organic tunnel, and widened toward the bottom into a kind of craw. It made his bones shiver, though it was only black stone, like the temple on Philae. Yet it exuded something. A terrible, indescribable intelligence and danger. It was like a sleeping tiger in a room.
"Petrified," said Trixie. "For uncounted ages. Can you imagine its hunger Bond?"
She said something in a language he couldn't identify, and someone from the crowd stepped forward, an old woman, sagging in her fishnets, bearing before her the Black Dodecahedron.
"When the Princesses' blood touches the Dodecahedron and the Seed is released, you will be among the first to see Ikla- Bafthgul live again. You will see it from the inside, James."
Then a shot rang out from above, and the old women grimaced and fell, a bullet in her back. The Black Dodecahedron clanked on the ground and rolled across the floor.
Trixie Treat whirled to see the shooter. It was Petra of course, crouching on the scaffold, aiming. The cultists slackened their grip for just an instant.
Bond gripped their arms and brought up his feet. He kicked Trixie square in her backside, and she gave a screech and fell into the well, into the petrified maw of her god.
He pivoted and threw the cultist on his right over his leg and into the well after her. His hand free, he drove his palm into the left-hand

man's nose, a crushing *atemi* blow that dropped him dead.
He straightened his tie and looked down into the well.
"After you, bitch."
The cultists swayed and moaned. These were cattle, ready to trample or flee. Bond drew his pistol and selected a few targets in the crowd, enough to make the mass back away. Not quite as fanatical as all that, in the end.
"Listen here!" he shouted. "In twenty minutes the house above is going to be hit with a barrage of cruise missiles from a ship off shore. So unless you want to spend the rest of your very short lives entombed with your precious god, off you go!"
Several of the men and women in the crowd broke and ran for the ladder. The two still holding the Princess dropped her and ran. One stooped down and grabbed at the ceremonial dagger Trixie had dropped. Bond killed him, and another who rushed at him swinging some kind of censer.
Seeing so many of their number killed broke the spirit of the rest and they joined their fellows in exodus. Petra picked up the ceremonial dagger and went to the Princess, using it to saw her legs free.
"There's not much time," said Bond, looking at the crowd climbing up the ladders. He took the Princess and hefted her in his arms. They moved toward the ladder, Petra examining the dagger with interest.
"Leave it," Bond suggested.
She dropped it and grabbed the ladder rung.
That was when one of the wall apertures burst open and Fesche came tumbling in, smashing through the sluice in a torrent of seawater.
He fell right before the Black Dodecahedron.
"My God," said Petra.
Bond passed the Princess to her, gave the girl a slight slap on the cheek to rouse her. "You've got to climb, Princess. Understand?"
She nodded, and turned to Petra.
"Miss Petra!"
"Come on. James!"
"Go!" Bond yelled, and backed away from the ladder.
Fesche got to his feet. The water was pooling around their ankles now, flowing into the well. Fesche turned the Black Dodecahedron over in his hands and looked at Bond thoughtfully.
Bond interposed himself between Fesche and the ladder.
"The Black Lotus was clever, Mr. Bond," he chuckled.

"Your lady friend taught me that trick."
"Where is Ms. Treat?"
Bond gestured to the well. "Making a wish. Why don't you follow her?"
Fesche stepped towards him, menacing, and Bond braced himself. He couldn't let Fesche retrieve the Princess.
Fesche stopped short. "I intend to." He stooped down and retrieved the silver-handled athame Petra had dropped.
Bond checked his watch. Fifteen minutes. Petra and the Princess were halfway to the surface, hampered by the crowd scrambling in front of them.
A few had seen Fesche appear, and turned on Petra with renewed courage. Two shots rang out and two bodies fell and crashed to the ground. This redoubled the progress of the survivors and Petra and the Princess made better time.
Fesche didn't move toward the ladder. He stepped back toward the well.
"This was not my first choice of deaths."
Bond looked at him strangely as he put the point of the dagger under his own chin and held the Black Dodecahedron beneath.
"And certainly not Ikla-Bafthgul's first choice either. But we must sometimes make do with what we have, Mr. Bond. I suppose it was inevitable."
He rammed the knife into his own throat.
Black, foul smelling, greenish blood immediately ran over his hand, and he leaned forward to let it dribble over the Black Dodecahedron. "Hear me, Osiris," he gagged. "This is the blood of an Emperor's house to appease and remove your ward. Hear me, Crawling Chaos! Hear me, Ikla-Bafthghul, Shatterer of Minds, Herald of Marshal Dagon! Hear me and wake!"
Then he pulled the dagger free and his blood gushed over the artifact, engulfing it. The glyphs on the stone glowed yellow and the whole affair rotated counterclockwise in his open hand. There was an accepting click as of a mechanism, and the Dodecahedron sprang into a stellated configuration, then something mustard yellow and luminescent as the guts of a firefly sprang from its points and coalesced into the wound in Fesche's throat.
The yellow stuff flowed upward into him, and streamed from his eyes, ears, from the corners of his gagging mouth, and oozed pus-like from

his nostrils.

He staggered and fell into the well.

Bond backed away as a sickly yellow light began to shine from the depths and the black stone lining the shaft cracked, shining yellow. The ground beneath his feet rumbled and shook.

Bond leapt to the ladder and clambered up for all he was worth.

The light below intensified and pulsed, illuminating the entire excavation, bright as daylight with a yellow tinge. It began to strobe, a disorienting effect.

Bond scaled higher, running along the scaffold, jumping to the next ladder.

The walls were shaking harder, threatening to dislodge the scaffolding.

There was a sound too, like an echoing, gasping and coughing, wet and monstrous.

He reached the top at last and checked his watch again. Five minutes to the strike. Although he didn't want to, he looked past his luminous dial down into the well at the bottom of the hole.

Something organic was oozing out, covering the floor in ponderous, writhing flesh, black and yellow and shot through with bioluminescent pustules that throbbed with interior light and burst with an audible pop and a flash of bright light like the bulbs of a bank of eager photographers.

In the center of it all was a great gummy maw, like the toothless mouth of an immense frog, working its jowls like a sleeper smacking its lips.

Bond shuddered and climbed the cellar stair, reached the door.

And that's when it started.

It began as a low thrum deep in whatever organ produced sound in the thing below. As it worked its way up the wet throat, it became a tone. Louder and higher and more intense than anything Bond had ever heard.

It made his skull bone tremble like a martini shaker. He felt it too in the pit of his stomach, in his chest, and it would not relent. He clamped his hands over his ears, more to steady his ringing head than to stifle the deafening noise. It was like the whistling of an artillery shell but emitting from his own brain, inescapable and unending.

He felt his hands grow damp with blood as he staggered into the foyer.

His eyes and nose were running now, and he could hardly see. He stumbled blindly, directionless. He couldn't find the door, slid along the wall.

The remains of glass in the windowpane blew outward and Bond cut his elbow on one. Desperate to escape the sound, he tumbled through the open window and fell into the wet grass.

He crawled, beaten flat to the ground by that sound, no idea where he was going. It was no better out here.

His heart began to hammer in his chest when he realized he could not escape the sound. He crawled on his belly, eyes clenching and unclenching to try and see.

It might have been raining. Every sense was stymied and overpowered by the overload of aural reception. His teeth ached so badly he wanted to dig them out of his mouth.

He kept crawling.

Then he nearly fell over the edge of the cliff, for apparently he had come out the back of the house.

He struggled to orient himself. His vision was melting; it was like trying to see through a waterfall.

He was looking straight down the cliff to the shore, thinking about hurling himself over.

Then he saw a flash on the horizon, and twelve bright lights arched up across the sky. It was strange to see the missiles flying and not be able to hear the scream of their approach, like watching a television program with the sound turned all the way down, except there was sound. Nothing but sound.

A heavy slab of sound pressing him down.

Lightning flashed. It was raining. It was storming. The sea was alive with it, raging. And there, scaling the cliff face, were dark figures. Hordes of them, emerging from the sea. Slick in the brief light, their hides dark and spined, incongruent combinations of man and sea creature, even less human than Fesche.

A few were quite close to gaining the top of the cliff, and these turned their bulky heads up as the missiles rocketed over them and then struck the house. The entire sky lit up with fire, and he felt the heat on his back. Bond saw wide, fish mouths lined with piranha teeth, and bulging black eyes, like the ones in the wood cut of D's old book, unfathomable for an instant before the shockwave of the thunderous explosion flung him head over heels off the cliff and he fell rapidly down toward the dark sea.

He crashed limply into the cold water and the tone was mercifully muted, but the dark, scaled bodies began to burst into the water all around him in clouds of bubbles. Some were dead, but some turned and undulated and fixed their faces on him and reached out with their webbed, clawed hands. He opened his mouth to scream and gulped seawater.

Then a huge boulder, a fragment of the cliff face, landed in the water, blotting out the firelight above him and driving him down to the very bottom.

He rolled out from underneath it, but another chunk of debris struck his head and he knew only that it was quiet wherever it was he went off to.

23. The Knight Who Would Have No Lady

The lift doors opened on the ninth floor and James Bond found himself face to face with a gentleman quite singular in appearance; early thirties, mop haired, black, prodigious horseshoe mustache dusted with premature streaks of grey. He wore thick dark spectacles, a cream, pinstriped Edwardian jacket and slim matching pants. Salmon ruffles poked out of the edge of his sleeves, matching socks above his white patent leather Chelsea boots, and a garish yellow marigold sprang from his breast pocket. The chap was fairly bursting with colors, like a little girl's sherbet threatening to melt over its cone on a hot summer day.

What such a fellow could possibly be doing on the ninth floor was a mystery to him. Another special consultant from Sotheby's perhaps? Bond excused himself and moved past the man.

The man smiled at him as he went past, and Bond looked back at him as the doors closed.

"Carry on, Mr. Bond," said the dandy, in an accent that smacked of the North.

Bond stood there for a moment, frowning. He didn't like being at a disadvantage.

It vexed him as he went off down the hall, and by the time he reached his office, he had convinced himself that the man was familiar to him, but couldn't deduce from where for the life of him.

Slipping, Bond, he thought. Old age setting in.

Or perhaps, more likely, one too many blows to the head.

His Corsican adventure, what little he remembered of it, had landed him once more in Sir James Molony's care.

Bill Ibaka had pulled him from the sea, he knew that much, and the recent news about an unaccounted-for missile strike on an abandoned house on the west coast of Corsica, which had effectively destroyed not only it but an entire picturesque point of land, had something to do with it, he knew.

He and Ibaka had foiled a ransom attempt by radical Middle Easterners, rescuing the young Princess Anne in the process. They'd both been offered a knighthood for the affair. Bill Ibaka had accepted his. Bond had refused. Again.

As he turned into his office, he nearly bumped into 006 on his way out.

"You lost the sweep, old man," he said with an oily, pompous grin. "You owe me five pounds."

"I never wagered," Bond said.

006 reddened and frowned as Bond went in and found the new secretary and subject of 006's ungentlemanly aside, Dolly Bird, giggling with Moneypenny, who sat on the edge of her desk, tucking a ten-pound note into her handbag.

"Good morning, ladies," Bond said, tossing his coat on the back of his chair.

"Hello James!" they said brightly, almost in unison, and still giggling.

"Did I miss something?"

"Only a ladies' wager, James," said Moneypenny, looking slyly aside at Dolly. "Confirming something about certain *members* of the Royal Marines."

Dolly Bird covered her face with her hands in an attempt to stifle the hilarity, but failed. "Oh my goodness Moneypenny, you're incorrigible!"

Bond smirked. He suspected he had heard the same rumor about the same Royal Marine.

"Well James," said Moneypenny, "another mission, another knock on the head. But still not enough of one to get you to accept a peerage. You're a knight in shining armor, James. Why don't you just accept it?"

"What's a knight without a lady fair, Moneypenny?" he said.

Moneypenny and Dolly exchanged looks as the former got to her feet. She paused in the doorway.

"A knight who's not looking!" she said in parting. Bond smiled and turned to the window.

It was a clear day and down in Regent Park and he saw a pleasant looking brown skinned girl with dark, curly hair walking slowly along the path.

"Is this really the second time you've refused a knighthood, Mr. Bond?" asked Dolly, chewing on the end of her spectacles suggestively.

Bond felt in his jacket pocket for the key to his desk, and flinched as something inside there moved.

"I don't go in for airs and titles, Ms. Bird," he said over his shoulder. But he must have imagined it. Feeling around the pocket he found a small hole in the lining. Something hard and pointed had slipped in there, and he worked it out.

It was an odd little stone carved into a pyramid, with some kind of tiny circular emblem engraved upon it. It seemed vaguely important. As he held it between his fingers, he got the fanciful sensation it was moving again, and turned curiously to the window once more.

"Nor do I," said Dolly from her desk.

Down in the park, the curly haired girl had sat down on a bench and produced a small paper sack. She began scattering breadcrumbs on the pavement at her feet.

Almost immediately a flock of pigeons descended upon the unexpected repast and began to peck at it and each other in a frenzy. Bond got out his key and opened his desk drawer.

"Then why do you keep calling me mister? I told you before, it's James."

"And I'm Dolly...James."

He dropped the little pyramid into the drawer and shut it, turning in his seat to smile at his lovely secretary, still nibbling on the end of her spectacles.

"Yes of course," he said. "How could I forget?"

ABOUT THE AUTHORS

William Meikle is a Scottish writer, now living in Canada, with over twenty novels published in the genre press and over 300 short story credits in thirteen countries. He lives in Newfound- land with whales, bald eagles and icebergs for company. When he's not writing he drinks beer, plays guitar, and dreams of fortune and glory.

Edward M Erdelac is the author of ten novels, including Monstrumfuhrer (Comet Press), Andersonville (Random House) and The Merkabah Rider series. His fiction has appeared in dozens of anthologies and periodicals including The Dark Rites of Cthulhu, After Death, Night Land Magazine, and Star Wars Insider. He accredits his lifelong lycanthrophilia to Lon Chaney Jr., Chuck Connors' short lived stint as a shapeshifter on TV, and well-worn boxes of Werewolf By Night comic books.
Born in Indiana, educated in Chicago, he resides in the Los Angeles area with his wife and a litter of pups. News and excerpts from his work can be found at www.emerdelac.wordpress.com.

Also by April Moon Books

The Dark Rites of Cthulhu - sixteen original tales of the Mythos in one horrific anthology.

Flesh Like Smoke - an anthology of original stories featuring shapeshifters and werewolves.

The Call of Poohthulhu – a terrible idea, really.

A Picnic at the Mountains of Madness - our first children's book. A delight for all ages.

The Short Sharp Shocks collection:

Vol. 1. AMOK! - an unnerving collection of murderous frenzy.
Vol. 2. Stomping Grounds - giant monsters on the rampage!
Vol. 3. Ill-considered Expeditions - foolhardy, doomed, expeditions.
Vol. 4. Spawn of the Ripper - our loving tribute to Hammer Horror.
Vol. 5. The Stars at my Door - optimistic Sci-Fi with a twist.

All titles available from Amazon.com
or directly from www.AprilMoonBooks.com

Printed in Great Britain
by Amazon